SHAPER'S DAUGHTER

RACHEL DEVENISH FORD

SMALL SEED PRESS

Other Books By Rachel Devenish Ford:

The Eve Tree: A Novel
A Traveler's Guide to Belonging
Trees Tall as Mountains: The Journey Mama Writings- Book One
Oceans Bright With Stars: The Journey Mama Writings- Book Two
A Home as Wide as the Earth: The Journey Mama Writings- Book Three
World Whisperer: World Whisperer Book 1
Guardian of Dawn: World Whisperer Book 2

First published in 2017
Copyright © 2017 Rachel Devenish Ford

ISBN-13: **978-0-9996061-0-0**

Small Seed Press LLC
racheldevenishford.com

For my father, who knows estrangement
and who has lost a lot this year.
I believe all will be restored.
I love you.

PROLOGUE

The man was trying to control his fear. He stood with one hand resting on the tall, ornate door to the king's chamber, wearing a long robe with a hood that hid his face. The king required hoods; he didn't want to see the faces of people who crept toward him like worms unless he requested it. It was almost never a good thing if the king asked to see your face. The hood was fine. With the hood, you didn't need to see him either. Not that he was ugly to look at—he was handsome in a deadly, ruthless way. But the eyes. There were rumors he could kill with his eyes alone.

The man's robe was a deep, brilliant red. Only five red robes existed—for the five closest servants of the king—but many, many people had worn them. Red robes didn't have a long lifespan and this man, standing at the door of the king's inner chamber, had lived much longer than any of his colleagues had managed. Today he had passed the guards at every entrance, walking deeper and deeper into the palace, until he reached this final door, guarded by nothing but the king's word. *Come in,* he would say. Or *Stay out.* If the king said stay out, the message would wait.

The red robe stood with his head down, willing the trembling in his arms and legs to stop before he raised his hand to knock. The king hated weakness of any kind, even the tremor of a shaky voice, and the man needed to make himself perfectly calm before he entered. Difficult, knowing as he did that the king would hate his news and that his anger could flare up suddenly, ruthlessly.

He raised his hand. It was mostly still, besides one wild tremor that he calmed. Today might be his last on earth, but he lived his life knowing every day was possibly his last. For a moment, the face of his father came into his mind, and he wondered what he was doing here, in this stifling hallway, shaking, serving this horrible man. Even these thoughts were punishable by death. He drew a deep breath and knocked. He had a brief flare of hope that perhaps the king would call *Stay out,* and someone else could deliver the message, later, when the king was ready. But the hope died at once.

"Come in," the king called, his voice low and deceptively silky.

The red robe pulled the large door open, walking through, no trace of fear visible now, he thought, to the slaves who stood in the corners of the room. The room was large, severe in its bareness. This was not the opulent throne room, but the quiet place where the king retired in times that he wasn't sleeping, judging, or spending time with one of his many wives. It was his own place, empty as his heart, the man thought, the hood hiding his face. The floor was shiny, black as a night pool, the walls draped in some kind of cloudy material, like a stormy sky. There was very little light. The windows were shielded from the heat of the desert by large wooden shutters that slaves had carried over half the world. Their desert kingdom had very little wood, and what wood there was had been hard won. The red robe bowed a full bow —bent in half at the waist— then approached, still bent with his face directed at the floor. The king sat at the only chair in the room, next to a table, eating a piece of fruit with a knife.

A slave stood nearby to wipe the king's mouth of the juices of the fruit between each bite. Another slave bathed the king's feet, smoothing soft, fragrant soaps over them. Both slaves were women. The king had only women and children in his inner courts. He didn't trust men to serve him closely, to sleep on his floor, as his slave women did.

"Yes?" the king asked. The red robe realized he had been quiet too long, still bent in front of the king, watching the slave who continued to wash his feet. She appeared to be holding her breath.

"I have news from Batta, Brilliant One," the man said.

The king kicked the slave away, not gently, splashing water over her robe.

"Oh?" The king's voice remained soft, but the red robe shivered at the masked anger. "Stand up and pull back your hood. I want to see which one you are."

Fear was like ice in the man's arms and legs, but he did as the king said, standing to his full height and pulling the hood away so the king could see that he was Herrith, oldest of the king's servants, the king's cousin, in fact, with the same dark brown skin and eagle-like face, long bones and immense height.

"Proceed," the king said, not giving any indication that it mattered who Herrith was. Herrith knew that being a relative of the king didn't promise any protection. He had seen death come to cousins and uncles of the king alike. In the silence, while Herrith gathered composure, he could hear the quiet sound of the slave crying. Herrith noted that the woman was a prior wife of the king's, who had done something that angered him and been reduced to the position of a slave. He took a breath and spoke.

"The high priest of the Worker city has reported that the girl entered their trap, that they had her and her brother in their prison..."

"Had?" the king said, and Herrith felt another shiver of fear. He smelled the strange, sweet smell that accompanied the king's anger, followed by the sharp burning that reminded Herrith of the aftermath of a lightning strike.

"They lost her, Brightness. She escaped with the Worker woman and her child. She is back in the cursed city."

The burning smell grew stronger and the king clutched the knife in his hand until the veins on his hands stood out like worms. Suddenly, with a growl, he threw the knife, not at Herrith, but at the large door. It narrowly missed the door slave, a child of about ten who didn't move a muscle, though his eyes grew wide and filled with tears.

The woman at the king's feet stopped crying. There was

absolute silence in the room. No one wanted to move, to draw attention. Herrith realized he was holding his breath. He let it out and went on.

"There is more, Brilliant One."

"Yes?" The voice was soft, menacing, ancient with hatred.

"There is evidence that she had help."

"Help?"

"From Abbaseet, the warrior. The traitor of the Karee tribe."

Nothing. No sound. No words. Herrith dared a glance and saw that the king was staring at the fruit in his hand, a frown on his face. Herrith felt the first stirrings of hope. He knew that look, the thinking look, not the look of blind rage that could have him killed in an instant.

"Abbaseet, you say? How did it come to be that he was able to assist the young lady?"

"The Worker priest," Herrith didn't bother to disguise the contempt in his voice, now that his breath had calmed a little. "The Worker priest didn't see him as a threat anymore, so he had him cleaning the prison room without chains or binding of any sort."

"Didn't think he was dangerous? We told the Worker pigs that he was dangerous."

Herrith said nothing. There was nothing to be said. Why hadn't the Workers heeded what the king's servants had told them about the traitor Abbaseet? The rebel Karee prince had been exiled as a slave to the Worker city, a horrible, smelly, demeaning place, with its stupid temple and streets running with filth, nothing like the beautiful Desert City. It was a fate worse than death, the king believed. But Herrith himself had told the head Worker priest that the warrior prince was dangerous, that he should be chained at all times, guarded every second. What had he been doing in that room?

"Idiots," the king said finally. "Have the high priest brought to me."

Herrith felt light-headed with relief, and with the relief was shame. The king's anger had turned elsewhere. But the king spoke again.

"As for the girl."

Herrith waited, cursing himself, wondering what his father would have thought of him. He didn't need to wonder. He knew.

Not the girl, please no. For a moment, the girl's mother was before him again, pleading. He was looking at her lovely face, he was overcome with love, he was unable to say no.

The king went on. "We'll wait and watch. She'll feel safe again. But then we will burn her out of her hiding place, and we'll have her. She won't be able to fight us; her power is not the kind for long resistance. She is too powerful to ignore, though. So we go to take her." He paused. "And then Abbaseet will burn too, like the desert dog he is."

Chapter 1

Sixteen looks a lot like fifteen, Isika thought, looking at her face in her bedroom mirror. Was she a little taller? Maybe. She stretched to her full height, admiring the shimmery fall of the turquoise tunic she would wear to her birthday dinner. The color was bright against her skin, as dark brown as the little velvety birds that lit on her windowsill in the morning. She had a new glow that Auntie said came from good food and a family that was hers, a place with lights that called her home in the dusk. Auntie had worked her hair into a hundred tiny braids with gold thread and jade beads woven throughout. The beads clicked softly when she turned her head from side to side.

She had the same face as always, but lately it looked more grown-up, more like her late mother's face. She didn't look as much like her mother as her sister Aria, who was an exact replica of their mother, Amani. There was something else to

Isika's cheekbones and wide-set eyes, her face less round than her mother's. She had angles that must have come from her father, though she couldn't know, never having met him. She placed Kital's birthday gift, a string of beads, over her forehead and straightened it so the long red stone hung in the center. Her little brother had been waiting from the moment she woke up, ready to give her his gift. After a moment of fright as she opened her eyes and found him an inch from her face, she had laughed and hugged him and fussed over his gift.

She gave herself one last look over, then turned and walked to the kitchen, slightly ashamed of spending so much time looking at herself. After living for so many years without a mirror, even five minutes looking at her reflection felt like too much.

But the truth was that she wasn't marveling at her own face (she still wasn't sure that she was pretty, despite Ibba and Auntie's opinions) or even her clothes, but at the fact that she no longer thought *outsider* every time she caught a glimpse of herself. She didn't think queen, either, though she would be queen someday. But the panicky feeling of being an outsider was easing day by day. She was starting to look at herself as someone who belonged: a Maweel girl, nearly a woman, celebrating her sixteenth birthday today with her friends and family. She looked Maweel. The people of Maween—except for the refugees they rescued from the evil of the Great Waste—were black-skinned, like Isika. But it was taking her a long time to feel that she belonged to Maween.

In the kitchen, she picked up a tray of Auntie Teru's berry tarts, carrying them out to the long table in the courtyard where Auntie buzzed back and forth, fussing over the placement of the various treats she had made. Jerutha, Isika's stepmother, sat in a swing chair, chatting away to Auntie while rocking Mesu, her sleeping baby. Jerutha's straight, light brown hair was tied up in a scarf—not ornate, she couldn't stand fancy things, but lovely against her pale skin nonetheless.

Out in the garden, Abbas, a Gariah warrior, was helping Uncle Dawit and Kital hang lanterns. Nearly a year ago, Abbas had helped Isika and her brother Benayeem escape the Worker city where they had been imprisoned, and rescue Jerutha, who had also been a prisoner there, destined to be the High Priest's wife—a fate Isika wouldn't wish on anyone. Since the rescue, Abbas was never far from Isika's family, revolving around them like a protector, but also pulled into the family love that emanated from Teru and Dawit.

Isika saw Abbas pause between hanging lanterns to watch Jerutha and Mesu. The tall warrior, wild-looking with his long black hair and patched desert clothing, was especially protective of Isika's stepmother. When Uncle Dawit wanted to hang another string of lanterns, he needed to call Abbas's name three times to get his attention.

He wasn't the only one who worried over fragile, kind Jerutha. Isika was also fiercely protective of her stepmother. Abbas's attention to Jerutha might have made Isika nervous, but Isika liked him. She couldn't help it. None of them could.

He was just so kind and intense, wanting to do the right thing for everyone. He looked a little odd in the garden scene, his warrior posture reminding Isika that he was trained to fight, dancing with his sword, his bright gold earrings swinging. But as he helped Uncle Dawit, he wore a smile that lit up his face.

It felt like a lifetime since Jerutha had helped Isika escape the Worker village where she had lived for many years with her stepfather, the priest, Nirloth. Isika's family was complicated, and her family was only the beginning of the intricacies of her life. After discovering the Maweel people, or being discovered by them, she had also discovered that she and her siblings were the descendants of their stolen queen. Isika was the heir of the kingdom of Maween, and she was also World Whisperer: the ruler who kept the peace of Maweel, and the direct link to the Shaper of the World. From the beginning of Maween, when the World Whisperer was ruling, the people were at peace.

But things hadn't gotten better for Maween when Isika stepped into the picture. The poison from the Great Waste had grown worse. Things weren't settled or easy, they were confusing.

Isika wasn't yet queen, but the Maweel tried to show her some of the same honor and respect they would have shown her grandmother, who reigned as queen. Some of this she simply refused. She didn't want to spend a lot of time in court. She didn't want the grand ballroom birthday party the elders had planned to give to her. She wanted her pottery workshop and the little party she would have here in the garden. That was all. Some of it she had to put up with. It couldn't be helped.

She set the tray down in the spot Auntie Teru showed her, dropping a kiss on the older woman's cheek as she passed. Auntie barely noticed, too busy counting the spicy fried mushroom balls and muttering about whether there would be enough. During her time living with Auntie Isika had learned she shouldn't try to stop the older woman's fretting. Auntie Teru enjoyed fussing over people and their stomachs, and there was nothing she liked as much as a lot of work. Teru and Dawit's son had been killed in a seeking journey many years ago, devastating them. It had left a scar that meant Teru didn't leave the house often anymore, getting shaky and panicky if she did. But she loved to have people over and to feed them until they complained that they couldn't eat another bite, then scolding them for not taking one last pastry.

Isika smiled at her foster mother as Teru chatted with Jerutha about babies and their sweetness. She felt a huge bubble of happiness floating around inside her as she went back to the kitchen to get another tray. It swelled a little more as her friend Jabari burst through the front door. She didn't examine the reason that she felt so happy at the sight of him. Instead, she fixed a frown on her face as he ran toward her.

"Do you have to gallop into a room like a donkey?" she asked.

He grinned at her and handed her a package wrapped in

brown paper and tied with what looked suspiciously like his headscarf.

She took it, unable to keep the smile back any longer.

"What is this?" she asked.

"A gift, of course, Squawker. What else could it be? I feel like I've been waiting to give it to you forever!"

She looked at him, a head taller than her now, the broad lines of his face creased in smiles. He had skin the exact color of their darkest sienna glaze in the workshop. He had turned seventeen not too long ago, and he looked like a man. He didn't act like one, though.

"Um," she said, untying the scarf from the brown paper. "Is this your *ser*?"

"Yeah, I'm going to need to get that back," he said. "But hurry!"

"Is it going to disappear if I don't open it?" she asked.

"No," he said. "Do you need me to do it for you?"

She laughed. "All right, hold on, I can do it."

They stood in the doorway to the living space of the house, and guests trickled past them, stopping only to smile and greet Isika as they aimed for the table outside, laden with Auntie's food. Isika carried Jabari's gift into the kitchen and laid it carefully on the cooking bench, turning it so the paper fell away. Her mouth dropped open. It was a pot. A clumsy little coil pot, slightly crooked and about the size of a cup to hold coffee or spice tea, but much thicker than the cups in their home.

She looked up at him.

"It's my first one ever," he said. "Tomas finally let me do something other than sweep."

Isika turned it over in her hands, feeling the smooth blue glaze under the pads of her fingers. Jabari had been working in the pottery workshop for almost a year, sweeping and cleaning kilns, hovering over her while she worked the pottery wheel, mixing glazes and getting underfoot.

These last months were responsible for the friendship between them, after their rocky start and the fact that Isika couldn't help using her many strong gifts, though Jabari was the more knowledgeable one and had trained his whole life. He had stopped scolding her so much and she couldn't help liking him. He was just so fun, a bright spot in the workshop. Isika found she hated the days that he didn't show up to work.

"It's beautiful," she said. She suddenly felt like she might cry. "I'll drink my coffee out of it every morning."

"Oh. Well... you might not be able to do that," Jabari said, clearing his throat. "It split in the kiln and there's a bit of a crack. But you could use it as a nice shelf decoration." He took it from her and carried it over to a bookshelf in the living space of the house. "Like this. See?"

She stared at him. She was still confused about the fact that he had chosen to stay home, rather than traveling this year. Jabari was a gifted seeker. His job was to find and destroy poison. He loved jungle and forest, rivers and swimming in moonlight. He was hardly himself in the confines of the city. And yet, here he was. And next week his brother, Gavi, was heading out on a seeking journey without Jabari, for the first time ever. Yet here Jabari was, making pots, excited as a child about it.

"Wow," she said. "Thank you." She left the pot on the shelf, smiling at him.

When she turned back to look through the back door to the garden, she realized opening the gift had taken longer than she thought. The garden was filled with people, and as soon as she stepped out, she was overwhelmed by hugs and blessings from the people who had come to celebrate her birthday. It made her teary and happy, but deeply sad at the same time, the way she had been on every birthday since her mother died.

KITAL RAN over and threw himself at her, with Ibba flying headlong at her soon after.

"Happy birthday, Isika!" they cried, and she kissed them both, laughing, wiping tears away quickly. She was pulled into the crowd. Already men pulled their drums out of the leather satchels that held them, getting ready to start the dancing and singing. Benayeem, her younger brother by a little over a year, came and stood by her. He slung an arm around her, squeezing her shoulder, and she leaned on him. The lights in the garden shone like the fire birds that lived in the forests of Maween.

"Happy?" he asked.

"So happy. I made the right choice."

As the heir to the throne, Isika was owed a birthday

banquet at the palace, a large, ostentatious affair with all the elders from different parts of Maween and as many Othra as they could entice. Isika had refused it all. She wanted a small party here, in her own garden, with the people who loved her. The four ruling elders were invited and would arrive at some point. But Isika knew them and they were less scary in her home than they were in the plush throne room.

Standing there, again Isika found herself wishing for something she couldn't have: to be a normal, non-royal Maweel girl. The last months had been the happiest of her life, uneventful and filled with long days in the pottery studio. There were, of course, the strange moments that came from being smack in the center of so many worlds. She was a girl who had grown up in the Worker village and had a sister who had been taken from her there, and a stepmother that she had rescued from the Workers, enemies of the Maweel people.

Plus she had Keethior, a magical companion animal who had chosen her. And a friend for life, a Gariah warrior who seemed to think his mission was to guard her; four elders who wanted to know what her intentions were; her own brothers and sisters; her adopted aunt and uncle; and all her traveling companions.

"It's complicated, isn't it?" she asked Ben, watching Abbas whirl in his own rhythm to the songs the drums were crying out, oblivious to the steps of the other dancers.

"Very," he agreed. "But wonderful." He looked around. "Where is Aria? She shouldn't miss this."

Their younger sister, whom they had lost when she was

seven and was now thirteen, lived with her own foster parents, one more complicated thing about their new lives. Isika wished their sister lived with them, but Aria was struggling and often pushed the other siblings away.

Isika shook her head slowly. "I don't know," she said finally. "I hope she finds her way here."

Chapter 2

The party went on all day. Isika ate, wandered, talked with her guests, accepted a lot of hugs, and bowed respectfully as the elders arrived. Ivram and Karah hugged her, and Andar and Laylit, Jabari and Gavi's parents, bowed their heads graciously in her direction.

Isika had just sat down to watch the dancers when her friend Brigid arrived, wreathed in smiles, and plopped a present into Isika's lap. Isika tore the wrapping off and found a dress, not the traditional tunic that she normally wore, but a robe that fitted at the waist and would flow all the way to the ground when she put it on, made of soft silvery grey weave. Her eyes nearly popped out of her head.

"This is too much," she told Brigid.

"It is not!" Brigid said. "You know my parents are weavers. This is some of their cloth."

That was only more impressive. Brigid was a rescued Worker, with long, impossibly straight brown hair, pale, freckled skin and deep blue eyes. Brigid's adoptive parents were Maweel master weavers, the best of their kind, steeped in the shaping magic that enabled Maweel to create the beautiful things they made almost effortlessly. The weavers had a large guild, and the gift for weaving magic usually passed from parents to children, but every so often, someone else in Maween would turn out to have the gift. Young Maweel children who would make good weavers were easy to spot, as they were always weaving grasses into baskets or hair into tiny doll shawls. Though not originally from Maween, Brigid had turned out to love weaving, and she was gifted at it. It was something mysterious and wonderful to the Maweel: the fact that their rescued children often found that a gift burst out of them when they were in Maween air. Brigid was also gifted with protection, so she had gone on a seeking journey to explore that side of herself.

"Thank you," Isika said, smoothing one hand over the dress.

"You're welcome. I'm so happy to know you, Isika. You're one of my dearest friends."

Isika smiled. She felt the same way about Brigid, but didn't know how to say it. She and the other girl had grown close after they returned home after their last journey. They rode horses for hours, or sat under Isika's favorite tree when both of them were done with their day's work. Brigid, like Jabari, had chosen to stop seeking for a time, though Isika knew it was because Brigid's parents were afraid, more than anything else. There was too much new danger, with more poison than ever coming from the Great Waste. They didn't want Brigid to go back to being a seeker.

"Let's go to your room," Brigid said. "You can try it on. I want to see what it looks like!."

"Right this moment?" Isika asked.

"Yes!" Brigid laughed. "I'm excited, I've been working on it for days. Mom helped me sew it, but it was my first fine cloth. Try it on just to see. You don't have to wear it if you don't want to."

Isika shrugged. "Sure." The dancing and music was still going at full strength and she liked the idea of a break.

On their way into the house Isika heard the voice that she'd been waiting for. Aria. *She came!* Isika thought, her heart leaping. Aria was in the entryway to the house, out of sight. Isika started to go to her, the dress forgotten, but then she heard Aria speak, and her heart sank back down into her chest. She put a hand out to stop Brigid before they turned the corner.

Aria was speaking in a low, intense voice. "She always needs attention. Look at this party! Lights, dancing, all for her. She couldn't have a perfectly good party at the palace, oh no, she had to have everything here."

"Isn't it simpler to have it here?" another voice asked. It sounded like one of Aria's friends from school.

"No, she would never do something because it was simpler, trust me. You should have seen her when we had to rescue her on the seeking mission. She made such a fuss about being hurt that Jabari did everything for her, running for everything she wanted, and then..." Aria took a gasping breath, "...at the very end she paralyzed us so she could do everything herself and take all the credit. She makes me sick."

Isika couldn't breathe. Pain radiated in her chest in a way she hadn't felt since her mother died. Brigid had a death grip on her arm, and Isika had no idea what Brigid was trying to do because she couldn't move if she wanted to.

"Aria, you're sounding bad again," the friend said in a low voice. "I'm going to get your mom. You need to go back to the healers."

Isika heard the sound of her sister sobbing, and underneath the pain she felt deep sympathy and love. Something was tightening around her heart, squeezing and squeezing. Everything in her wanted to go to Aria to comfort her. But just before Isika burst into the room to throw her arms around her sister and beg her to feel better, Jabari walked up behind Isika and Brigid in the corridor.

"What's wrong?" he asked, and Isika shook her head wildly, putting a finger to her lips. Brigid grabbed both of their wrists and pulled them into a nearby room, closing the door behind them. For a moment, Isika stared at the room without recognizing where she was, but eventually she came back to herself and saw that they were crowded into the bathing room. She blinked and put her back to the wall, slowly sliding down until she was sitting on the floor, staring at the stone tiles, worn smooth by years of people walking on them.

Brigid whirled to face her. "It means nothing, Isika," she said fiercely. "Don't think about it for even one more minute, it means nothing, do you hear me?"

"How can it mean nothing?" Isika asked. Her voice sounded strange to her, as though it came from far away. "Did you hear her? I've never imagined that she could feel so much... contempt..." her voice broke and she couldn't continue. She buried her face in her hands.

"Is anyone going to tell me what happened?" Jabari asked.

Isika couldn't explain or feel anything but pain. Brigid filled him in quickly.

"You heard what Aria's friend said," she said to Isika again when she had finished. "She's not well. You know that!"

"The arrows," Jabari said. "Why can't anyone heal them?"

"Most of them are out," Isika said. "But one is different, and no one can touch it. The healers said it's stronger because it pierced the wound that never healed. The one from her sending out, when Nirloth threw her away. Oh, I hate that this travels with us. I wish we could be finished with the evil of that place forever!"

The arrows that poisoned Aria weren't literal arrows. Aria had been sacrificed, sent out in a tiny boat by the Workers, to what they assumed was her death among the waves. But Aria, at nearly eight years old, became the oldest rescued child ever found in one of the tiny boats. She was traumatized when they found her, because she hadn't been asleep like most of the children who were sent out, but had lain there awake, terrified of the water. The Maweel had rescued her and brought her back to the city, where Aria had been

adopted by parents who loved her. Then, on their last journey, Aria had stumbled into a trap meant for Isika, and the
trap had recognized Aria as someone of Isika's blood. It sent
the poison arrows into her instead. She was already horrifi-
cally wounded from the betrayal of being sacrificed, so when
the arrows found her, the poison had nearly killed her.

"Her parents told my parents that she's barely the same
girl," Jabari said, sliding down to sit against the wall across
from Isika. "It's not your fault."

"It is my fault! Those arrows were meant for me! And
they hurt her instead. It's the same thing that happened when
our father chose to send her out and I stayed."

This was the most painful part, more agonizing than any
beating she had ever received from her stepfather, more
painful even than her mother's death. She had helplessly
stood there, watching, when Aria's boat was pushed out into
the waves.

"The healers are searching for a cure," Brigid said. "And
they're treating her often. It helps."

"But they say that every time the poison floods her, it gets
a little worse," Isika said.

She couldn't say any more, and the silence grew heavy
in the little room. It was breaking Isika's heart. And Ben was
barely able to talk about it. Aria was a gorgeous, lively girl
who was being consumed from the inside. Even though Isika
knew she shouldn't take the things her sister said personally,
she couldn't help hearing the words over and over in her
mind. She wanted Aria to know how much she loved her,
wanted it badly, but it seemed that there was no way to

make her feel loved. She was wild with the desire to help, but Isika was the last person in the world Aria wanted to talk to.

Aria trusted Brigid, so Brigid had become their link. She kept Isika filled in on how Aria was doing, and dropped hints to Aria about how much Isika cared for her.

Isika saw then that Brigid hadn't told her everything Aria said about her. She looked at Brigid, suddenly sure there had been more harsh words than Brigid had passed along. She had a sense of what it had been like for Brigid to be in the middle. How kind her friend was, to be willing.

Isika jumped to her feet and hugged Brigid hard, stepping away to look at her two friends; short, dreamy Brigid and tall, energetic Jabari, frowning slightly as he looked back at her. She found she had tears in her eyes.

"I don't even want this! You know it's true, Jabari. I never asked to be World Whisperer, all I want to be is to be the same as everyone else. Nobody believes me, but you two have had years of being normal Maweel kids and as soon as I get here I'm caught up in all this..."

"Stop right there," Jabari said. He leaned back and folded his arms over his chest, and didn't say anything else. He just looked at her. If he had said something, argued, Isika could have pushed back, using the anger that was roaring like a furnace inside her, but his silence and his gentle eyes made her feel suddenly, hugely ashamed, and she sighed. Her anger grew cold and turned to sadness. Brigid's eyes were wide and suspiciously shiny.

"I'm sorry," Isika whispered, wrapping her arms around

herself. "I'll find a way to be the right thing, to do the right thing. I don't—"

"Today is today," Jabari said. "No one is asking you to be World Whisperer today. You only have to go out there and be somewhat sane around all these people who love you. That's probably enough for you to deal with."

"*Some* of them love me," Isika muttered, but she smiled at him as he put a hand on her shoulder, jerking it back quickly at the shock of colliding magic they felt whenever they touched. "You're right, Yab," she used Gavi's pet name for him, something she'd started doing recently and had continued when he didn't object. "Having you, this family, is a gift. What would I do without you? If you hadn't found me on that beach, I would still be in the Worker village, gathering wood every day and working in a temple I despised. Or I would be dead."

She wiped at her face and took deep breaths, standing straighter, preparing to go back to the party that celebrated her small, conflicted self. She wished above all for her mother. Brigid linked arms with her, and they walked out to the party, Jabari just behind them.

"Oh, you didn't leave the dress on?" Auntie asked, when they arrived in the courtyard. Isika shook her head. She didn't tell Auntie she hadn't even tried it on.

"I forgot about it," she said. Auntie gave her a quick look and Isika knew she saw that something was wrong. She smiled at Auntie to reassure her, and searched the crowd, but she didn't see Aria anywhere.

"Aria's family took her home," Auntie said in a low voice.

"Her mother said to give you a birthday greeting. Aria wasn't feeling well."

Isika nodded, not daring to meet Auntie's eyes again, and after a moment, Auntie squeezed her shoulder and put a fruit pastry into her hand, continuing on her way to hand out food. Isika ate the delicious pastry, and stood trying to get her face under control. She hadn't even finished chewing the last bite when her hand was caught and she turned to see Gavi, pulling her into the mass of dancers.

He laughed at the expression on her face, and she shoved away the sad, grieving parts of her that missed her little sister and her mother. She smiled back at him, and she danced.

Their dance followed the drums, and Gavi had always been good at dancing. Isika followed his steps, trying to remember what she had learned in the last year. Nearby, she saw Ivram dancing with Karah, Jabari dancing with Ivy, Auntie leaping higher than Isika had thought possible. Kital and Ibba jumped around to their own rhythm, in the middle of the floor. The drums picked up speed and suddenly Isika was laughing, she couldn't have stopped dancing if she wanted to. The evening light made everyone beautiful, the trees swayed overhead, and the thankfulness that she had tried to force before welled up without effort, filling her whole soul until her dance felt like a prayer.

Chapter 3

Jabari yawned as he brushed the last of the clay dust out of the kiln, and unfortunately, Tomas caught him at it, marching into the kiln room with a tray of pots ready to be fired, just as Jabari was thinking the yawn would crack his face open.

Tomas lowered his eyebrows. His grizzled white hair had the same dust in it that Jabari had been cleaning for hours, and Jabari found himself thinking about how he could use the kiln broom on his master's head. He blinked, coming back to reality. Oh, he was tired.

"Is this so boring to you?" Tomas snapped. "Do you need to find apprentice work somewhere else?"

Jabari shook his head quickly, and stood a little straighter. He thought maybe Tomas was joking, but the master potter was notoriously hard to read.

"No, I love working here, Uncle. Forgive me. I was up late at Isika's party last night." He winced as he rolled his shoulders. They had been dancing until the sun came up, and his muscles were sore. "Why didn't you come to the party?" he asked.

"What makes you think I wasn't there?" Tomas asked, holding the platter of cups out. Jabari took them and loaded them carefully into the kiln, one by one.

"I didn't see you."

"I was there. I was eating Teru's cake and watching you young ones dance. In fact, I saw Isika dancing with many people; her brother, your brother, Ivram, that new Gariah man..."

"Abbas," Jabari murmured, not liking where he saw the conversation headed.

"Abbas," Tomas said agreeably. "But I didn't see you dancing with her."

"I danced with her. Well. I danced near her. We had a good time." He picked up one of Isika's cups. She had a new style lately; etching delicate leaves and flowers into her pots, then filling them with red paint. It was stunning.

"Tell me, Tomas. Is this good work? Is it as good as I think it is? Or am I just easily impressed?"

Tomas looked at the cup Jabari was holding. "It's very good," he said. His tray was empty, so he went back out into the drying room to fetch more. Jabari placed the cup very carefully into the kiln and followed him.

As Tomas began loading the tray again, testing the pieces carefully to make sure they were ready, Jabari leaned back and thought about what Tomas had said. He scowled. It wasn't that he was avoiding dancing with Isika. It just hadn't happened, that's all. And there was that magic sparking thing that happened when they touched. It could make dancing... difficult.

"Where is Isika this morning, anyway?" he asked.

"I gave her the day off. She needs to get ready for the ceremony at the palace. Surely you haven't forgotten."

Jabari had forgotten.

"Me? Of course not!" he said. The ceremony. Of course. She would have the first ceremony for ruling, the way he and Gavi had, though they weren't royalty the way Isika was. How would it be for her? She didn't like a lot of people looking at her. Tomas stared at him under lowered brows, holding out the tray that Jabari hadn't noticed was ready.

He held his hands out. "You know I want to be here, right, Uncle? Were you joking when you said I should find another place to apprentice?"

It was true that Jabari wanted to be there. He wasn't the natural potter that Isika was—the type of building magic needed for pottery seemed to have evaded him completely—but he did love the pottery workshop. It was challenging to try things without any benefit of a gift, and he liked the difficulty. Most things in life came easily to him. Before Isika came along, he had been the most gifted person in his generation. He had always liked to push himself, to run for miles and to do things that didn't come naturally. Pottery was turning out to be one of those things. No matter how hard he tried to build pots symmetrically, they always came out crooked or cracked in the kiln. It was maddening and fun. And the workshop was a pleasant place; it smelled good, it was full of light, and there was Isika to walk home with every day.

He couldn't explain what it was that had changed in the last months, or exactly the moment when he had become so totally and completely on her side. It had started on their last journey, when he rescued her from the Worker city, only to see her immense power against Mugunta in the desert. She had fought alone, while the rest of them were helpless. He had never seen such a thing before, and beyond the initial embarrassment, he knew that what he needed more than anything was to be on the side of the person who could do that. Keethior had declared himself to her; the Keerza came to her when she needed them. These were not small things. But there was something else, something in her, that he recognized. He supposed it was royalty, and he knew that he wouldn't dream of challenging her right to the throne ever again. In fact, he was frustrated with his parents for not acknowledging her clear inheritance of power. He was annoyed with her for not appreciating the inheritance. He was frustrated with everyone, a clear sign that he needed to go for a long run.

"I do know that, young one," Tomas said, breaking a long silence. It took Jabari a second to remember what the master potter was talking about. *Oh yes, wanting to be in the pottery workshop.* "But we haven't ever talked about why you are here. I know only that your parents thought it was a good idea if you stayed in Azariyah for some time. But—you're the last person I could ever imagine giving up seeking, so I'm not sure why it's necessary. And your brother has such a clear gift with his garden, yet he's going out seeking again next week and you're staying."

Jabari smiled to himself. It did seem strange, when Tomas put it that way.

"That's it exactly," he said. "Gavi wants to become head gardener in Azariyah one day. I want to become a ranger. So my parents asked him to continue as a seeker so he can learn more about the surrounding villages and farmlands before he settles down for good. They asked me to stay here, so I will learn to love Azariyah, the city I will protect as a ranger." He shrugged. "Of course I already love it, so it's probably overkill, but you know my parents."

"I do know your parents. But you don't seem too upset."

Jabari thought about it. That was complicated. He felt unsettled, worried about Gavi leading, nervous about being left behind. But Tomas was right, he wasn't too upset.

"It's easier to go along with my parents than to fight them," he said.

"So you came to my workshop," Tomas said, and he raised an eyebrow at Jabari again.

"Yes," was all Jabari said, and Tomas shook his head, but he was quiet after that.

Jabari continued to load the kiln, then filled it with red rock fuel, muttering the fire words over the rocks to ignite them. The work was duller without Isika there, and Tomas's implication began to push its way into Jabari's brain, forcing him to think about his true motives for choosing this work-shop as the place he was working. He knew that Isika was part of it. He had never truly considered just what an art pottery was until he heard her raving about it. He went to knead clay, sighing at the sack that needed to be done before the end of the day.

Yes! Of course he came for her. He wanted to get to know the girl who would be queen, to see if she was someone he could get along with even when they weren't fighting or running for their lives.

And those things were true. But it was also true that today Isika wasn't here, and he was itchy and irritable, bored with pots, uninterested in talking to the other apprentices. He glanced up from the clay he was pummeling and caught the older man's eyes. Almost as if he knew what Jabari was thinking, Tomas grinned at him. Jabari was shocked, Tomas was stone-faced even when he was having a good time.

"Finish that last batch and you can go for the day," Tomas said. "You must have lots to do to get ready for the ceremony."

Jabari wedged the clay twice as fast, turning it and pushing down with his palms to work the bubbles out. He wondered again about Tomas. The master potter was known for being a hard teacher, relentless in his passion for the perfect pot, and unwilling to take on apprentices who didn't already show skill or at least passion for the craft.

And yet Tomas had taken Isika as an apprentice. She also had no experience, though her gifting made up for that. And then he had taken Jabari into the workshop, even knowing Jabari didn't really care about pottery, at least in the same way Isika did. Was it because of Jabari's parents, his connections? The other apprentices thought so. Some of them were against Jabari being there and weren't quiet about the fact that he wouldn't be if his parents weren't the rulers of Maween. But was it really that? Or something else?

Their land was changing, now that Isika was back, and things were at once more hopeful, with a queen in their future, and more challenging, as the Great Waste seemed to grow stronger. Poison crept in quickly—whispers of it even into the city itself. The healers struggled with patients they couldn't seem to cure, and poison walls were stronger. Maybe Tomas, quiet and obsessed as he was in his small domain, could feel the world changing too. Maybe he sensed Isika's need for support and the way that Jabari could help her, if he could be a friend to her.

Jabari shook his head as though he had come out from under deep water. He put the clay away in its stone pot, hung up his apron, and paused at the door to wave goodbye to Tomas.

"Are you coming to the ceremony?" he asked Tomas, interrupting the apprentice who was asking the master potter for instructions. The apprentice frowned in disapproval. Jabari winked at him. All the apprentices except Isika took themselves far too seriously.

Tomas snorted, barely looking up from the pot he was etching to talk to Jabari *or* the apprentice.

"What do *you* think?" he asked in response to the question.

"Yes, you're right, never mind. But then, I wouldn't have thought you'd come to Isika's party either."

"I go out if Teru and Dawit will be there," he said. "If not, well, Isika has plenty of other people looking out for her."

If it was meant as a warning, Jabari didn't need it. He looked out at the valley spread before the door, rising up to where he could see the tip of the palace shining over everything.

"I wouldn't be so sure of that," he said. "I think she needs all the allies she can get."

Tomas did look at him then. "Expecting trouble, are you?"

"Let's just say that after her last foray into an enemy city, I'm shocked that we've had this much peace at all."

"It must be hard to always be on guard," Tomas said.

"It must be hard to always be aiming for perfection," Jabari said. And then, at the flash in Tomas's eyes, he realized he had gone too far. He took that as his cue to leave.

Ten steps out of the workshop, he breathed the scent of the trees and grass. He broke into a run, appreciating the burn in his sore muscles. Ah, he missed the road, and Gavi was leaving so soon. Seeing him go was going to be a lot harder than he let anyone know. And Aria was going. That had been decided by the elders and Aria's parents, and Jabari still didn't understand it.

"But why?" he had asked. "She's still sick."

"That may be, but the travel will be good for her," his mother told him. "They'll be steering clear of the most troubled areas—we'll send rangers for that— and she feels safe with Gavi in a way that her mother says she doesn't with anyone else. We don't like sending her so far from Gavi when she's feeling so bad. His healer gift helps her almost more than the healing tents do. It's not a long trip, either, they'll be back in three weeks."

"Gavi can heal her temporarily. This is madness."

"It's all madness, Jabari," his mother had said. "We're just beating back the madness as best we can. We don't know how to heal Aria's sickness either, but letting her sit and stew in it isn't helping, and she does much better in the outside air."

"But what if she gets injured further?"

"She won't!" his mother cried. "It's just a simple seeking trip! And we're trusting Gavi not to lead her into more danger."

It was a jab, a reference to the way he had led the seekers off course the last time they were all out together. Jabari had winced. But she was right, most likely. Gavi would be wiser and more conservative with his choices. Perhaps too conservative, without Jabari there to encourage him. Would he know when to move? Or would he always hold back?

Jabari ran and ran, trying to outrun his irritation, his questions about Gavi as a leader, his fear for Aria, his fear for the way he was already so tangled in Isika's future, his long day of working with dusty clay. And every step took him closer to the ceremony, where he would need to be vigilant if he wanted to be a good friend to Isika.

Chapter 4

Kital skipped ahead of Isika as she walked arm-in-arm with Auntie Teru. She could hardly believe that Auntie had agreed to come to the ceremony. As far as Isika knew, it had been eight years since Teru had traveled farther than the pottery workshop where she still sometimes went to visit her friend Tomas, and even that was rare. Auntie grew all of their food in her own kitchen garden. When she needed something she couldn't grow, first Uncle Dawit, and now Isika or Ben, bought it at the market. After their son, a ranger, died eight years before, in a fight on one of the borders, Auntie Teru had only felt safe at home.

Isika felt guilty for the effect of her last two big adventures on her foster mother. She knew Auntie didn't sleep very well when Isika was away—Ibba told her she sometimes found Auntie in the kitchen in the middle of the night. But Auntie Teru never said a word to hold her back. She encouraged Isika and she was a supportive mother. But she couldn't put herself in situations that were unfamiliar. The house was safe, beautiful, filled with food, filled with love. Other places were unpredictable. So Auntie kept her circle small and strong. And then there were days she didn't come out of her room, and when she did she looked as though she had been crying, but she always started a big pot of spice tea and a batch of flat bread.

Walking down to the palace, arm in arm, Isika kept stealing glances at Auntie, because she looked so beautiful. After braiding Isika's hair into countless tiny braids with gold threads running through them, she had disappeared into her room and emerged a while later in a gorgeous, embroidered robe. It was a different style from the beautiful robes Karah and Laylit normally wore, and it looked antique. It was covered with hand embroidery in shades of the sunset, in intricate shapes of flowers and animals.

Isika could have stared for hours, but after doing Ibba's hair in four long braids that she coiled around her little sister's head, she had to get dressed herself. She wore a tunic and loose pants like usual, but the indigo tunic was sleeveless, with cutouts on the shoulders. It shimmered as she walked, the gold beads sewed to its collar twinkling in the afternoon sunlight.

Auntie was taller than Isika, though everyone said Isika was still growing. Teru was the same height as her husband, statuesque, strong from her work in the garden, but soft and rounded as well. She was stunning in the embroidered robe, her bright *ser*, the color of a pink and orange flower, wrapped around her hair, up on her head, rich and shiny with scented oil.

Uncle Dawit walked on Auntie's other side. He stood tall, as he always did, but he glanced at Auntie every few minutes, until she said, "Dawit, you are killing me. Stop staring, will you? I'm not that nervous. You, on the other hand, have enough energy humming through you to light the palace without using red rocks."

Dawit smiled, rueful, but said, "You're so breathtaking I can't pull my eyes away," and then tripped over Kital, who wore his best clothes and ran in circles around them while they walked.

"You'd better pull your eyes away and watch your feet," Auntie said, but she squeezed Uncle's arm and dropped a kiss on his cheek. Uncle was as wiry as she was plump, a retired ranger who still spent time guarding the palace, an uneventful job because Maween was never attacked. It was difficult for unfriendly magic to find its way through the heavy, bright magic of the Shaper that surrounded its lands. Only the trickles of poison that created walls got through, and they never came as far as the palace.

"Kital," Isika said. "Calm down."

"I can't. I'm so excited!" he said. "You always get to come here but I never do."

He wasn't wrong, but there was no way a five-year-old could understand what a mixed blessing it was to be here. Isika loved the palace and its beauty. But she didn't love being involved in palace things, in the heaviness of the thoughts and the elders and their eyes.

She sighed now, as they drew close to the palace steps, then blinked and smiled. An enormous black bird, half the size of a man, perched on a pillar beside the steps to the sprawling white stone palace. When the bird shifted its wings, deep red and purples glinted from every feather, glowing in the late afternoon light.

"Keethior," Isika said. "How wonderful. Where have you been? I haven't seen you in a long time."

"You haven't needed me. And anyway, I don't answer a human's questions about my whereabouts."

Isika's smile grew. The bird was one of the Othra, ancient, magical creatures that spoke and appeared at times when the Maweel needed them. Last year, Keethior had declared himself to Isika as her personal servant, and then spent every possible moment making sure she knew that didn't mean he was at her beck and call.

It's good to see you, friend, she told him in her mind speech.

And you, he answered. *Although I hate these large human gatherings.*

"Even the singing?" she asked aloud. He gave the Othra equivalent of a sniff.

"I like the singing," he said. "Is young Benayeem singing today?"

"Yes," she said. "Ibba too. They're already here. I've barely seen them this week. They've been practicing for ages."

"None of them practice as much as our teachers made us study," Auntie said, as they walked up the stairs to the palace doors. "Back when the queen was here, we practiced all day, every day, for weeks on end before a ceremony. But I'm telling you just how old I am, aren't I?"

"You're eternally young, Auntie," Isika said.

The guards bowed a little deeper than normal when they reached the top step. She smiled at them, then inhaled as the palace reached out to her. It had always responded to Isika in a way she could feel: an embrace, a settling of stones, a sigh. More recently she had felt the palace's sense of welcome singing around her whenever she was in the large, beautiful building. Every crevice and alcove, the carved details in the white stone, the paintings on the walls, they hummed at her as she walked down the long halls under the gentle arches.

She knew it was because she was the heir, World Whisperer, the link between the Shaper and the Maweel, the one who could call the earth back into rightness, all of that. But today the feeling was much stronger. She felt as though she had stepped into something as unlike air as water, though there was no danger of drowning. If anything, she was lighter, taller, ready to face the ceremony she had been ever-so-slightly dreading, especially since she had heard Aria's hurtful words the day before.

The air seemed to bend for her, warmth spread into her from the places her feet touched the palace floor as she walked. She looked around in wonder, and Keethior gave a chirping call and flew ahead of them, into the great room.

Isika stopped. She turned to look at Auntie. Even the warmth of the palace couldn't take away the trepidation she felt at walking into that room. The day was a precipice, a moment of turning she wouldn't be able to revoke. She was afraid.

"Come, young one. Do I have to be the one to pull you in?" Auntie smiled into her face, and Isika read so much love in the lines around her eyes that she took a breath and reached out to grab Kital's hand. She thought about Ibba, singing today. Her lilting, soaring voice was one of the most beautiful things Isika had ever heard, and keeping that at the front of her mind, Isika walked into the great room as the palace guards bowed low on either side of the doors.

THE FIRST THING she saw was the Othra on their pillars. Keethior wasn't at court regularly, so he didn't have his own pillar, but Nirral, Efir, and Eemia, the three Othra she knew well from previous adventures, all stood on their pillars, facing the door. Keethior perched on a round table near the aisle that led to the platform at the front of the room, where the elders sat. Isika saw a servant eying the giant bird, possibly wondering whether he could dare to shoo away an Othra who was shedding small feathers on some of the better furniture.

Just try it, thought Isika, smiling to herself. Even she, the supposed master of this giant, unruly bird, wouldn't dare try to make him do anything he didn't feel like doing. The servant apparently came to the same conclusion, because Keethior continued to perch on the table, undisturbed by him or anyone else.

She knew she was distracting herself with these thoughts, so she walked a little taller, held onto Kital's hand and Auntie's arm a little tighter, and walked through the crowds of people, nodding at people she recognized or knew, to the raised area where the four regents sat, the highest elders in the land. Other people in the room also held the title of elder, but it was these four who made most of the decisions, or were responsible for the unfolding of the decisions that the group of them made.

They were regents, running the kingdom, because Isika's grandmother had been kidnapped over thirty years ago and Isika, her heir, was still on probation, being measured by these very intimidating people before her. Andar and Laylit, both tall and striking, their skin as black as a night with no moon, their robes stiff and sparkling. They both offered friendly smiles when they looked at her, and that surprised her. Ivram stood and walked to Isika, kissing her on both cheeks gently, but Karah came and took both of Auntie's hands in her own. With a shock, Isika realized that in the past it would have been common for Auntie to be here.

"Welcome, Elder," Karah said. "It is so good for our hearts to see you here."

Isika gave a little start of surprise. Elder? She turned to Dawit, who stood just behind her, but he didn't look at her— all his attention was focused on Teru. Teru bent forward and kissed Karah on both cheeks and then her forehead.

"My heart has come home," Auntie said, in the traditional greeting, but with a catch in her voice. "You know my love has been with you all these years. Now I have finally found a big enough reason to come to the palace again."

Isika ducked her head. She felt unworthy to be that reason. She knew the sorrow that Auntie felt over losing her son; she had felt the same sorrow after losing her sister and her mother. She understood the safety of Auntie's house. But they had all lost something in losing Auntie, she realized.

She looked around the room, already close to tears before the ceremony even started. There was such a stir over Auntie coming back that no one had even greeted her fully, despite the fact that this day was in her honor. She didn't mind; she was thankful for the time to look around and get used to where she was.

The great room was gorgeous and imposing, with a row of white stone columns on either side of the room, leading to the raised platform on the far end. Beyond the columns were tables and rugs scattered throughout, with low seating areas formed by low tables surrounded by cushions woven in deep, rich colors. The walls were painted in miniature scenes from the history of Maween. Isika's grandmother and her ancestors before her were featured in several of the frames. Isika still hadn't fully studied them, as she wasn't in the great room very often. But they were familiar to her now, and she felt the welcome of the palace settle around her like a cloak as she walked with Auntie toward one of the low seating areas.

Jabari approached from where he had been standing with Gavi and Ivy. He wore a brilliant white shirt, and blue pants embroidered with a pattern that looked like hundreds of small linked triangles. Isika had never seen him looking so formal, and she felt a little tremor of nerves. *It's only Jabari*, she told herself. Still, she couldn't help noticing how tall he was, how the lines of his jaw were strong and his face was intense. *He looks like a king*, she thought, and she felt a familiar longing that he would rule Maween after his parents, instead of her. Jabari looking formal made it feel as though this whole ceremony was very, very serious, but then he grinned as he came closer, his smile brilliant in his face, his eyes crinkling at the edges. She found herself returning the smile as he transformed back into her friend Yab from the pottery workshop and two intense journeys. He turned to give Auntie Teru a hug.

"Honestly, young one, if everyone is going to make such a fuss about this, I'm going home," Auntie grumbled, but Isika heard the pleasure in her voice.

"You look beautiful, Auntie," Jabari said. He looked at Isika. "Happy birthday again, Isika."

It was nearly time to begin and the choir came to stand directly in front of the platform. Benayeem and Ibba there, standing with the others. Isika waved at them, and at her friend Deto. Ibba was nervous, Isika could tell, because she couldn't stop moving when she was nervous. She hopped on one foot until the choir leader motioned for her to be still.

They sang, and goosebumps erupted all over Isika's arms as the voices blended together and rang in the huge room.

For the endless sea
For the fragrant night

For the breath of new life
We thank you, Oh Uncreated One
Oh Shaper of forever
A circle that never ends
Running forever in time
For sun and shade, fire in the stars
Our hands at rest and at work
For love in the eyes of the Maweel
We thank you
Nenyi, Nenyi, Shaper of forever
Our hearts have come home.

Isika heard Ibba's sweet voice soaring through the other voices and she thought the music would pick her up off her feet, but somehow they stayed on the floor. Tears threatened, but she smiled and looked at the pillars that disappeared into the distant ceiling.

Oh Nenyi, she thought.

The song finished, and she looked around, wondering what came next. They hadn't practiced any of this. The beads in her braids clicked softly as she turned to look at Ivram. He nodded at her and gestured for her to come forward. She let go of Kital's hand as she walked to stand beside the choir.

She stood before Andar and Laylit, and Laylit held something in her hand. Isika tried and failed to get a look at it, before Andar reached out to put both his hands on her shoulders. He was slightly shorter now than Jabari, she realized, looking into his face, not very far above hers. She was distracting herself again and she forced herself to concentrate.

"You are our beloved queen's granddaughter, and we honor you at your sixteenth birthday, for now you are grown and ready to walk as a woman. We honor you for the future, when you will learn more of your grandmother's ways, we honor you despite your coming to us as a stranger. Here is your first circlet, which you will wear when you join us in hearing those who have need of help in our lands."

Isika took a step back. *What?* She thought this was just a simple recognition of her birthday. Was something changing? Why had no one told her? Laylit was moving toward her with her hands stretched out—Isika could see now that the thing she held was a silver circlet much like the ones that Andar and Laylit wore, but this one not much thicker than a thread —and placed the circlet gently on her head. It moved like a living thing on Isika's forehead, adjusting itself until it sat perfectly on her brow. She reached up to touch it and felt a buzz of magic like the earth magic that sang through the trees.

She opened her mouth, because everyone seemed to expect her to say something, ready to give a speech of thanks when there was a commotion at the door. She felt a faint buzz of relief to be saved from speech giving, and turned with everyone else to see who was there.

A guard ran into the room, shouting. "Fire on the plains! Fire on the plains! Elders! It's huge, you can see the light and smoke from the city."

Instantly the room buzzed with groups of people talking

and pushing. The noise grew. Isika left the front to look for Teru, reaching her and finding her foster mother staring at Uncle Dawit in horror. She looked like she wasn't breathing.

"This... is, oh no, it cannot be. This is his work." That was all Isika heard before Teru fainted.

Chapter 5

After the guard's panicked announcement, the room became unbearable for Benayeem. The group of people turned into a seething mass of thoughts and emotions, and his gift caused him to hear them all as strands of sounds and music, all different, all insistent. Any large place with a lot of emotional people was hard for him, but a closed room with over a hundred people was excruciating. He wanted to curl up on the floor with his hands over his ears.

Instead he did what he had learned. He forced all the sounds, the clamor of music and the beating of drums into a room in his mind, and shut the door. They were quieter, though he could still hear them. He listened through the door in his mind for one specific, dear thread of sound. Auntie Teru.

Benayeem had not been at all sure that she should come today, knowing as he did the battle she fought every day. Teru was the bravest person he knew. She spent her life taking care of them while fighting a fear so intense that he could hear it clearly. On hard days, when she went to cry in her bedroom, he could hear the sound of the terror that overwhelmed her, the drums, the discordant, driving music that taunted her. Sounds of death and hopelessness. He knew what she had battled just to get here today.

He found her music through the crowd now, sounds like nothing he had heard from her before. Stark fear. He pushed through the crowd to get to her. By the time he got there, she had fainted.

"We need to get her home," he said to Isika and Uncle Dawit. Uncle Dawit's face looked gray and stricken, deep lines furrowed into his brow. Isika also looked worried, but she nodded and put her arm around Teru's shoulder. Auntie began to wake, her eyelids fluttering, and Isika bent close.

"Let's go home, Auntie," she said. "But we need to walk, so I'm going to do what I can to take the fear away, is that okay?"

Auntie nodded, but shut her eyes tight. Tears rolled out of the corners of her eyes, making tracks through the deep wrinkles in her face. Benayeem felt sick to his stomach. Dawit went to Auntie's other side, and he and Isika supported Teru as they walked out of the great room, down the corridor to the door that led outside the palace. Ben called to Kital and Ibba and they came quickly, puzzled looks on their faces. As they passed through the crowd, people kept running by, faces tense with worry. Jabari ran past, glancing once at them, concern evident on his face. He must have decided they had it under control, because his face cleared and he kept running, out into the night to help with the fires.

Benayeem wished he could go as well, but he dismissed the thought almost as soon as it came. There was no way the elders or rangers would allow them to be there. He walked behind Isika, Auntie, and Uncle, feeling useless. He could hear the song inside Auntie changing as Isika worked to heal and protect her from the fear, drawing magic up from the ground to do it. The way his sister could bring Nenyi's life magic out of the ground and offer it was incredible to Ben. Isika could heal people, heal the seas, the land. She was a mystery.

Dawit and Isika put Auntie in her favorite chair when they got home. Uncle wrapped blankets around her while Isika went to put a kettle on the fire, to make her some spice tea. Soup was simmering over the red rock fire already, their dinner for late in the evening, after the ceremony. Dawit ladled a bowl of it and carried it over to Teru's chair, where he began spooning the broth into his wife's mouth. She took several sips, sighed, and took a deep breath.

"All right, all right," she said. "I need to finish this batch of flat bread. Help me up, would you?"

They watched, worried, as she stood on shaky legs. She squared her shoulders, nodded, and went to retrieve her bowl of dough, rolling out the flat bread that was part of nearly every meal in Maween. Ben knew this routine well, having watched Auntie do it many times before. It was how she gathered herself back together, her hands in the dough, shaping and flattening it. She would be all right.

Across the room, Isika rounded her eyes at Ben and gestured for him to join her in the courtyard. He sighed as he went to her, recognizing her music as the intense sounds that meant she was plotting something.

"We need to go down to the fire," she said. "We need to be there."

"They'll never let us go," Ben said, already shaking his head.

"We're not going to ask permission, silly." She crossed her arms over her fancy clothes, glaring at him. "Listen. Right before Auntie fainted, she said, 'this is his work.'"

Ben stopped shaking his head, remembering the strange, intense fear he had heard from Auntie.

"Whose work?"

"I don't know, but it must be magic that's familiar to her."

"She was very afraid of it, or him, whoever he is." He looked up at the darkening sky.

"We have to go. Ben, you know I have to help."

Ben looked back at her, listening to the drums that beat an insistent rhythm in what he was coming to think of as her World Whisperer music.

He could see a pattern forming. Isika said she wanted to settle in and enjoy a normal life, but the minute there was trouble, her magic hounded her, telling her it was her duty to protect and save the Maweel people. Since the day they had arrived in Maween, there always seemed to be some trouble or another. Ben didn't think his sister would ever be able to settle down and be normal, not as long as there was a Maween to protect.

THEY WALKED BACK DOWN the hill toward the palace. Ben had been willing to concede this much. They would go to the center of action and find out what was happening with the fires in the plains. Ben knew Isika still had other plans brewing, that most of all she wanted to go and see if she could discover who Auntie was talking about. Who made Auntie this afraid?

Benayeem hoped someone at the palace would stop Isika from going any farther. He shivered as they walked. The night was eerie, the trees were outlined in light, and Ben realized that the whole western sky was glowing. He stared as they walked, entranced by the orange color in a sky that should be black and filled with stars, so distracted that he crashed into Isika when she stopped walking.

"Ben," she hissed, "pay attention. Look up ahead, what's happening at the palace?"

They had reached the long, tree-lined street that led to the palace. It was buzzing with people, most of them unfamiliar to Ben. As they watched, at least forty men and women gathered at the base of the steps. The elders stood together on the top step, and as Ben watched, Ivram kissed his wife, Karah, and walked down the stairs to join the people there.

"Rangers," Isika breathed.

They had traveled with a few rangers on their first journey with the Maweel, back when Kital had been kidnapped. But Ben had never seen so many together before. The rangers were mostly very tall, men and women dressed in dark gray traveling clothing, so that they blended into the night sky. They wore their *sers* wrapped around their heads, bows on their backs and long knives in glinting sheaths on their waists. Among the dark-skinned Maweel, Ben saw one or two Rescued Maweel with pale faces glimmering beneath their *sers*. The music of the rangers was strong and orderly, mostly unafraid, intent and brave.

"Andar is making a speech," Ben said to his sister.

"Andar is always making a speech," Isika muttered, but they walked near the little crowd that hovered at the edges of the ranger unit, so they could hear what Andar was saying.

"As always, Rangers," Andar called, voice ringing, hands spread. "We fight poison, not men, so avoid bloodshed if at all possible. This fire reeks of poison, so be on your guard; there is great evil behind this. Fight the fire to protect our farmers and protect Azariyah! And beware," he added. "Let us not lose anyone tonight, anyone at all. High Elder Ivram goes with you to battle the magic of the Great Waste. Those of you who are gifted this way, battle with him. The rest of you, fight the fire."

"How are they going to fight it?" Ben asked Isika in a whisper. She shushed him, listening hard.

"Jabari, Gavi! Deto!" Andar said. A little way away, three figures moved and in the light of the red rock torches, Ben saw his friends. "Go with the rangers, but hold back. Support them if they grow weary. Bring food and drink when they need it. This will be a long night's work." He turned to the side for a moment, and Ben could see tension in the way he held his head.

Benayeem felt his sister shift beside him, heard a slight change in the music that emanated from her, and braced himself.

"Uncle!" Isika called into the night, causing every ranger to turn and look at her, as well as Jabari and Gavi, standing close together. "I would like to go and support as well."

Andar's mouth formed into a line before he answered her.

"Absolutely not, Isika. You are the heir, and you are untrained. You will remain in your home until the fire is taken care of."

Isika's music trembled, then blared in a rush of sounds. "What?" she shouted. "Just now, during the ceremony, you put a circlet on my head. Does it mean nothing? Is it only for show?" Ben heard the crowd's hiss of indrawn breath and the unsteady music behind it. No one spoke to the First Elder that way. Even the World Whisperer should show more respect. He stepped on his sister's foot, but she nudged him away.

Andar's face was angry. "If it helps you to think of it like this, Isika, then certainly you may think of it as a show. It is not the circlet of a ruler, by any means, so you are, in effect, accountable to me. And as such, you will listen the way I expect my own sons to listen to me. Is that understood?"

Isika looked as though she had a lot more to say, but she clenched her jaw and folded her arms. "I understand," she said.

The music shifted as the rangers and observers sighed

and relaxed again. They turned their attention to Andar, who dismissed them.

Ben heard the angry music radiating from his sister. He knew they weren't done for the night, that they were now locked into something he wouldn't escape easily, but he couldn't take his attention off the rangers. He watched them stride away, faces lifted, bows on their backs, toward the fire that threatened the plains and the harvest. Torchlight glinted in many sets of eyes, and some of them glanced their way, full of curiosity for the girl who dared to shout at the High Elder.

Ben felt a strange longing as he watched them. One of the rangers spoke a short command, and in unison they broke into a run. Rangers fought the more dangerous magic, broke it, restored the lands in places where people were stolen and lakes were poisoned. And their music was ordered and gentle, not the music of those who loved harm or violence. Not chaotic, the way his could be sometimes. Since he had arrived in Maween, Benayeem had only ever wanted to be a singer, but watching the rangers run, he felt something new; a desire to protect Maween, to be strong and ordered like them. He wondered if he could be a ranger. He wanted to see how they fought the fire.

So, when Isika turned to him and said, "We're taking our horses," he didn't argue. Together they slipped off toward the horse barn, and the last thing Ben saw before they left the light of the the palace steps was Jabari watching them go.

Chapter 6

They ran to the horse barn, Ben trailing after his fast, determined sister while he silently dreaded the night ahead. Wind and Night, their horses, were waiting for them at the fence. Ben knew Isika had been calling to them in her mind as they ran. He reminded himself that he wanted to see how the rangers fought the fire, even as his stomach dropped with anticipation of the trouble they were going to be in.

Where were the Othra? Where had they disappeared to, when the guard came in and announced the fire? Keethior would be a huge comfort right now, but he was nowhere to be seen.

Ben stood with the two horses while Isika went to get the saddles, listening to their music as they tossed their heads and danced away from the glow in the sky. Panicky notes were threaded through their calming song. Ben loved to listen to the music of animals; so much more than merely peaceful. It was like a clear pond. The notes didn't tumble over one another in a web of sound, the way human music did. The sounds were distinct and clear, different for every kind of animal, and within the types, different for individuals.

But the horses were clearly afraid. Isika came around the corner, carrying the saddles, and Ben told her what he was hearing.

"Are you sure you can calm them?" he asked. "This is a lot of poison."

Isika furrowed her brow. She turned and held her hand out to her tall, gray horse, Wind, who walked to her and laid his muzzle in her hand. Immediately his music changed. The panicky notes disappeared, and he whuffled a sigh.

"I think so," she said, stroking his nose. "If there is trouble with the horses, though, we can come right back."

Ben nodded. Isika reached out to his black horse, Night, calming her. They saddled up with the cloth saddles the Maweel used, mounted, and were soon on their way, heading in the direction of the enormous glow. The fire was outside the city, and Ben was surprised by how far they had to go, considering how huge the ominous light was. He shuddered to imagine a fire any closer. They crossed the long meadow that took them on a roundabout way to the north road, past fields and farms Ben had never seen before. Isika seemed deep in thought, quiet as she rode.

The color of the sky was like nothing Ben had experienced, orange and deep purple, glowing as though it were alive. He heard tendrils of deep, disturbing music, that seemed to be coming from the smoke itself. His stomach hurt.

They drew close to a farm and a little stand of trees, and just beyond, the first sight of the flames themselves, like a slap in the face. Ben reeled from it, tears springing to his eyes.

"Isika," he murmured, but she was ahead, she didn't hear him, so he followed, hoping to call to her, to warn her. There was a roaring, the flames and the wind were loud, and underneath the fire, the music he had been trying to escape his whole life. Why was it so familiar? Ben didn't understand. He needed to stop and think, but Isika's horse was far ahead, and Night needed to be in Isika's presence, the only thing that could calm the horses when they were this close to poison. He pushed his horse to catch up.

Just beyond the next stand of trees, Isika halted. Beyond was a wall of flame, and Ben saw the dark silhouettes of the rangers working at the fire, but he couldn't tell how, because his vision was blurring, lights crackling at the edges of his sight.

"Isika," he croaked, and this time she heard him, her face full of worry as she turned to him.

"Your room, Ben," she said. "Put the sounds in your room."

He shook his head, frantically, eyes wide. This was not that; this was something different. He had enough sense, as his vision swam again, to slide down the side of his horse before he fell off. He leaned against Night's side, but the horse was skittish and danced away from Ben as though his hands were sparks. Isika reached out to try and calm the horses, and Ben couldn't help it, he crumpled on the ground, cursing his weakness as he did.

Then all was fire and noise. He heard horrible, discordant music. Wave after wave of sound and memory hit him, things he hadn't remembered since he was a small boy.

He saw bright colors, white sand. Dunes that stretched until forever. Hands, reaching for him. Saying goodbye to his mother, never enough time. Pain as blow after blow hit the backs of his legs. A caning, he remembered, huddled on the ground. Watching another slave boy being caned. Crying in his bed. Sleeping in a tangle of other boys. Plucked from sleep in the night to scrub floors after the king had a party. The king! The Desert King. Ben had been one of his slaves. He remembered. Remembered the face of the man he was never supposed to look at, but couldn't help seeing. Then, even then, Ben had heard the music, had looked around its source as it taunted him and made him crazy.

The king kicking a slave away. Dropping more wine on the ground and ordering the woman caned for clumsiness. Ben sitting in the corner, exhausted, trying to keep from falling asleep.

"And this one?" The king saying, pointing at Ben. Dread and terror. "What will we do with this one? Bring him here."

Hands again, pulling him from under his arms, dragging him across the floor to the king. Ben limp with fear, the horrible music growing louder, filling his mind.

"What is he doing? What's wrong with him."

"This one is always afraid, Brightness."

"Boy? Boy?" Lying with his face on the floor, unable to look up.

"Worthless. He'll be a cleaner all of his life. What a waste."

And then, the man who once again plucked him from sleep. But this time, no more scrubbing, only a quick walk into the women's quarters, where perfumed smells came from every corner and there was his mother. Walls that billowed with fabric, sounds unlike any he'd heard. Sounds of sorrow and beauty. His mother, her beautiful face. Running to him, holding him close.

A quick intake of breath from her, a tight squeeze, and then her face, scared and gaunt. Her round belly.

"You think we can make it?"

"Yes, lady," a voice, the voice of the man who had taken him from sleep. "We will go at night. I know someone who will help us get out."

Behind his mother's robe, the girl, his sister, someone he had only seen a handful of times. Her eyes big in her face, her music soothing, even then. Rounded cheeks, happy eyes. A fierce stab of jealousy. She lived with their mother. And he had scrubbed floors under the eye of the terrifying king. His mother held another sister; a sleeping toddler. *Family,* he thought, and the word was strange in his mind.

They left through a secret door in the walls of the city. Then, the desert. For months and months, the desert. Sand and heat, night cold. The infinite sky. Happiness.

The desert was clear of poisonous sounds, and he was with his mother. He learned to lock away the memories of the city, of pain, of the cruel king. He wanted to be friends with his sister, who seemed to be afraid of nothing, so he locked away his jealousy, too. He stayed close to his mother, touching her at all times, if he could, so nothing could ever pull him away from her again. Her face, smiling down at him. Gently tugging his hand from her robe so she could adjust the little sister on her back.

Another memory, then. The sand rolling down. The man saying farewell. The little tent. The four of them, alone. Ben's perfect happiness.

"Benayeem," a voice called. "Ben, come back."

He heard Isika but didn't want to follow the sounds of her voice. He didn't want to leave his mother there, in the desert, but it was too late because his eyes opened a crack and she was gone, her face disappearing from sight, and someone else's face was very close. It took several heartbeats to understand where he was. The sounds were so loud, the music of his nightmares, the fire licking at the edges of his vision. But the music was muffled, he realized as he came back to where he was. Isika. She was holding onto him, holding the music away.

Benayeem remembered. He wasn't a five-year-old boy anymore. He wasn't helpless. His mother was long gone and he was a singer. He was nearly fifteen and he was taller than his foster father. He had learned to control the terror and fear.

He took a deep, shaky breath.

"What happened?" Isika asked. Her eyes were huge, her

mouth a line in her face. "You were talking, you were calling out to Mother..."

He shook his head once, hard, focusing on pushing the sounds back.

Ben saw how shaken she was, and the firelight reflecting in her eyes. He collected the fear, the sense of helplessness, the longing for his mother, and he put all of it into the room he had built in his mind. He sat up.

"This is the magic of the Desert King," he said.

She stared at him. "What? How do you know?"

"I think I was one of his slaves, in the Desert City, when I was a small boy."

"What? Didn't you live with us?"

"You really don't remember?"

"I've told you that a thousand times... no I don't remember. You know I wanted you to tell me, because I can barely remember anything. It's all... blank. Like an empty wall."

He was silent, looking at her. He knew now, why he refused to remember, all those times she begged him to talk about it. It was the misery beneath it all, the fact that she had been with their mother always, and he living with a lot of other little boys, beaten for mistakes, always in the presence of the terrible king. Deep under everything, the pain of those days could still break him. Somehow, deep inside, the jealousy and anger still lived. His pain had nothing to do with her, he knew it, she had barely been older than him. So he had pushed it away, so the anger couldn't ruin the friendship they had formed, out there in the desert, playing with sticks and the baby goats of the nomads. They had been like little goats themselves. They had learned how to be friends.

"I remembered a lot," he said, "just now. I wasn't with you. I lived with the slave boys in the palace, and you lived somewhere else, with a lot of women and our mother."

He turned to look at the fire. "It doesn't matter now." Though his mind seemed to feel differently. "But this is his work. What does he want? Remember, the priests said they captured us for him. What does he want with us? Do you think he knows we escaped?"

Was all of it some wild plan to get back an escaped slave boy? But his voice, when he said Ben was only good for cleaning. Why would he care?

Isika stood, offering Ben a hand. He took it and stood beside her, feeling his strength coming back to him, feeling himself return. He was Benayeem the discerner, the gifted one. He had helped save them in the Worker City. He wasn't that same little boy, hearing the word, "worthless," echo in his head again and again, wondering why it mattered so much.

Just then, voices, nearby.

"Oh, you two, here? Really?"

He turned just in time to see the look on Jabari's face when Isika's full anger turned on him. The look returned Ben to himself, as did the sight of her stomping toward Jabari.

"Don't you dare say a word, Jabari, you hypocrite. You know we should be here."

Ben smiled.

Chapter 7

Isika looked into Jabari's face with as much indignation as she could dredge up, worried as she was. He looked back, not with anger, but a sort of resigned irritation that stung her more than anger would have.

"You brought your horses," he said, his voice flat. "To a fire."

"I can protect them," Isika said, bristling. "Ask the horses, if you want. They're doing fine."

Jabari put a hand on Wind's muzzle, lifting his eyebrows at the horse as he spoke in animal speech from mind to mind. He didn't shield it from Isika, so she could hear his question, as well as her horse's response.

Is she right? he asked, his thoughts gentle and probing. *Are you okay?*

Wind blew into Jabari's hand. *We follow her,* he replied. Isika's face grew hot. She heard what her horse wasn't saying. The animals were suffering, pushing back fear to follow her.

"I can protect them," she said again, aware that she sounded petulant. She crossed her arms over her chest, refusing to back down, glaring into Jabari's face, daring him to send her home. He watched her for a moment. His mouth twitched upward, then he held out his hands, palms up.

"Ivram is here," he said finally. "You're not going to be able to change his mind, even with your fiercest Isika face."

"Maybe he won't find us," she said, relieved that she wasn't going to have to fight Jabari. She knew she needed to be here, felt it deep within. She was pulled in a way she hadn't been since... well, never mind, it happened often. But she listened to the feeling when it came, and it hadn't led her wrong.

"You might be underestimating her Isika face," Ben said, his voice wry.

Jabari turned to smile at him, and flinched. Benayeem's eyes were rimmed with red, as though he hadn't slept in days. Isika balled her hands into fists, wishing she could undo the memories that had finally come back to him.

"What happened to *you?*" Jabari asked Ben. "You look like you saw a mud demon."

"I'm just afraid of Isika's face," Ben quipped, avoiding Isika's surprised look at his evasion, "like you." He was silent for a moment. "Wait. What on earth is a mud demon?"

"You don't know— well, I'll tell you another time," Jabari said. "I always forget how little you two know about life in Maween."

"Yes, do that. Sounds like a story for a smaller fire, like a camp fire," Ben said.

Behind the forced lightness of Ben's tone, Isika heard him struggling not to fall apart. She turned to him, catching his hand.

"Ben—" she said.

"Oh, you're not going to send me home," he said. "Don't even think about it. And I'm immune to your Isika face." She looked at him for several moments, then shrugged and turned away.

"Come on then," Jabari said. "You can see how rangers fight fire."

The light grew brighter as they came closer to the fire. Jabari walked ahead, Isika and Ben just behind him, leading their horses. Isika clung to Ben's hand, trying to send him waves of healing. She sensed he was too exhausted to receive much. He squeezed her hand gently and let go as they got to a narrow place and he had to drop behind with Night.

Isika kept twisting to look back at her brother. His forehead was furrowed with anxiety and pain. She didn't like seeing his face that way. It reminded her of how he looked all the time before they left the Worker village. What had he heard? What did he mean, he was a slave boy? Was it true, that they hadn't lived together in that other place? She couldn't remember a time without Ben in her life, but then, she could remember almost nothing before they had left the city. Only bits and pieces, colors, smells. Her mother. Oh, her mother. Had Ben been separated from their mother? Tears sprang to her eyes as she tried to imagine it.

But it was true that the Desert King had been looking for them. He had tried to trap them in Batta, the Worker City, by kidnapping Jerutha. Isika hadn't heard a lot about the Desert King, but she didn't think he would be happy that his slave had escaped. He was looking for Ben. She grew angry, thinking about it. She would protect Ben with her life if she had to.

They arrived at the fire and she gasped.

The plains opened up before them, and where it should have been dark under the night sky, the fire had turned the horizon red and orange, the sky grimy brown and gray, obscuring the stars. The fire felt malevolent to Isika, like a living thing growling with hatred. It was a peculiar shape, square at the edges, straight lines along the top, like a wall of heat rushing toward them. They were near the river and she felt a sudden urge to jump in, hide herself under the water, away from the searching, angry eye of the fire. She turned her attention to the rangers and drew a breath.

They stood in a line, shoulders strong against the fire. She had seen rangers before, of course, when a few of them accompanied her and the others to find Kital and rescue him from the sea people. She had even seen a ranger die, poisoned by terrible waters, so she knew they weren't invincible, but now, watching them, she had the feeling that they were stronger than anything she had ever known. They were like the myths of giant beings sent from Nenyi, to roam and protect the earth. Rumors Dawit shrugged off every time Isika tried to ask about them.

The rangers stood with their hands out, and as Isika watched the man nearest her, water from the river rushed toward him in a long tongue, touched his hands, then hurled itself away and threw itself on the fire. Where the water touched the fire, it faltered, hissing. Isika yelped, then clapped her hands. Jabari smiled at her.

As she listened more closely, she realized the rangers were singing. She walked closer to hear better, stopping only when Jabari held his arm out to keep her from going any farther. The singing surrounded her, and Isika was close enough to see the sweat dripping down the weathered face of the nearest ranger. He was tall, taller even than Jabari, with deep black skin and a touch of gray at his temples.

He stood like a rock, holding his arms out. The scene took her breath away. The line of rangers, arms outstretched, water leaping from the river to meet them, rushing back to hurl itself at the angry fire. The mighty sound of their singing. Isika caught a sense of the whole world, the battling forces, the heat of the evil and the cool water of Nenyi, the rangers at peace, collected and strong. She heard a whisper, caught a sense of Nenyi himself, a cool presence she had only felt in dreams. She turned her face up to it, heard her brother singing beside her, the same song the rangers were singing. She stepped forward, ready to join them, but an angry voice broke into her reverie.

"Isika! What are you doing? Jabari, son of Andar! What in Nenyi's world are you thinking, bringing them here?" Ivram strode toward them, as mighty as a ranger himself, his staff in hand. It glowed, the way it always did if Isika was near.

"Uh, oh," Jabari murmured beside her.

"It's okay," she whispered back to him, "Ivram will let me stay. He understands."

"Not this time, I don't think," Jabari said as Ivram came near and they could see the terrifying look on his face. "He looks like he's going to beat us with that staff of yours." He coughed and stepped forward. "Fancy meeting you here, Uncle!" he said in a cheerful voice, smiling widely.

"This is not the time for play, Jabari," Ivram said. "Take these two back to the city immediately."

The grin disappeared from Jabari's face. "Me? I'm here to support the rangers. And I didn't bring Isika and Ben here. They came on their own."

"You should have sent them back when you first saw them."

Jabari looked like he had more to say, but he deflated, nodding. His voice was quiet when he spoke again. "You have to see how I have no good place to stand, Uncle. It's either your anger or hers, and she's World Whisperer."

Ivram's face softened. "When Isika is queen, you can obey her wishes every time. But she is still guarded by us, preparing for that day. Mugunta wants to kill her before it comes to pass, can't you see?"

"I'm standing right here," Isika broke in, feeling distinctly uncomfortable at the talk of Jabari "obeying" her. "I can hear you. But you don't need to worry yourself about taking us back, Jabari, because I'm not going."

Jabari sighed, dropping his head into his hand. He took a step back as Ivram moved closer.

"You will go back to the city," Ivram said. He didn't

change his face, didn't threaten, didn't speak louder. But Isika felt his authority, she felt the staff glowing brighter. She heard a whisper of sadness from Nenyi as she and the second elder argued. But she couldn't give in. She couldn't.

BEFORE SHE COULD SAY it again, the wind shifted, sending a hot, malevolent gust of air toward them. It grew and grew and they all turned to look.

Isika saw something move in the upper corner of her vision, and she turned to see a shape plummet out of the sky in front of her, landing at her feet. It was Keethior. He landed, tall, feathers out with all reflected red and purple lights, brighter than ever in the glow of the fire.

"Leave, Isika," he said for everyone to hear. "Daughter, you must go now."

She had never heard him sound afraid before, and she flinched at the intensity in his words. There was pressure from the fire and the two wisest beings in her life. The rangers' song grew louder and Isika bowed her head, listening, knowing she could pull water from the river too. She could help, she knew how to do it.

Isika, Keethior said, this time in her head, so only she could hear. *You don't understand. This fire is for you, to trap and kill you. You need to go now, you must leave, flee, go to the city where it is safe!*

Okay, okay, Isika grumbled back at him. Beside her, Wind rippled his coat and blew, pawing at the ground. He felt the meaning from the bird, even if he didn't understand the words. She sent more calm to both the horses, feeling responsible, now, for all of it. The tired, straining rangers, the horses and their fear, Benayeem's collapse. Was it all to trap her? Why did her presence bring so much trouble?

"We'll go," she said, trying to make her voice sound gracious and like it was her own idea, rather than like she was being herded like one of the simple cattle on the outskirts of the city. "But you don't need to come, Jabari. We have horses and we know the way."

"No," Ivram said. "Jabari will go with you to make sure you reach the city safely."

Isika opened her mouth to protest again but another wind picked up, even hotter and more full of hate than before. The rangers had been advancing on the fire, putting it out steadily, during the conversation, but under the wind, their singing faltered. The wind plucked the water out of their hands and dried it instantly. Then the fire began to move oddly, forming tongues that rearranged themselves into shapes.

"What under Maween skies?" Jabari breathed.

Isika took a step closer to Ben and held his hand again. She reached out for that same whispery presence she had felt before, needing to be reassured by Nenyi. But she couldn't feel anything near except hatred. The air burned with the poison of the fire. And then there was a shift. She felt a call, like incense in the wind, not hatred but something that tried to pull her away from the others. The shapes of flame turned into letters, the letters formed a word, and the word was her name. *Isika.* She heard a gasp from many dry throats, a scream, a shout as people read her name in the poison flames. She heard a voice hoarsely calling her, shouting at her in her mind. *Isika! Isika!*

The voice was horrible, something from a nightmare. Ben cowered with his hands over his ears and she wanted to put her hands over her own ears, but she couldn't move. The rangers shouted with rage, then began singing more loudly than before. As one they took more water from the river, joining it until it looked like a great pond floating in the air, then they flung it at the fire.

And then Isika was on the ground, everything quiet as the light flickered and dimmed. The voice called her name, over and over, the air sucked the moisture from her mouth until she couldn't swallow. A huge wind roared and the last thing she knew was Jabari picking her up and flinging her over her horse's withers, jumping on behind her while Ivram shouted, "Ride, Jabari, ride!"

Chapter 8

When she woke, it was to magic, sparking like crazy. She was slumped against Jabari, on Wind, galloping down the road in a headlong rush. The trees stood on either side of the road like rangers, and for a moment Isika relaxed, her head fuzzy, feeling the sparks as a sort of pleasant buzz, before she remembered what had happened. She sat forward with a gasp, causing Wind to skip sideways, nearly stumbling as the horse realized she was awake.

"Wait—Isika, don't," Jabari said, but he didn't finish because they pulled up at the palace steps and Isika nearly threw herself off her horse, sliding down his flank, peering into his face to make sure he was all right. He shuddered with fear and exhaustion and she cupped his nose in her hands and blew on him, feeling the fear ease as his nostrils quivered at her smell. She was going to burn up with embarrassment. She had collapsed and Jabari had carried her home! They must all think of her as such a weakling.

Jabari dismounted more slowly, patting Wind's neck absently as he watched her.

"Are you okay?" he asked. "You were out for a long time."

Isika grimaced and shook her head. "I don't know," she muttered. "I don't understand what happened." She breathed quickly to keep tears from coming and Wind turned and lipped her shirt on the shoulder. She sighed. "I think I'll go home."

Jabari looked up at the sky suddenly. "Ivram said to wait for him," he said.

That couldn't be good, but since Isika had already defied enough orders for any night, she heaved a deep sigh and walked over to the palace steps. She nodded at the guards at the top of the stairs. Wind followed her, sniffing at her legs as she walked, then hovering above her as she sat down on one of the lower steps.

I'm okay, she told him. *Don't worry.*

The voice, he said. *It screamed for you. I was afraid for you.*

You heard it? She asked, stunned. *How did you hear it?*

It spoke our language, he said.

She stared at the horse.

"What?" Jabari asked. "I didn't hear what he said, what's the matter?"

"He... Wind said the horrible voice was using animal speech."

Jabari rubbed his forehead and pinched his lips together

before answering.

"Yeah," he said. "I thought so. I think we were the only ones there who could hear the voice, actually. We don't have many animal speakers left in Maween, you know."

"I didn't even realize I was hearing... and my name... in the flames." She looked at him, feeling sick to her stomach. He stared back at her, his eyes wide and troubled. "Who was that? What can it mean?" she asked, hoping he had some idea.

He shook his head, looking away. She saw that he had ashes caught in his short hair and smeared across his face. He shrugged, keeping his eyes trained on the road, watching.

"Here he comes," he finally said, and Isika looked up to see Ivram striding toward them, with Benayeem by his side, leading Night.

"Oh, desert sands and spines," she murmured.

"You'll be okay. He looks scarier than he is."

But Jabari must have underestimated how angry Ivram was.

"I'm taking your horse," he said when he reached them, his eyes blazing, his voice angrier than she'd ever heard. "You've shown that you're not responsible enough to have one."

Isika was on her feet in an instant.

"You can't take back something you gave me!" she said, clenching her teeth to keep from shouting.

What's wrong? Wind wanted to know.

He wants to take you from me, she told her horse, thoughtlessly.

There was a space of one breath, then Wind reared up on two legs, coming down on his front hooves hard, dangerously close to Ben's feet. He did it again and again, neighing in panic, shivering. Isika tried to speak to him, but she couldn't reach him. Night broke away from Benayeem and ran off toward the stables, and after a desperate look at Isika, Ben chased his horse.

Still Isika's horse reared and kicked, screaming wild horse screams. The noise brought people out of the palace and soon Andar, Karah, and Laylit were standing on the steps above them. Isika tried to calm her horse. He was beginning to tire, flecked with foam.

Wind... she said. *Wind, come back to me. He can't take you. He won't. I'm sorry. I'm sorry. Wind, lovely one, come back to me.*

She focused all the warmth and comfort she had within her and sent it to her horse, sending images of his stall, the horse meadow on a warm day. She showed him pictures of the two of them riding together over the small flowers that dotted the fields. Slowly, slowly, he settled, his coat still rippling. She went to where he stood, a few feet away, and laid her cheek on his sweaty shoulder. He sighed and twitched, then stopped pawing the ground, torn up now with his hoof marks. He sighed, shuddering, nearly asleep. Isika kept her face pressed against him. She was ashamed and exhausted, and didn't want to face the small crowd that included Gavi and Ivy now too.

"Isika!" Andar said. "What have you done?"

She turned, keeping her back against her horse, sending

him wave after wave of comfort. If Andar knew, if he had any idea how much the poison took out of her, how hard it was to see it, surely he wouldn't question her at times like this.

"I went to help with the fire," she said.

"You were told to remain," Andar said. "And once again you have endangered our people." He crossed his arms over his chest, looming from the upper steps so that Isika had to crane her head to look up at him. "What's more... I've had a report from some rangers who were at the fire. It seems that you are the one who has drawn this poison fire toward us. Tell us, Isika, why was your name in the flames?"

"How would she know that, Father?" Jabari broke in, his face turned up to his father. He came to stand next to Isika. She blinked up at him. In all the confusion, she hadn't realized he was still there beside her, not with all the others on the upper steps. "She's as confused as any of us."

"If I want your opinion, Son, I will ask for it," Andar said.

"Forgive me Father, but can't this wait?" Jabari persisted. With one hand he indicated the night, still hazy with smoke, the shivering horse beside Isika, the crowds of people who had gathered to watch the altercation. Ivram was half slumped over, the staff glowing brightly in his hand.

Isika was so tired she didn't know if she could even make it home. The whole world seemed to be filled with smoke; it was in her nose, her mouth. The flames with her name danced before her eyes. Tears came suddenly, and she ducked her head to hide them. Jabari took a step closer to her, not touching her, but standing with her. She drew in a breath at the kindness of it.

Andar seemed frozen, then it appeared as though he came back to himself. He shook his head, then stood tall and spoke again.

"No one will take your horse from you, Isika," he said, and she couldn't keep a sob back. Wind put his nose on her arm. "We'll discuss this at another time. For now, sleep. Sleep well, all of you. News from the rangers is that the flames have been put out. Sleep in peace."

Isika turned toward the horse barn, her feet heavy as stone, but Jabari put his hand on Wind's bridle, stopping them.

"I'll take him," he said. "You look like you're going to collapse. I'll get him dry and fed, don't worry."

She stared at him, then nodded, thankfulness welling up.

"He likes the *burta* grain in his trough," she said. "Especially after a long ride."

"I'll do it," Jabari said.

Wind whinnied nervously as Jabari started to pull him away.

He'll take care of you, Isika told her horse. *I'm so tired, I must sleep. Don't worry, he is very kind. I'll see you tomorrow.*

See you, she heard, and she was halfway up the road to her house before she realized that the words hadn't come from Wind, but Jabari.

THE NEXT MORNING, she woke slowly, a taste of ashes in her mouth. Her room was bright in late morning sunshine, the light cloth at the window waving slightly in a breeze. She blinked for a minute at the bright light of morning, wondering why she had a feeling of dread in her stomach, why her head ached and her mouth tasted like a fire pit. Memory came slowly, and she groaned and turned over to bury her face in her pillow. Tears came and she let them come, finally, sobbing at the shame of the night before.

She couldn't ignore the calls that came to her. As soon as she felt the tugging of danger, the evil of poison, she needed to go to it, she needed to protect the land she had inherited as World Whisperer. Did it mean she would always be in trouble with the elders, that she would always be a figure of suspicion, a stranger here? Maybe, but it was more than that.

It wasn't supposed to be this way. She was in tune with the needs of the land. She was meant to be a help for the people, linking the earth and the Shaper. She wasn't meant to be dangerous or scary. Why had the fire come for her, with her name written in the flames, so everyone knew just who it was for? Why were things getting worse instead of better? Why did Aria hate her?

More than anything in the entire world, she wanted her mother. Oh, if only her mother was alive, if she had come back to Maween with them. Isika imagined her mother here, rounding out after the starvation of the Worker village and the desert, helping Isika know what to do. Making things right with Aria. The elders would listen to Azariyah's daughter more than her granddaughter, wouldn't they?

She couldn't have her mother back. It was something that simply couldn't be. Isika turned over and looked around the room, using the palms of her hands to wipe the tears off her cheeks.

The room was beautiful, and its loveliness, after the ugliness of the night before, was more soothing than usual. The walls were the white washed earth of the whole house, rounded and rippling, almost living. Along the top, a painted vine dripped leaves and flowers, and the windows were paned with clear glass. Light blue curtains moved in the morning air. Isika and Ibba's beds were simple wooden frames with a single mattress and a few pillows, with soft woven sheets, likely made by Brigid's family or someone in their workshop. Ibba wasn't in the second bed. Isika assumed she had woken long ago, and was already in the garden, ignorant of the trouble her older sister had caused in the night.

In the corner stood a wooden chest of drawers, her sixteenth birthday present from Uncle and Kital. The two of them had worked together, putting the chest together and polishing the golden *hoona* wood until it gleamed with light. She stood and went to the chest, lightly brushing her hand along its smooth surface. She opened each drawer slowly, feeling a spark of pleasure at the love Uncle and Kital put into it, at having something so beautiful that was all her own.

Last, she saw her new circlet, sitting on an embroidered mat on the dresser. Isika didn't remember anything after coming home last night, and she certainly hadn't set the circlet on a special mat. She realized Auntie must have taken it off her head and found a place for it, and her eyes stung as she thought of the kindness of her adopted family. She took a shuddering breath. She belonged here, here in this home. If only she could always stay here and never have to protect or deal with the elders afterward.

The circlet was made of delicate strands of silver, woven together, swooping and curling like leaves or vines. She touched it with the pads of her fingers and it buzzed against her, filled with magic that recognized her. The magic felt friendly, like talking to Wind, or like the trees that filled her and called to her. She sighed. Something hurtful had entered her heart the night before, when she saw her name in the poison flames. That hurt sighed and lay down inside her at the touch of the circlet. She felt belonging settle back around her like a cloak. She thought of Jabari, his kindness in standing beside her last night. And then she remembered the fact that he could speak to her in animal speech *in her mind*. What was that?

Just then, as she was coming back to herself, the door opened, and Auntie stood there, wrinkling her nose.

"You'd better bathe, daughter, you smell like a wood fire."

Isika rushed to her and was enveloped in a warm, padded Auntie embrace.

"There, there," Teru whispered. "It will all come right in time. Nenyi promises that. We can believe her."

A small weight caught them around the waists and Isika heard a small voice.

"You slept so long, Isika! I missed you! Come play with me!"

She bent down and kissed Kital on his fuzzy head, her sorrow easing, ready now to meet the day.

Chapter 9

When Isika reached the pottery studio later in the day, she lingered at the doorway to read the feelings of the room. Did the apprentices know that Ivram and Andar had shouted at her from the palace steps? She wouldn't be surprised if some of the apprentices had been out there watching the scene. But people looked up from their work and nodded, then ignored her. She relaxed. If they knew, they weren't going to say anything.

Tomas sat at his wheel, throwing pots. He glanced at her, but looked back at the pot he was making. It wasn't until he finished, cutting the pot away, that he looked up to see Isika tying on her apron. He cleared his throat loudly. Isika froze.

"Hi Tomas," she said.

"So nice of you to join us," he replied.

"I uh... had a late night," she said.

"So I heard."

She glanced up at him, but he didn't go into detail.

"However," he went on, "you might try to remember that we have the four-year commission to work on right now, and your presence is desired. If you deem us worthy, I would ask you to remain within the walls of the city and go to bed on time so you can be here just after dawn. Not after noon." He looked at her from under his eyebrows. "Don't forget that you are *my* apprentice."

Isika scowled and stalked to the clay bench, where Jabari was busy wedging air out of mounds of clay. He looked as exhausted as she felt. He widened his eyes at her, and she smiled a little, moving her shoulders to get rid of the tension she felt. She could take Tomas, she told herself. Under the sarcasm, she heard his concern for her. Also, a subtle warning. Tomas was reminding her that she was under his watch, and that it was not okay for her to leave the city again. But at least he wasn't punishing her.

Okay, she thought. *I got that already, there's no need to convince me.*

She picked up her tools and a jar of water for slip, took a big lump of the pale colored fine clay marked for the four-year commission, and went to her wheel.

"What are we doing?" she asked.

"You're on plates," Tomas said. "I want thirty of them from you today."

Her jaw dropped. "Thirty? You've got to be kidding."

"Thirty."

Isika glanced at the light outside. She was going to be here into the night. Forget what she had decided about him not punishing her. Tomas knew that plates were her least favorite thing to make on the wheel, and thirty was more that she would be expected to make even if she hadn't arrived two hours past noon.

She sighed and leaned into the wheel, feeling determination flood through her at the challenge. She'd show him. She would get them done and be finished by the normal workday. Maybe she could even learn to love making boring, flat plates.

The four-year commission was when the palace replaced every bit of crockery in their kitchens with a new set. Tomas came up with a different design every time, and he had been working on this design for two years now. Isika had caught on quickly; she was the only apprentice allowed to throw the palace commission with him and the second and third potters. Some of the apprentices were jealous, especially the ones who had been there a long time without being promoted to the four-year commission, but they focused on mixing glazes and forming handles for cups, doing the first glaze, and Isika and Tomas worked the second glaze, which was a bit tricky.

One of the apprentices told her that the master potter had never before allowed an apprentice to throw with him for the four-year commission. But Isika was a good potter. She knew it, so it wasn't that surprising. She also knew that she couldn't take credit for throwing beautiful pots. Building was part of her gift.

The new set would replace the last, which had a lot of missing dishes through the breakage of four years, no complete set of plates or bowls anymore. The pottery would be given to the weavers' guild, or the builders or growers. And they would have a sale of their old pottery to raise money for resources, selling their plates cheaply to families who only needed five matching bowls instead of fifty or a hundred. The four-year commission was a celebration for everyone.

Isika threw plate after plate, making sure they were equal in thickness and width, sculpting the tiniest of lips around the circumference, the way Tomas had shown her. They were simple to make. Too simple. She yawned, exhausted, but she buckled down and soon she had finished the first two large trays, ready for the drying room. She looked around for an apprentice to carry them, but Tomas spoke before she found someone. He had been silent, focused on the soup bowls he was making. They were difficult because of the inward curve at the top.

"Bring them yourself. You need to get up and stretch."

Isika stood and realized he was right. She felt creaky and sore. She picked up one of the heavy trays, laid with five plates, and carefully carried it to the drying room, where floor to ceiling shelves lined the walls, full of pottery that would dry before the first glazing and firing.

She was looking for space for her plates on the very full shelves, when Jabari came in, carrying her second tray.

"He let you carry that for me?" she asked, certain that Tomas wanted her to do as much work as possible.

"I didn't ask him," Jabari said, smiling at her.

Isika felt embarrassment flood her as she remembered her weakness, the night before.

"Thanks for bringing me back when I collapsed," she

said. "And thanks for taking care of Wind." She paused and cleared her throat. "That was kind of you."

"Well, I expect you to get Auntie Teru to make me a plate of berry sweets."

"Better yet, I'll ask Ibba to do it. She's getting really good at baking."

Jabari moved several pots over on one of the shelves and fit one tray of plates in the space left over. "Is she? I miss her. I haven't seen her in forever. I saw her at your party, but she was too busy flitting around serving *baltani* to talk to me."

"See what I mean? She made that dessert."

"That's what you can get her to make me, then."

The thought of *baltani*, layers of thin pastry around yogurt and honey, made Isika's mouth water. She watched Jabari carefully placing the second tray on a lower shelf. She needed to get back to the wheel—and make twenty more plates— but she could tell Jabari had something on his mind. When he straightened and turned to her, his eyes were serious.

"Why did you go out there? You must have known you would get caught."

She thought of answering flippantly, but Jabari was king of deflecting questions with jokes, and she knew he wouldn't be deterred.

"I wanted to help protect Azariyah," she said. "No, that's not quite it. I feel compelled to protect Azariyah."

"The rangers don't necessarily need you to protect Azariyah."

At her raised eyebrows, he scowled. "They've been

protecting Azariyah for a long time, since way before you arrived."

She blew out a breath, clenching her fists.

"Then what is the *point* of me, Jabari? Why even have a World Whisperer if you can do perfectly well without her? And I get it. Now that I'm back, things are worse than ever."

He looked back at her, his face softening.

"There is a very definite point to you, and I don't know why things are worse, but they'll change. Something will change. And we'll understand. But the elders won't let you protect Azariyah until you're queen, you know."

"Why? They should be training me now. What, suddenly I'm going to be queen and I'll know nothing?"

He shook his head slowly, rubbing the top of his head with one hand. "I think... it has something to do with trust."

"They don't trust me. I get that too; I've only heard it a hundred times." She paused, picking at a fleck of dried clay on her arm. "Do you feel the same way?" she asked, hating how wobbly her voice was.

"I want to see you have an easier time with the elders," he said. "So I want you to start *listening* to them." He paused and looked up at the high ceiling in the workshop before meeting her eyes again. "It's strange, because these are heavy things we're talking about, and I don't really know why I feel so certain. But yes, Isika, I trust you."

The odd thing, Isika thought, back at her wheel, throwing more boring plates, was that she knew how he felt. Because she trusted him too, and she didn't know why.

THE SUN MOVED through the sky as she bent over her work. She was on her last five plates when Tomas hung his apron by the door and gave her a last look.

"You did well," he said. "I wasn't sure you could do it. You don't complain, daughter. That's something I learned today."

Isika bit down hard on her bottom lip. She'd beat him at his own game, but it wouldn't be a good idea to smile about it now. He could always assign her more.

"Sweep up before you leave," he said. "Especially under the carving table. I'll see you first thing in the morning. Jabari's going to lock up, so don't take too long."

Isika's hidden smile disappeared. Trust Tomas to push his point. Surely it was overkill? Auntie would be angry when she heard.

"I already spoke to Teru, by the way, so don't even bother sending her down to me."

"I would never—" Isika cried, outraged.

"See you tomorrow!" he said, sauntering out into the night. She heard him whistling a Maweel song.

In the drying room, Jabari picked up the song in his deep voice.

"I forgive, I forgive
For all the wrong done to me
I forgive, I forgive
For all the ways people erred
I forgive, I forgive..."

DRAT TOMAS, Isika thought darkly. He never did anything by accident. A song as a parting shot.

She finished making the last plates, then stood, pounding her fists into the small of her aching back. Tomorrow she would feel as if she had fallen off her horse, she was sure of it. Jabari came out of the drying room and picked up the last tray.

"I'll put these away and finish up in there. You sweep."

Isika dragged the broom along the rough earth floor, picking up little pieces of clay and dust, pulling them out of the corners. She felt worse than she would if she fell off her horse. She felt deeply exhausted, worn thin and empty. Maybe all this punishment was right. Maybe it had been incredibly foolish for her to go last night. But how could she hold herself back when the earth was calling her?

She was sweeping the last of the mess into a dust pan when Jabari came out of the drying room, still humming the forgiveness song under his breath and jingling a set of keys in one hand.

"Ready?" he asked, as she dumped the dust into the small trimmings basket.

She could barely nod.

"You look terrible," Jabari said, looking startled.

"Thanks," she mumbled.

"No, really, you do. What helps when you feel like this?"

She thought for a minute, and when the obvious answer came to her, it was enough motivation to get her out the door and halfway up the hill before Jabari finished locking the big doors and ran to follow.

The night was cold and black, the sky filled with stars beyond counting. Isika imagined they were Othra, thousands of them, all out there, eyes bright with kindness. She sniffed at the air but she didn't smell any more than a whiff of smokiness, left over from the night before. No new fires had started. A small part of her relaxed.

"Wow, thanks for waiting," Jabari said when he finally caught up to her. "I really appreciate it. Where are we going?"

Isika pointed at the tree. The ancient market tree was the oldest in the city. Its branches reached over the day market, closed now for the night, so that everything was quiet and still.

"I'm climbing the tree. You don't have to come if you don't want to. It doesn't appeal to everyone."

"I can feel the trees too," Jabari said, his voice quiet. "A little. Not like you can."

"You're welcome to come with me. Right now I think it's the only thing that will help me feel better."

"Even more than food?" Jabari asked, his voice wistful.

Isika laughed. "Are you hungry? Go, don't feel you have to wait for me!" Maybe she needed to be alone. She had been thinking while she threw plates, but the motion was fast and there wasn't time to puzzle out the events of the night before.

"I'd like to come, actually. I'm pretty tired too. Maybe it will help."

Isika glanced at him. He had been out possibly later than her, and he hadn't been late to the workshop today. Of course he was tired too. She felt angry at her own insensitivity.

"Well, come on then," she said. As they came to the tree, she reached out for it. As she touched it, her breath caught, and she exhaled. This tree was different from any other she had ever touched. She began climbing, feeling the ancient weight of its age. She knew, just from listening, that it had been here before the Maweel had ever ventured onto these lands, before people had come. She felt the strong life of Nenyi in the tree, and wondered, without ever being able to find out, whether the tree had been made by the hand of the Shaper herself, when the world first began.

She climbed onto a broad branch and leaned against the trunk of the tree. Its hum felt like a river, like water flowing and flowing, soothing and restoring every aching muscle and every hurt part of her mind. The questions remained, but for the first time that day, she believed they might not break her open. The tree's song felt like honey, like water, brilliant like the stars. She sank into a kind of stupor and shapes passed behind her eyes.

Flames, higher and higher until she thought they might devour her. She ran from the flames and saw a small black-skinned boy hiding under a table. With a shock, she realized he was Ben. She saw a man with a brown cloak, his hood covering his face, and somehow she knew he was crying. She saw herself on Wind, running faster than they had ever run before, and then she saw Abbas and Gavi whirling and dancing, and she realized they were fighting an enemy that she couldn't see.

It was a while before she came back to herself, sitting in the tree with Jabari in another branch somewhere beside her.

The night was very dark, but she caught the flicker of his eyes as he looked over at her.

"Are you okay?" he asked. "You weren't answering and I was getting worried."

"I'm fine," she said. "Better than fine. I'm full again. I hadn't realized how empty I was feeling until this moment."

"That's amazing," Jabari said, and Isika heard something like envy in his voice, but he didn't sound bitter or mean. It shocked her to think he could be envious of her, the unknown girl who was such a threat to the elders. He was Jabari, son of the high elders.

But then she thought of how she would feel if she couldn't feel the tree in this way, thought of all the times she couldn't feel anything from anywhere, and she understood. "I heard you in my mind last night," she said.

Jabari snorted. "I wondered when you would bring that up."

"Why do you think we can do that?"

"Because we can use animal speech in our minds, unlike others," Jabari said. "It makes sense, I guess, that the pathway is open for us as well."

Isika rubbed her arms, chilly in the evening coolness. "It could be useful, I would imagine."

"Yes."

"But the Desert King can use that pathway, too, it seems."

"Yes."

Isika bit her lip, unhappy at the thought of the Desert King. "Jabari, I see.. visions sometimes, when I'm in a tree."

"Visions? Of what?"

She didn't want to talk about fire anymore, or tell him about Ben as a slave boy, or herself riding on Wind. So she told him about Gavi and Abbas.

"I saw Gavi and Abbas together, fighting something I couldn't see. It looked like a battle."

He was silent for a moment. "That's interesting. You know Gavi is going out on a seeking journey tomorrow, right?"

"It's tomorrow already? I did know that. Aria's going too, right?" She felt the kicked feeling she always felt when she thought of her sister, fragile and on a seeking journey. "I still don't understand that."

"I don't either."

"And Abbas? Have the elders decided he is trustworthy?"

Jabari was quiet for a moment. "I think they spoke to Benayeem, asked him what his gift was telling him about Abbas. Ben said he'd always felt purity from the warrior's soul. Not deceit or malice. So they trusted him." He paused again. "Ben didn't tell you?"

Ben had certainly not told her. Isika shook her head, though she knew it was doubtful Jabari could see it in the dark. She knew why Ben hadn't told her; it was easy to guess. Her brother loved her and didn't want to hurt Isika with the information that the elders were working with him, trusting his gift before they trusted hers.

"Speaking of trust," she said, trying to keep her voice steady. This was the thing that had been pricking at her all day, the thing with the ability to hurt her terribly, so she spoke slowly. "When you said you trusted me, did you mean before or after you saw my name in the fire?"

Jabari was quiet for a long time.

"It was a decision I made these last months, while we worked together, after we got back from Batta. So I guess it was before I saw your name in the flames, and it's true that I don't know what the name means..."

"Jabari, just tell me. Can you still trust me?" This time she couldn't keep her voice level and it broke, embarrassing her. She felt Jabari's hand come near and then rest on her shoulder.

"I'm trying. I'm fighting to trust you, Isika. And the thing I keep going back to is that you don't know what those flames were, any more than I do. So whatever it is that's coming for you, you don't have a part in it. And it doesn't seem to have a part in you. The things that are going on lately are strange and terrifying, but I still trust you."

Chapter 10

On the day he was supposed to set out on his seeking journey, Gavi was still working in the garden, bent over his garden bed. He had packed weeks ago, long before his mother reminded him he needed to, long before the servants thought to pull out his travel pack. He had packed without trouble or drama, and that was how he wanted to keep the journey. He was ready. He straightened, arms crossed in front of him, and looked at his work. There were only a few more things to do.

He picked up an empty basket and carried it over to the straw pile to pick up some mulch. The beans were about to flower, and he knew the heat of the midday sun would be too much for the casual watering the other gardeners gave them when he was away. More than once he had come home to find that his plants had withered. No one took care of them the way he did.

The head gardener had shaken his head at Gavi when he saw the beans sprouting again.

"We're too far south for them to grow well, son," he said. "I don't know where you got the seeds, but this region is too dry."

Gavi had picked the seeds out of a traveling peddler's collection a few years ago. The peddler, Gariah, had been riding a camel laden with shiny strings and gold necklaces, vests made of the teeth of some strange fish, gems, and seeds from across the water, from places Gavi had never heard of or visited.

He bought the seeds and grew them carefully, in tiny pots. They grew with the shooting climbers of beans, but their light green leaves were a different shape, and lightly streaked with purple. He had tried growing them without success a few times, and now Gavi had planted his last two seeds. They had sprouted weeks ago, and were climbing quickly.

He was hopeful this time because he had moved banana trees nearby so the beans got a half day of shade, and he had planted seeds of a spicy flower that pests hated. The head gardener had suggested both ideas—for someone who didn't think the beans would grow, he was awfully involved in Gavi's efforts.

Gavi filled the basket with straw, then lifted it easily to his head to carry it back to the corner of the huge Azariyah kitchen gardens, where his beans and other odd projects lived. He mulched the two precious bean plants, covering the earth around them with straw to keep the soil moist, then did the tomatoes and the spicy *zita* greens that the scalding *zita* curry was made from. His mouth watered as he thought of it. He had many weeks ahead of him of eating potatoes, rabbits, wild birds, and fish. He could use one last *zita* curry.

The tomatoes were leaning too heavily on one of the stakes, so he pulled some twine out of his bag and got to work, reinforcing it with another stake from a pile nearby.

He heard footfalls on the dried leaves between the garden beds. Though he didn't look up, he knew who it was.

"I thought I might find you here. Do you have any idea what time it is?"

"Yab. Hello to you too," he replied.

"Hello and goodbye. You need to get down to the meadow immediately, they're beginning the journey blessing and why are you still here?"

Gavi stood. His knees were stained with dirt now, but then they usually were. He turned and hugged his brother without a word. When he pulled back, he had to look away from Jabari's face quickly. It was too hard to see his brother acting as if not going on the journey didn't bother him. It was too hard for Gavi to act as if his brother acting didn't bother him.

He shrugged. "I'm packed. All I have to do is walk down there." He gestured at the pack that leaned against the short wooden fence.

"Hey!" Jabari said, laughing. "I was looking for that. I need to go through it and get rid of what you don't need!"

"Not this time," Gavi said, smiling. "This is my trip."

"Oh," Jabari said, a tone in his voice that Gavi had never heard. Gavi shot a look at his brother.

"Don't worry, Yab," he said, "We'll probably be back with our tails between our legs before long. You'll barely miss us. I don't even know how we're going to leave without you."

"You'll be fine," Jabari said. Gavi paused to study his brother's face for a moment. He saw sadness, but no bitterness. He saw that Jabari meant what he said, that Gavi would do fine. Gavi wished he believed the same.

He started walking again, heading toward the entrance to the gardens, down to the meadow.

"There's no way you can know that," he said, attempting to joke about it. Now his voice sounded like Jabari's had a few moments before, like someone trying to hide feeling bad. What was wrong with the two of them? It was as though they thought they were saying goodbye forever, like this little blip in time was way bigger than it was. Since they were small boys, they had known that Jabari would be a ranger and Gavi would be a gardener, that they would be separated one day. So this was no big deal, though it was opposite of how they imagined.

But they had been together since Gavi was adopted. Jabari had been two years old, and Gavi was somewhere around two—no one knew his actual age. No one except the parents who had cast him away, and they couldn't ask them. Jabari and Gavi were like twins who looked nothing alike, Jabari tall and rangy, dark-skinned, built like a running cat, and Gavi broad in the shoulders and light-skinned, tanned from hours in the sun, with intense blue eyes and blond hair that never lay flat.

They fell into step, walking down the hill. It was the fire that was throwing them off, Gavi decided. No one knew what to do about the fire, and one thing Gavi had taken for granted, these months that he was preparing, was that Jabari would rest easy in his mind, safe while they were separated. He had felt a little sorry for Jabari, who might worry about the seekers, but then, Jabari wasn't much of a worrier. It wasn't in his nature. He was explosive and forgot things quickly. Gavi was the worrier, the quiet one who brooded forever.

Gavi had never imagined that a threat would come so close to Azariyah. Now he did worry about Jabari, about what would happen in his absence.

"No Lightwalker antics while I'm gone, okay?" Gavi said.

The Lightwalker of Nenyi was someone they had invented when they were boys. They took turns being Lightwalker in their games, and Gavi couldn't remember which of them invented Lightwalker. It was most likely Jabari, though. Even back then, Jabari wanted to protect Maween from all harm. He ran around pretending to fly and tear down walls, while Gavi spent hours staring at the algae floating on the surface of the pond, entranced by other plants that grew on air alone.

Lightwalker was the protector of Maween. He strode around making everything good again, made of Light. His footfalls shook the ground, and plants grew in his footprints. He could save a whole village at once. Nothing could harm him. Gavi felt a brief stab of longing for those days, the days they played at it and never imagined they would have to face trouble the way they did.

"And try not to let Isika be Lightwalker either," Gavi added.

Jabari snorted. "Let's face it Gav, she's Lightwalker in the flesh. We just didn't know Lightwalker would turn out to be real."

It was true. And both Gavi and Jabari knew it was hard to keep her from being Lightwalker. It was as if their daydream had come to life and was a stubborn, beautiful, gifted girl, not the man they had imagined, whose head brushed the clouds.

The meadow was near. Soon the journey blessing would start. And then Gavi would just... walk away.

"You'll have Abbas," Jabari said.

Gavi's eyes widened as he looked at his brother. "How am I supposed to talk to a warrior prince? He's the only other guy in the group. And he's a prince. And a warrior."

Jabari grinned. "Being the only guys should make it easier, right? You'll be fine. You're the one with real tact out of all of us."

They walked silently again for a moment. Then Jabari spoke quietly. "Take care of Aria, Gavi. She's not well. I don't care what the healers say."

Gavi nodded, with a now-familiar sick feeling in his stomach. He knew Jabari was right. Gavi was a healer; he could feel the not-rightness in Aria. Something was eating her from the inside. He wished she could stay back. His mother had explained why Aria was coming, that all four of their parents felt she would be better off with Gavi nearby. But it still seemed strange to start a journey with a girl who was suffering from a wound. Several times over the last weeks he had thought that he should call the journey off, stay home so he could be near to Aria without needing to take her on a long journey. But every time he came close, he realized how badly he wanted this journey. He didn't want to call it off. He wanted to try a journey without Jabari. That was the truth, for better or worse.

As they got to the meadow, with the choir in place and many people gathered around, he thumped Jabari on the back, and Jabari stopped and hugged him again.

"Be safe, big little brother," he said.

"Of course I will," Gavi told him, hoping it was true.

AFTER THE SONGS WERE SUNG, the blessing was spoken, and about a hundred hugs had been given, causing Gavi to smell like twelve different kinds of perfume, he stood around waiting. *When are we going to leave?* he wondered. *It's getting late.*

He was still wondering, looking around for the signal to begin, when he realized with a shock that the signal was supposed to come from him. He flushed with heat, knowing he was bright red. He needed to call the seekers together and begin the journey.

He took a few long breaths, pulling himself together, then called to Ivy and Aria. He watched as Abbas bowed to Jerutha, a deep bow that brought color to her face. Gavi smiled. It wasn't hard to see how Abbas felt about Jerutha. She seemed flustered but pleased to have a warrior bow as though he was promising to come back to her.

Ivy and Aria walked to Gavi after they finished their goodbyes.

"Ready?" Ivy asked.

"That's my line," Gavi said.

She looked startled. "Oh, well then. You say it."

"Ready?" he asked, grinning.

"Ready," the girls said, and as Abbas strode over to join them, they began walking, followed by the cheers and waves of the people who loved them.

They took the stone road. A few people stood on their porches or outside their gardens to wave them off, but not many. This was a routine seeking journey, an ordinary thing, and people didn't usually stick around to watch.

Gavi was thinking of the look Isika had given him, which said the same thing Jabari had said in words. *Take care of Aria.*

He dropped back to walk with her, letting Ivy and Abbas walk on ahead. He searched his mind for a way to ask without being annoying. *How are you doing? How are you feeling?*

"Was it different, saying goodbye to your parents, after last time?" he finally asked.

She glanced up at him. Her eyes unsettled him. They were the eyes of someone who had suffered too much. Even Isika, who had been beaten in her old home, who had lost her mother and seen both Aria and Kital put in the sacrificial boats, didn't have eyes like that. Something horrible had happened to Aria the day she was sent out to die in the waves. And that something had never healed.

Her hair was in hundreds of tiny braids with stones that clacked softly as she walked. She was nearly fourteen, he realized with a bit of a shock. He was seventeen, and used to thinking of her as a child, smaller than the other Maweel children. She was the first black-skinned outcast they had ever found, and she had been malnourished; she was a full head shorter than all of her classmates. When they found her, she had staunchly insisted that she was almost eight, despite the way she looked. Her face was more oval-shaped than Isika's, her cheekbones wide, but not as sharp, her eyes long and wide-set. She was still more petite than her siblings, too, though Gavi didn't think it was lack of nourishment anymore. Isika was tall and strong, looking like someone to be reckoned with, and Benayeem was tall and imposing, despite his gentle nature. But Aria seemed delicate and fragile, as though a strong wind could carry her away.

"It wasn't too different," she said, shrugging. "My parents always cry. But the healers convinced them that I was nearly well and that this was much better for me. So here I am, doing what I've always dreamed of doing." Her voice carried no excitement.

Something in the angle of her head confirmed Gavi's worries. She wasn't doing well. He had to admire her tenacity, though. She was strong, a weaker person would have been killed by those arrows. There was some silvery core of strength in her, and he didn't think she even knew it was there.

But he didn't know why he didn't send her home right now, before they left the outskirts of the city, before they came across any poison. If she was on the journey, he would have to put half his energy into watching her. He knew he would need to use his gift to heal her, probably often, offering strength and taking out the poison that the arrow was leaking continually. He really should make her go home, despite what his parents wanted, despite what the healers said. But he saw her face, hopeless but resigned, and he sensed that silvery strength in her, malleable but persistent, and he couldn't do it. He couldn't turn her away. He would have to make sure she was safe with them.

And, he thought, walking with his friends, one of them a mere shadow of who she should have been, perhaps there would be a cure out there somewhere, something just lying on the road, ready for them to find.

Chapter 11

Two days later, the seekers reached the crest of a hill where they could see farmland stretched out before them. Aria inhaled and the air tasted like journeying. She was beginning to love the road, the way Jabari had always talked about. He had been the first person to ever tell her about loving the road, and at the time she had thought it was crazy. Why would you want to leave home? And not that Jabari had told Aria about it. It was more that she overheard him talking with Deto. He said it was as though there was a connection between him and the land, but the only way he could find that connection was when he was running, when the trees were a blur rushing by.

Aria couldn't believe that instead of being here on the journey, Jabari was back in the pottery workshop with Isika. She felt betrayed in a way she didn't know she could still feel after all this time. She should know better by now; there were hundreds of ways people could betray you.

Jabari was the reason Aria had become a seeker, and she had thought that he would always be here. But she was laying it to rest. It wasn't Jabari's fault. He hadn't said or done anything to make her think she should become a seeker for him. It was just the kind of stupid thing she would do. She sighed.

The Maweel were a running people, and on Aria's last journey, she and the other seekers had run nearly the whole way to the Worker city, Batta. On this journey, with Gavi in charge, they were running less. It had become noticeable over the two days they had been traveling. Aria knew why they weren't running. She saw the concerned glances from Gavi. She smiled at the back of his head, now, his hair that stuck up all over like long yellow grasses.

"What are you smiling about?" Ivy asked from where she was walking, beside Aria. "Not that I'm complaining, it's nice to see you smile, little sister."

"I'm smiling at Gavi's hair," Aria said, honest before she could stop herself.

Ivy glanced up at Gavi. "Yes, it does seem to defy the laws of nature that say we remain on the earth. It's always been like that."

"Has Gavi always been this way?" Aria asked.

She was obsessed, lately, with the ways people changed and didn't change. She herself had become so changeable, ever since the arrows entered her. It had happened in the village where she had been cast away like leftover scraps of food. She was happy one moment, then sad, then angry. She couldn't read herself anymore, couldn't count on herself. She didn't know whether she would be this way forever, or whether it was a passing thing. She desperately wanted there to be some consistency in her world, she was always quizzing her adoptive parents about it. *Is there anything that is ever the same? Will you be the same? Will you send me away when you are sick of me?* She knew they grew tired of her questions, but they always answered her the same. *We will never send you away.*

Too bad she couldn't trust it.

"What way?" Ivy asked.

"I don't know. More restful than his brother, unhurried, liking to eat."

Ivy laughed. "Oh, that. Yes, he has always been the same. Always been kind and considerate. He's not too troubled. He likes to eat and make food. But he's growing. Look at his shoulders, they're massive! He's strong and brave."

Gavi turned and gave Ivy an odd look. "I can hear you, you know."

Aria felt heat coming into her face, but Ivy laughed again, her eyes glowing.

"Eh! Little brother, you have become a man!" She imitated her father's voice nearly perfectly and Aria laughed.

Gavi shook his head and cocked an eyebrow at Aria. "Never take your cousin on your first leading journey. She will not respect you."

Ivy turned suddenly serious. "No, cousin, I respect you. And this is not your first time. You and Jabari have always led together. I saw that many times. I am not joking; you have become a man." Her eyes lit up with humor again. "A respectable man."

Gavi reddened slightly and gave Abbas a look.

Abbas looked seriously between the two of them.

"I did not know you were cousins," he said. His voice seemed impossibly deep, with strange rolling consonants and curving vowels.

"We're not," Gavi told him. "But Jabari and I grew up with Ivy in the palace, and we are all the same age, so we are as near to cousins, or even siblings, as people can be."

"How is it that you came to be the brother of a black man?"

Aria nearly choked. Had no one filled Abbas in on the customs of the Maweel? Gavi didn't look taken aback, though Ivy covered her mouth to hide her smile. Gavi walked with Abbas and explained the way the Maweel took children in, children who were outcast from their villages. Aria felt the familiar prickle of shame and sorrow come over her as she heard him speak. It had been with her since the day the bells rang, letting the whole village know she would be given over, but the arrows had made it worse.

"Will you marry Ivy then?" At this, Gavi nearly choked. Ivy, however, threw her head back and laughed a long, loud peal of laughter.

"No, never! Not Jabari either! I could never marry men who are like my cousins."

Abbas looked at her oddly. "You don't arrange marriages, then?"

"Not if we can help it," Ivy said. Abbas looked confused.

"Sometimes, if someone really wants to marry and hasn't found someone, the parents will step in and help. But it's always by choice."

Abbas looked like he was thinking hard. Aria was fascinated by him. He was such a wild-looking person, with a contrasting gentle nature.

They walked a while longer.

"What will the journey be like, do you think?" Aria asked Ivy softly. She didn't want Gavi to overhear. But he was up ahead, talking to Abbas, who walked with a swinging stride that suggested he might start dancing or fighting at any moment. They were an interesting looking group. Gavi with his tanned white skin and shock of wheat colored hair. Ivy, beautiful, light brown and built like a water bird of some kind, long-limbed and startling. Aria, skin black as purple night. And Abbas, brown-skinned, a giant who was unquestioningly a warrior, with gold ornaments in his ears and on his wrists, a long, swinging stride, black hair that was braided to his waist, and deep-set eyes under black eyebrows. He looked like a hawk to Aria. She wondered if there were more people in the world who looked like him.

"Mostly standard, I guess," Ivy answered. "The way it's been so far."

They had pulled down two poison walls and stayed in two homes over the last two days. Aria frowned. Even she knew that wasn't quite standard. There were too many walls.

Ivy went on. "But I do know that Gavi's parents asked him to find the source of the fires and if possible, destroy it."

"What?"

"Yes, that's asking a lot of a seeker. I'm surprised, and I'm used to the way Uncle Andar and Auntie Laylit ask too much of their boys. But never mind. I shouldn't speak this way."

Aria thought about that. She thought about the not-so-standard seeking journey, and she thought about her secret. She wondered how it would affect them, because the truth was that she couldn't keep it hidden much longer. Gavi would find out that she was still sick, sicker than the healers had known.

Late in the afternoon, they came to another farm. First Aria saw the house, and sighed. More walls. The she noticed the bean field. She stopped dead in her tracks, shocked. All over the field, threads of smoke were winding their way into the air. Tiny fires, so dangerous for the people in the house. Behind the poison walls, the people would be in a stupor, doing the same meaningless tasks over and over again. They couldn't know their farm was in danger.

It was always sad when a farm house was poisoned. If it was remote enough and poisoned for long enough, the crops would die in the fields. If it was near a village or town, the neighbors might try to keep the farm up for the poisoned family, but it was hard, because they had their own work as well. Poison hurt everyone.

Aria knew the Maweel were confused. It was true that Isika showed some very powerful traits, but they had been longing for the return of a World Whisperer because when the World Whisperer was there, the walls didn't come. Now she had returned, but there were more and more walls, walls that grew back almost as soon as the seekers tore them down.

"Gavi!" she shouted on ahead at her friend, who was walking toward the walls with Abbas. Gavi looked back and saw the smoke, then he and Abbas ran back to where she stood with Ivy.

Aria stood, transfixed by the fires, sure that she and the other seekers would never be able to put them out. For a moment, the edges of the world went black and fuzzy and she saw as though down a long corridor. She blinked and the world was right again. Gavi was speaking.

"Fires first, then walls. Abbas, look for pails in the shed. Ivy, run and see if there's any water in that well. And Aria, come with me. Let's look at these fires."

Aria followed Gavi into the field as the others ran off. As they rustled their way over to the first thread of smoke, she thought about the lack of hope in herself, wondering when she had become this way. She had always been hopeful. Even though she had been betrayed, she had expected better in the future. Now it was as though she knew that there would never be anything better, as though all there was right now was all there would ever be. Even the World Whisperer wouldn't turn out to be much of a World Whisperer. She thought of her secret again, wondered if it had anything to do with the bleakness she felt.

Gavi was speaking to her. Aria tried to look as though she had been listening. They stood over a small fire that was about the size of Aria's hands if she cupped them together. The smoke coming off the fire smelled like despair.

"Wait here," Gavi said. "I'll check on the pails and the water."

He walked back through the bean plants, the way they had come, reaching out to heal a bruised stalk after he bumped into it.

Aria stared at the small fire. It wasn't real fire, she realized. It could become real fire, if it had the chance. Her vision grew dark again, and as though in a dream, she reached out and cupped her hands upside down, as though she was trying to contain the smoke, keep it from reaching the sky. In her hands she felt all the bitterness and grief that came to her in dreams. It angered her, so she leaned forward.

Vaguely she heard footsteps and yells, but it was too late, she squatted down and put her hands directly on the small fire, feeling cold sparks within her responding to the flames, and a sharp stab from her belly, just near her ribs, where her secret was lodged; the one, last arrow the healers hadn't been able to remove, that pained her with every breath she took. The arrow protested, shrieking near her ribs. She gritted her teeth against it and the fire went out.

She lifted her hands. There was the tiniest bit of ash on the ground. Her hands were unscathed, not even ashy or charred, as clean as though she had just washed them. She looked up. Gavi, Ivy, and Abbas stood there with pails, staring at her.

"It's not hot," she told them.

Ivy walked over to a nearby tiny fire and held her hand above it. She pulled it back with a yelp. "It's hot to me," she said, sucking on a finger.

Gavi was still staring at Aria, his green-blue eyes looking a little too closely. Aria looked away.

"Okay," he said. "Ivy, Abbas and I will use water. Aria, you... do it your way. Let's get this field rid of poison."

Chapter 12

Benayeem was in the palace library for the first time, and it was nothing like what he had expected. The walls were high and glowing with paintings, with more history of Maween depicted on every inch. But he stared at the stacks of books, piled on every surface, so thick he could barely see the tables underneath. To be honest, he would have imagined it neater. Apparently, there was some sort of order in the madness, though, because as soon as he put a finger on one of the stacks, a short, thin man hurried toward him. The man's white-streaked hair was in locks that cascaded down his back. His dark skin was scattered with even darker spots, concentrated on his cheeks and nose. He was vibrating with irritation, and the music coming from him was quick and complicated.

"Is there something you needed, Young One? I would be happy to find it for you."

"Oh," Ben pulled his hand back from the book he had been reaching for. "Am I not supposed to touch the books?"

"Well. Hm. Well. There is no rule against it, but I have them all in order, and if my order gets disturbed, riffled or ruffled, it will throw off the workings of the library system."

Ben's eyes grew wide. He looked around the room, at shelves sagging with books and tables with stacks as tall as a man.

"Oh," he said again, "oh." After a short pause, he realized the man was waiting to hear what he needed. "I would like to read about rangers," he said.

"Origins? Historic battles? Or rules of?"

Ben stared. "All of those, I suppose," he said.

He watched as the man scuttled to a nearby table, sweeping his hair, which reached nearly to the floor, behind him as he went. He attached a large eyepiece to his face, stood on the table, and quickly ran his hand down the tallest pile, stopping at a book halfway down. Ben was about to offer help taking the books off the top, when the man chopped sideways with his hand to knock the book out of the middle of the stack, catching it with his other hand on the other side. The top books settled without tipping or falling.

If Ben's eyes had been wide before, they were bulging now. He watched in wonder as the man hurried to a few more tables, repeating the procedure at different levels in different stacks, then returned to Ben and offered five books. They weren't dusty, as Ben had expected. Instead they seemed pristine, as though they hadn't been left in piles in an old library.

"Thank you," he said, feeling bereft of words.

The man bowed.

"What is the... protocol... for checking them out?" Ben asked.

The man looked at him oddly. "No protocol! We don't have many rules here. Just bring them back within a moon's length."

BEN LEFT the large library at the top level of the palace, and walked down the stairs to the front entrance. He glanced over the books, and saw that indeed, the librarian had given him one of each of the books he specified, as well as one he hadn't specified, called, *"The Nature and Magic of Caring for Books."*

When he reached the ground floor he looked up to see Jabari approaching, a wide smile on his face.

"Benayeem!" Jabari said. "I haven't seen you in ages."

"A week," Ben said. "Though it seems longer. My teachers are keeping me in the school room at all hours as punishment for going out to the fires last week."

Jabari nodded. "Sounds like them."

"But I'm done now," Ben said.

"So you thought you'd get a little more study material?" Jabari asked, grinning.

Ben felt heat come into his face. "Kind of," he said, hoping he could keep from telling Jabari the nature of his study. For some reason it felt private. He didn't want anyone knowing how badly he wanted to be a ranger.

However, Jabari was bending over the books, reading the titles.

"I met the librarian," Ben said, hoping to distract him. "He's an odd one. Funny that I've never met him before. I would have remembered meeting him at one of the feasts."

"Olumi?" Jabari glanced up from reading the books' spines. "He never leaves the library. He has a room for sleeping, a bathing room, and a kitchen there. Sometimes Ivy brings him food from the feasts. I've known him all my life. But here—" he pulled out the book on the care of books. "He's slipped this one in. I'll return it. I can distill the information for you: don't read them in the bath, don't read them while eating, don't shelf them on one end. You know, the way books are meant to be stored. Olumi thinks books should be stacked flat."

Ben grinned. "That explains the towers of books in the library," he said.

"Exactly," Jabari said. He tossed the book, catching it in the air and whistling as he walked away.

"See you," Ben said.

Jabari turned just before heading up the stairs. "Ben?"

"Yes?"

"I think you would make a great ranger. Most who are gifted with justice become judges, boringly enough. It would be helpful to have someone with a justice gift helping to see into the minds of people when we're on tough journeys."

Ben ducked his head, his face growing hot. "Thanks," he said.

HE READ the books every chance he got, while the fires continued on the plains. Every day there was news of more fires, always just outside the city, as though the poison was trying to wear the people down and make its way inside. The winds picked up whenever there was a fire, so that the smell of smoke came into every corner in the city, casting a shadow of fear over the Maweel.

Ben read about the origin of the rangers, how hundreds of years before, a nearby emperor had been giving the Maweel so much grief, they formed a force of warriors who were trained for peace. Rangers disabled, rather than killing, using magic to bind rather than destroy. Ben read histories of battles. He read about present-day rangers. He stopped for dinner, feeling that somehow Olumi would know if he ate while he read. And when he saw Isika shelving his ranger books with the others in their house, he shrieked, "No!" and ran toward her, pulling them away so she couldn't set them on one end.

Uncle Dawit looked up over his own book. "I see you've been talking to Olumi," he said, smiling, then instantly absorbed in reading again.

One day at dinner, Uncle Dawit told Isika and Ben that the elders wanted to talk to them the next day. Isika looked at Ben across the table.

"What?" Ben said, when Isika didn't stop staring at him.

"What did you do?" Isika asked.

"Why are you looking at me?" Ben asked.

"Because this time I didn't do anything," she replied.

"I got in trouble from Auntie for washing the windows

with jam today," Kital piped up. They all laughed, but Ben saw the way Isika's face grew sad and distant as her thoughts curved in on themselves and she folded herself away.

They went the next morning, after Isika and Ben ducked down to tell Tomas that Isika wouldn't be there this morning. He wasn't pleased. He shook his head, grumbling at them.

"They want me to take you on as an apprentice, they should let me take you on as an apprentice and stop interfering every single day."

"Who called you?" Jabari asked, holding a tray of pots.

"The elders," Benayeem told him, when it seemed Isika wouldn't answer, as she was trying to soothe the master potter.

"Funny, they forgot to tell me," Jabari said. He disappeared into the drying room, clattered around for a few moments, then reappeared, his apron already off. "I need to go, too, Tomas. My parents forgot to tell me we were having a meeting."

"What?" Tomas exploded. "I would imagine that if they forgot, they had a good reason to forget..." his voice trailed off as he and Jabari looked at each other for a long moment. "Fine, go," he said. "But be back immediately after, and same quota today, Isika."

Isika shrugged, her face impassive, but she groaned as the three of them walked up the hill together.

"I don't even know what I'm in trouble for, and I feel like I'm being punished by both sides," she said, scowling.

But Benayeem felt warm at the thought of all of them surrounding his sister, all these unspoken guards. It seemed that Jabari had joined her other guards: Auntie Teru, Uncle Dawit, Ben, and Tomas. Jabari was one of her silent protectors now. Ben glanced at him and saw that Jabari's jaw was clenched. Maybe he wouldn't turn out to be so silent.

"What do you think they want to talk to me about?" Isika asked Jabari.

"They're not done with the night of the fire," Jabari said in a low voice. "I think they want to ask you more questions."

Ben glanced at Isika and saw that her shoulders were tense. At the top of the hill, they spotted Kital and Ibba running toward them.

"What?" Isika said, catching their hands so that one walked on each side of her. "Why aren't you in school?"

"Auntie said the elders wanted to talk to us."

"But I thought they only wanted to talk to Ben and me," Isika said, looking at Benayeem with a frown.

"Auntie was in a mood, you know how she gets when she's cutting vegetables, but she's doing it really hard," Ibba said, "and then she told us to go along to the palace, because surely the elders wanted us there as well."

Jabari shook his head, smiling. "This should be fun."

THERE WAS a moment of stunned silence when all of them

entered the great room, and then Ivram gave a bark of laughter, shaking his head.

"Teru," he said, and laughed again. "She has her ways."

Andar's face was more serious.

"I don't recall inviting you here, Jabari," he said from where all four elders sat on the raised platform at the end of the room.

"I thought you must have forgotten."

"This isn't a trial," Ivram said quietly.

"It isn't? Then why are you all up there? Can we sit somewhere else?"

Benayeem felt a flash of gratitude as the elders looked at each other, then gestured for them to sit in one of the cushioned sections of the room. His shoulders relaxed when they were all on the same level. He was practiced now, at keeping the sounds he always heard back in his mind, especially when they weren't too pressing, but he listened now.

The music in the room was tense and, Ben would say, frustrated. It didn't seem malicious, but Ben did hear something strange from Jabari's mother, Laylit. He listened harder. Her music was low, sad, straining, and in the midst of the notes were bitter, sharp chords. He watched her for a moment. She was very lovely, and she kept her face very calm, but she was distressed. She kept looking from her son to Isika, and when she looked at Isika, the bitter chords twanged like shrieking birds.

Andar was speaking and Benayeem realized he hadn't been paying attention, but then there was a little commotion in the doorway to the great room and Keethior swept in, flying low above their heads in a circle, then landing on a pillow. The elders stared at him.

"Welcome, Othra," Andar said finally. "It seems this party is much bigger than we expected."

"A party?" Keethior said. "For whom?"

"You are welcome to perch on one of the Othra stands if you would like," Laylit said, staring at Keethior's claws, biting into the silk pillow he was perched on. He fluttered his wings and a few feathers and leaves fell on the pillow.

"Thank you, Elder, but I prefer cushions. So soft. They remind me of my first nest, lined with the feathers of my mother."

Jabari grinned and Isika hid a smile behind her hand. Ben was too tense to smile.

"Well, let's continue, before more people join the party," Andar said. He glanced at Kital and Ibba, who were busy playing a game with polished stones set out on one of the low tables. Andar lowered his voice anyway. "Ivram and many other witnesses saw your name outlined in the flames the other night. We need to ask, Isika. Are you certain that you know nothing about why it was there?"

"I'm as surprised as you are," Isika said, a tremble in her voice.

Laylit shifted in her seat and Ben could almost hear her thoughts. *I'm not surprised.*

"Do you know of any connection between you and the Desert King? Because this is almost certainly his work."

Isika turned to look at Ben, hard, a firm stare, and it was his turn to shift in his seat. She wanted him to tell them what he had told her. He knew his sister, it wouldn't occur to her to hold back the information, even though it could hurt her.

Ben sighed. "You know, because we told you, that we lived our first years in the Desert city, before our mother escaped with us," he said. "Isika has almost no memory of that place, but I know that I was a slave to the Desert King."

There were gasps around the room as people took in what Ben said.

"You mean, you know him? You've seen him face to face?" Ivram asked, his face intense.

"How could you not have told us this before?" Karah asked, her soft voice full of reproach. Ben's heart sank, then sped up. It was so ugly, the stench and blame of serving such an evil man.

"You know who else served the Desert king?" Keethior said suddenly. "Do I need to remind you? Azariyah, stolen queen of the Maweel. Do not blame the child for being born a captive."

Everyone was quiet. Jabari's fists were clenched, his face hard.

Isika spoke. "We told you that they were looking for us, when Jerutha was taken to Batta. Looking for me. It seems they still are. I believe it is because my mother left, taking Ben, a slave, with her. But that is only an idea. And it's all we know."

Benayeem heard the way she avoided the word "he" as though everything would collapse if she even sent one thought toward the Desert King. He understood, because his mind avoided the man, skittering away in panic if Ben even tried to imagine him. He watched the elders and listened to the play of emotions in the music of the room, knowing that there were many unanswered questions among them.

Andar leaned forward on his cushion, then spoke. "We do not know how to fight a fire we don't understand. There seem to be many forces trying to tear Azariyah apart with whispers and suspicion as well as fear." He lifted his hands, and his weariness was visible. Next to him, Ivram nodded.

"We're trying to do this well," he said, "to help the people get to know you, Isika, but then there are strange signs and odd magic around your name, in the very flames that plague us. We need you close to us so we can show that we're on the same side."

"Please come and sit with us for petitions a couple times a week," Karah said, "so the people of Maween can get to know your face and learn that there is no danger in you." She continued in a low, urgent voice, her face creased in worry. "We want to do right by you, Isika. Please help us by trying to work with us."

Ben felt a twinge of guilt that wasn't entirely his to own, as he thought of all the times Isika had publicly argued with the elders. Her face was anxious now, and her music a mixture of quick, angry notes and sorrowful wails, the kind he heard when he knew she was thinking of their mother. She nodded, though.

"Of course I will come, if you think it is best."

Ben saw Jabari slowly relax his fists as Keethior opened his wings and let out a long note of music.

Chapter 13

Life in the city went back to something approaching normal, though there was unease everywhere and in everything. In addition to her work at the pottery workshop Isika began work with the elders at petitions, listening to the complaints and needs the people brought before them.

On her first day, she put on the new palace tunic Auntie had bought her. It was gold, with swirls of darker gold embroidery, and deep red, loose pants went with it. She set the circlet on her forehead and felt it buzz as it settled against her skin. *Hello*, she thought as she looked at herself in the mirror. The circlet didn't answer, and she laughed at herself. It felt so alive, like it changed her somehow.

Petitions happened in the great room, and the elders in their chairs on the platform at far end of the room, while the people lined up between the white pillars that reached to the hidden recesses of the ceiling. Servants milled around, serving water or crumbly cheese and flatbread. That was a nice touch, Isika thought, struck again by the hospitality of her new land.

Ivram had told her there were usually the normal farmer disputes about property lines or water. But that day, there was fire, only fire. Tiny fires had begun igniting from nowhere, all over the Maween, in the fields of the farmers and around their houses.

The first farmers who came were a husband and wife with desperate, sooty faces and dirty clothes. It seemed they had come directly from fighting the fires in their fields to the palace to find help.

"Please," the woman said. "We can't keep up with the fires. As soon as we put one out, another starts."

"We will send rangers to you as soon as we can spare them," Laylit told the woman.

"When will that be?" the woman asked.

Isika's heart begged the elders to do something.

"There is an order of rangers traveling to fight fire," Laylit answered, "and a group of seekers as well. Perhaps they will come to your farm soon. But we cannot spare more, because the rangers are busy protecting the city."

Large fires had continued to erupt very near, threatening the palace and everyone who lived in Azariyah.

"Can we send Deto to this woman's farm?" Isika broke in, her voice echoing in the large room. "Maybe Brigid can go with him?" She didn't dare ask for herself. She knew what the answer would be. But she saw the gratified look that the couple sent her way.

The looks the elders gave her weren't as pleased. They put their heads together to confer.

"We will send seekers to you," Laylit said, straightening from the huddle. The couple laid their hands on their hearts in respect for the elders, turning to bow toward Isika as well, touching their foreheads with their fingers in a sign of high respect, startling her.

That was when Ivram asked her to watch and listen rather than interjecting in Petitions. She did, though it was hard for her to keep her peace.

As the days went by, stories began to trickle into the city, of Gavi and Aria and the other seekers putting out poison fires in the fields. There were tales of one girl, the youngest, who could put them out with her hands.

Well done, Aria, Isika thought, when she heard it. *Be careful.*

The elders began telling the petitioning farmers that the seekers would surely reach them soon.

Isika saw the looks the people gave her when they left Petitions room. Sometimes the looks were puzzled, sometimes disappointed, sometimes suspicious. The people of Maween had thought the troubles would be over if they had a new World Whisperer. Isika heard the same words over and over in her mind. *It's only getting worse.* The words felt like an indictment, but she didn't know what she had done wrong. *I'm just as confused as you are,* she wanted to tell them. But she sat silent and watching, trying to learn.

Every night, Benayeem pored over huge books about rangers. Isika was pleased that he had found something he was interested in, but when she looked at the pictures of the wide-shouldered, strong rangers—built more like Jabari—and then looked at Ben, his thin frame and fragile mind, she worried for him.

One day, she was in the workshop making cups for the four-year commission, nearly finished with her quota for the day, when Ben rushed into the workshop.

"I have an idea about how we can protect the city!" he said, pulling up beside her wheel.

Heads in the workshop swiveled toward him as the other apprentices paused to listen. He fell silent, his shoulders drawing in on each other as he realized he was the center of attention. Isika knew he hated attention unless he was singing. Beside her, Tomas glanced up at Ben, then went back to his work.

"Can it wait?" he asked. "Isika's nearly done for the day."

"Yes. Of course. Sorry. Where's Jabari?" Ben asked Isika in a low voice.

She gestured at the kiln room with her head, her hands busy forming another cup. Ben disappeared into the kiln room, where Jabari was busy loading the huge kiln with all of the pots they had made in the last week, ready for the first firing. Isika could hear them talking, an excited rush from Benayeem, and quieter interjections from Jabari. She frowned, annoyed. Thanks to Tomas, Jabari was hearing Ben's idea first.

The other apprentices began trickling out of the work-shop, hanging up their aprons as they went. Late afternoon sunshine flooded the workshop through the windows all along the tops of the walls. Isika finished her last cup and set it on the tray. She washed her hands, then walked back to the wheel to get her tray for the drying room. Jabari came out of the kiln room and got there first, lifting the tray easily.

"Tomas," he said. Tomas was still at his wheel, throwing bowl after bowl. He regularly worked longer than any of the apprentices. "If you have a minute, you should hear this idea too. I think it can work, but we'll need your help."

Tomas sighed, then nodded without looking up. "Give me a minute to finish this bowl and wash up," he said. "And I'll hear the young one's idea."

Isika, Ben, and Jabari were all gathered around one of the workshop tables when Tomas joined them.

"So, young ones, you're going to protect the city? Let's hear this idea."

Ben cleared his throat. "I've been researching the rangers from long ago," he said. "Long ago, there was an emperor from over the sea who wanted to take the city. He was a great sorcerer of Mugunta's magic, sending arrows into the city from afar. So what the rangers did was form a protective magic barrier from inside the city. Not a wall, nothing that would keep people out, but a barrier like a bowl, upside-down over the city, against the sky, to keep evil magic from attacking them." He grinned and sat back. "I think we should try it."

Isika's eyes grew wide. She hadn't known what to expect, but this idea actually sounded good. Jabari sat forward.

"I think we should do it," he said. "I've been bound by my parent's desires and my word not to go back out to the plains to fight fires. And it's driving me crazy because all my gifts tell me to protect the city. It's what I do." He glanced at Isika and she nodded. She knew how he felt. He spread his hands on the table, palms down, and leaned farther forward. "This could be a way for us to help without going against their wishes or leaving the city. And it could be a part of our apprenticeship too."

Tomas looked up, his thick brows drawing together.

"Part of your apprenticeship how?" he asked.

Isika drew circles on the table with her finger, her mind busy trying to figure out how to build protective magic like a pot.

"We would need to sculpt," she said. "And you could help us understand how to sculpt magic like clay. You know how, don't you? You were a ranger once."

Tomas squinted at her. "How did you know that?" he asked.

She shrugged. "Auntie told me," she said. She didn't have to add, *of course.*

"It's difficult magic," Tomas said, looking at them all. "And I think only you two," he gestured at Isika and Jabari, "would be able to do it."

"Why?" Isika asked. "Because we're potters?"

Tomas snorted. "No, daughter, think. Only you and Jabari have the life gifting, the combination of all the other gifts. You will need to combine building and protection to do this magic."

"I knew that," Ben put in. "It's only the idea that is from me."

"But don't underestimate him," Isika said. "He can learn anything."

Ben looked doubtful. Tomas looked thoughtful.

"We have this commission due..." he said.

"What good is the commission going to be if the palace burns down?" Jabari burst out.

"I didn't say I wouldn't do it," Tomas said, warning in his eyes. "Settle down young one." Jabari sat back, his face repentant, but he couldn't stop his grin.

And so they began. Every morning at dawn, before it was time to be in the workshop, Jabari and Isika went to the farthest barriers of the city and worked on a protective dome. They first made it out of a feathery magic that Jabari had used as a seeker before, guarding horses in fields that were under attack from poison. Then they worked on reinforcing it, much the way Isika would build a pot, except that they needed to add layer after layer of thin magic. Cracks formed, and they patched the cracks. It was invisible to most people, but if they wanted to make it visible for others to see, they could. She began wearing her circlet to work on the dome, because as it buzzed and hummed against her head, she could see more clearly how to build and reinforce the magic.

Tomas came out to observe sometimes, always sharp, always critical of their work. Isika could read him well, though, and she knew he was impressed. Often, the more impressed her teacher was, the more critical he got, so she didn't feel too badly.

She did feel tired, running from the workshop to the elders for Petitions, back to building the protection, back to the workshop. She fell into her bed at night, utterly exhausted. Auntie Teru, who knew what she was doing, wouldn't allow her to help with cooking or cleaning anymore, and Isika started to feel guilty about the burden she was on her adoptive mother.

But Jerutha, who was feeling better after her ordeal in the Worker city, came over one day and saw how hard Isika was working, and how Auntie needed help. Her eyes lit up.

"I'm bored to death in the palace," she said, "With all the servants there. Mesu is old enough to lie on a cushion and tell stories to the sky while I help Teru with cleaning. Don't feel badly, Isika. You're doing something good for all of us.

Teru snorted. "Yes," she said. "Just ask yourself, child, what good is a clean house if it burns to the ground?"

It was a near echo of Jabari's question to Tomas, and Auntie meant to be funny, but a cold wave of fear broke over Isika as she looked at Jerutha holding Mesu and Auntie sitting beside her. She worked harder than ever the next morning, patching holes in the protection, which always seemed to be under attack from the outside. Before the dome had been up, Isika hadn't realized just how much unfriendly magic was flying in their direction. It was a problem she frowned over when she woke in the night. She had thought Azariyah was so safe, when she first arrived. But it seemed they were in danger, too. And they shouldn't need this dome, as the elders reminded her when she overheard them whispering. She should be protection enough.

"Is it because she isn't queen yet?" She heard Andar ask Ivram in a low voice.

"Possibly. We can't know, this has never happened to us before. We always had one World Whisperer installed before the other came in. We have to be patient."

"But why is it getting worse?" Andar insisted, and then they noticed her sitting at the bottom of the stairs and became quiet. Both elders smiled and nodded at her, but Isika felt like some kind of toy, sitting there, mostly useless but meaningful because her position had been meaningful long ago.

It was nice to see more of Jerutha. Often, when Isika came home in the evenings, Jerutha was still there, and Isika could hold Mesu and sniff his neck, which always smelled like cinnamon. She cooed at him to make him laugh, while Jerutha bustled around the kitchen with Ibba and Kital close behind her, putting dishes on the table and cleaning up after Teru's wild bouts of angry cooking. Teru was angry, there was no doubt about it. When Teru was calm, her kitchen was calm. When she was angry, it was a storm. She flung spoons at the washing basin, rather than laying them carefully inside. She chopped wildly, so that bits of herbs flew through the air.

One day, when it was particularly bad, Isika held Mesu and watched Jerutha run around after Teru, cleaning the sauce that was trailing from her spoon. Isika was exhausted. That day, an entire piece of the dome had come down after a bad attack of fire in the east. They had felt the bite of the magic immediately. She and Jabari had worked to sculpt again, but they only got a thin layer done and they would need to be back out first thing in the morning. Isika felt as though her eyes would drift shut before food was even ready, but she couldn't watch Teru's sorrow and anger any more.

Enough, she thought. She stood, holding Mesu on her hip, and walked to the kitchen, a space open to the rest of the room, divided by a curving bench that was now covered in pots and pans.

"Auntie," she said. "Why are you so upset?"

Teru whirled, and from the sitting area, Isika saw Dawit set his book down in his lap and take his reading lenses off.

"Teru," he said, his voice a gentle warning.

"It is not you," Teru said. "It is only Azariyah, dear one. Not the city, but the woman. Our lost queen. Your grand-mother. I am angry again, now that these fires have come. I am angry that we lost her. I am angry that since we found you, we haven't done right by you. It seems that Mugunta is having his way after all, despite the fact that we found you again. Why must he poison everything? Why did we lose our son? Why do I have to sit by and watch you in danger every day, know that Gavi and Aria are out fighting fires and there is nothing I can do, nothing I can do..."

Dawit was there now, taking Auntie, who was sobbing, into his arms. He tried to lead her to her room to rest, the way he did when she was having a bad moment. But she shook her head wildly at him.

"No, my love, I don't want to leave. I want to be here; I want them to see how sad I am. They have to know all of me, to know the sorrow of me. Maybe they can love that too."

Jerutha made a short, low exclamation like a hurt animal, and Isika moved toward Teru.

"We do know, Auntie, and of course we love you. Mugunta is not winning, because there is still so much love here."

"You know I carry so much sorrow too," Jerutha whispered. "It is why I feel safe with you, Teru. Because you understand."

Dinner that night was late, but quieter and more peaceful than it had been in weeks. The family was a little group of refugees, people who had been through something terrible together and were happy to simply sit and eat, looking at each other from time to time, making sure each one was okay.

Chapter 14

Aria sat on her sleeping mat, staring at her open hands. She had the strangest feeling, as though she had never seen her hands before, never known what they were capable of.

It was Abbas and Gavi's turn to hunt tonight, so Ivy and Aria set up the sleeping mats, filled a pot with water, and chopped potatoes. Soon Gavi and Abbas returned to the camp, Abbas holding a large hare. Abbas was skilled at hunting, and on the boys' hunting nights, they returned quickly. Ivy had always been their best hunter, and she was determined to beat Abbas's speed at finding a meal for the group. Aria raised her eyebrows at Ivy—tonight may have been the fastest ever. Ivy smiled back at Aria, her face rueful.

Gavi shook his head with a smile as they walked to the fire.

"Abbas is the one you want with you on a journey," he

said. He opened his hand and showed Aria a cluster of what looked like tiny sticks. "Taste one," he said.

She picked up one of the sticks and put it in her mouth. It was spicy, an explosion of flavor that reminded her of something she couldn't quite place.

"He knows all the forest spices," Gavi said, moving toward the cooking pot while Abbas dressed the hare. "Our food will taste like palace food on this journey."

"I'm glad you came with us," Ivy said to Abbas. "Not just for the spices. You're a good travel companion."

Ivy sat across from Aria, building the fire between them. She did it quickly, seemingly without thought, her slender hands assembling a little tent of thin sticks, then pulling a red rock starter out of her pouch, to spark the fire in a nest of grasses. Aria shivered, thinking of all the grasses they had seen burning on this journey. But this was not that kind of fire. This fire was small and friendly, without malice.

"It's good to be here," Abbas said in his mild way. His accent curved and lilted the words so that they sounded like a song, Aria thought dreamily. He went on. "I was tired of being indoors. I have always been on the move, all my life."

"You are Gariah, right?" Aria asked, her voice surprising her. She hadn't spoken much that day, and it was rusty. She cleared her throat. "Do all the Gariah travel all the time?"

"I'm from an outer tribe," he told her. "We are the Karee, the moving ones. The Gariah live in the city, like the King. But many of them hate him also. Many fight from within, but he is very powerful."

"I heard you are some sort of prince," Ivy said, chopping

pieces of root that Abbas had found the day before. They were nutty, filling the soup with rich flavor.

"I am a prince; my father is the Karee king. But we are a small people without a permanent place. So I am a prince of tents." He stripped the meat from the bones of the hare, chopping it into a metal pot.

"Do you want to go back to them?" Gavi asked. The question had just occurred to Aria as well. Why had Abbas stayed with them, if he was a tribal prince?

His face grew sad as he walked to the soup pot, squatting to toss the hare meat into the water. "My people fight and lose," he said. "They have fled to the far edges of the desert. I was captured and made a slave." He stood up and flicked his long braid behind him. "I have seen the power of the World Whisperer, so I follow her now. I will help my people again one day, but beside the World Whisperer. I have seen it in my future."

Aria stared at him, her hands empty and open. She knew she should be helping with dinner, but she couldn't bring herself to move at all. She was bone weary, the kind of tired that you feel you will never recover from. She knew from talking to the others that they didn't feel like this. It was the arrow that did this to her.

And there was Abbas, also talking about following her sister. Isika, who had abandoned Aria and sent her in a boat to die. Didn't anyone care that Isika had sent her out? She caught herself. No, Isika hadn't sent her out. Isika was only a child when Aria was outcast at the shore of the village. Isika wanted to be her friend.

But she hated you. They all do.

She didn't know where the voice came from. It came out of nowhere, lately, whispering to her about her own unloveliness, the fact that nobody wanted her. She clenched her hands tight. When she looked up, Gavi was watching her.

"Having a hard time again, tonight, little bird?" he asked. The kindness in his voice was too much; tears sprang to her eyes and she nodded without words.

Abbas pulled out his pack of spices, so Aria knew it would be stew with zing again tonight, tasting like the far-off desert where Abbas came from. He was older than them, close to thirty, she thought. He was someone who had seen a lot, and for a moment, all the sorrow he must have known threatened to overwhelm her, but then Gavi came, sitting beside her on her rock. She sighed.

Gavi took her hand, and she leaned on his shoulder, exhausted from fighting the arrow, fighting her mind. Every few nights, when the arrow became too much to battle, he used his healing magic to help her. The healers in Azariyah had been baffled by this arrow, dug deep into her. They didn't understand why they couldn't pull it out. Before she left they had been confident that they had taken care of it, that she would absorb the poison and get rid of it. But she wouldn't and she knew why they couldn't remove it, though she didn't know how to explain. The poison arrow was wedged in tight, near her ribs, into the place that had never healed, the part of her that had been sent away.

Gavi's magic felt like her real mother stroking her forehead when she couldn't sleep. Like her mother's voice, as she sang in the evenings. After she had been sent away, Aria had cried and cried for her mother. She had wept until it felt like she would die. She longed for her in a way that she had never longed for anything since. And some tiny dream in her, that she would see her mother again, died the day she found Isika again and her sister told her their mother was dead.

She bowed her head as Gavi's magic soothed her. It filled the empty spaces, and she felt hope returning. Maybe there was a place for her. Maybe she wouldn't always be cast off and abandoned, motherless. She remembered her foster parents, how they took care of her, loved her, joked with her. She smiled.

"Little bird?" she asked, her voice hoarse. "I'm more like a little broken duck, with an annoying cry."

"There's our girl," Gavi responded. "But no, you're our little bird. We need to keep you well until we figure this out and you can fly again."

Tears sprang to her eyes again. Gavi was so kind. A lot of time had passed while she dreamed of her mother's voice. The soup was bubbling. Her stomach rumbled at the fragrance. Ivy bent over the pot and began to fill bowls. Gavi was still holding Aria's hand and she felt even more strength coming from him. All at once, the circle seemed friendly again, and she couldn't wait to eat and talk over the day with them, the way they did in the evenings. She loved her friends, and she loved Maween. She pulled away and looked at him.

"Thank you," she said. His eyes had flowers in them. Most people in Maween had dark brown eyes, but Gavi's were blue like the sky, with rays that bloomed out from the dark centers.

He smiled, touching her face, once, lightly. "It's an honor to help you, Little Bird. You're stronger than you know."

He stood and took a bowl from Ivy, wandering over to another stone and perching on it, his long arms and legs folded up. Ivy came and offered Aria a bowl of stew, and she took it, holding her face over it, breathing it in. It smelled like far away, like running across the desert, like being under night skies.

"Thank you, Abbas, for gathering things for us to eat," she said. He looked up, his earrings gleaming in the firelight.

"You're welcome. Little Bird. It suits you."

"Yes, it does," Ivy added. "And this soup is ridiculously good. How are you even real, Abbas? Gavi, a prince has made us soup. We've really come up in the world."

"Well, an almost-queen makes us our bowls, so you're right," Gavi said.

They all laughed, even Aria.

AFTER THEY HAD FINISHED and were sitting around feeling the excellent feeling of being full, Gavi asked the question Aria had been wondering about.

"What do we do?" he asked. "We have walls and fires, everywhere we go. Do we ignore the fires and work on the walls? Or do we need to put fires out first? Or do we have to do it all?" He shook his head.

"I think we should split up at each house," Aria said. "I

will take care of the fires, and you can take care of the walls and the people inside."

They were all shaking their heads at her, instantly.

"Nope," Ivy said.

"No, Aria, we're not splitting up. But it doesn't work for us to do it so slowly. What is it you do, when you're putting those fires out? How do you keep from being burned?"

Aria looked down at her hands again. She thought about it. Part of her wanted to hold it back, to keep it as her own gift, something special for herself. But then she thought of all the fields burning, slowly dying, with the people locked inside their houses by walls and poison, losing everything. So she tried to understand what she was doing, when she put the fires out.

"The fire is not actually hot," she said slowly. "Though it tricks us... I think I see it as it truly is. Malicious. Poisonous. But not a true fire. It burns because we let it. Our fear of it gives it heat."

She looked up to find them all staring at her.

"Who are you, Little Bird?" Gavi asked. "How did you know that?"

She flinched, wondering at the question, but he saw her face. "I'm just kidding with you, I know who you are, Aria Rescued One. But this is amazing, that you understood this. Of course. A poison fire is not really a fire, just as a poison wall is not really a wall. It is fear that makes it real. Fear of something that isn't actually there."

Ivy was shaking her head, her eyes wide. "We have to

write this down or something, Gavling, she's cracked some kind of code. She's a genius."

Aria grinned at them. "You two are crazy," she said.

"Crazy in love with you," Ivy said, and Aria laughed then.

Abbas broke in. "I don't actually understand yet. Forgive me."

Gavi looked up from scribbling something in a small book he always carried with him. "The walls we see can be broken easily, because they are not real walls, they are poison walls. It is fear that makes them real. Fear of others, fear of the poison that makes them. So when we come and we do not fear them, when we have this gift, we can pull them down, turn them to dust."

Abbas nodded, his dark eyes thoughtful.

"These fires are the same, but this time, the fear gives them heat, makes them real. They burn because we see them. That's why they can sit there for so long without actually burning anything away. But when we see them and fear them, they turn into real, burning, hot fire. So the answer is to go to the fire without fear. To fight them as poison, not as fire. The way we take down walls as though they are nothing."

"Because they are nothing," Aria said. And maybe it was because they were around the warm, real fire, maybe it was because Ivy had said they loved her, maybe because Gavi had just used his gift to heal her, but she felt a sudden, hot surge of hope that they would overcome the poison, even the poison arrow in her. Because they would not fear.

Chapter 15

The next day, Gavi woke Aria and Ivy at dawn. Abbas was already up, going through his paces, swinging his staff in arcs with the rising sun illuminating him. Abbas always woke earlier than anyone else, practicing staff work, or archery, or footwork. He seemed to be perpetually in motion and always aware, and Gavi was beginning to understand how disciplined he was, to continue in that way. He paused to watch the warrior prince for a moment.

Spines and stones, he needed to learn from Abbas. Abbas looked up as though he could sense Gavi watching. He whirled one more quarter circle and lunged with his staff, then relaxed, placing the staff point down and leaning on it.

"Can you teach me how to do that?" Gavi asked.

Abbas's eyebrows shot up and he smiled. "Yes. Should we start now?"

Gavi laughed. "No, not now. Today we need to pack up and test our fire theory."

He was more than ready to move, to get to work on the problem of the fires with a new theory in mind. He had barely been able to sleep after Aria opened up the concept of poison fires for him. Nearly every house with walls also had a fire in the fields nearby, and he couldn't stand the thought of so much poison just sitting there, unchecked. They would send it back to the Great Waste, where it belonged.

"Nenyi help us," he whispered.

They ate cold soup and packed away their bedding, then they were walking down the road. Aria's braids stuck up on one side of her head after the hasty morning, and Gavi smiled at her, though she didn't see him. His face fell as he thought of the arrow that hurt her. He could feel it every time he took a moment to send healing magic toward her. How had she hidden it so the healers sent her on the journey? What could heal it? Would her poison theory work in the fields? Would Gavi be able to put fire out with his hands?

It wasn't long before he had a chance to try. Mid-morning, they came upon a long, long wall that had erupted around a large earth house, one with enough space for a big family. All around the house were fields of short, newly planted bean seedlings, and streams of smoke lifted into the sky from spots scattered through the field. Short flames flickered in every direction, and as they watched, the flames burned higher. Aria met his eyes and nodded.

"It's true," Gavi said. "They burn higher when we see them."

He waded into the middle of the field, the others following, avoiding the fires as they walked, then stood, looking around at the rows of beans and flames.

"Now's the time to test Aria's theory," Gavi said. "A theory my gut believes is right. So let's go. North, East, South and West, kids."

Gavi went West, his face toward the distant, invisible sea. He walked toward the first column of smoke he saw and immediately he felt it, the hot hand of poison fire. The flame leapt up in response, becoming real, singeing the edges of the plant, until the little thing wilted and fell. He stared at it in consternation. How could he not fear this thing?

Behind him somewhere, he heard music. Ivy, walking to the south, was singing.

"Out of the cracked earth
Out of the fire
Out of the flood and storm
Out of the desert
You bring light
You bring light"

GAVI BEGAN to sing as well, and he heard Aria's sweet voice joining from the northern side.

"Oh the earth cries
Oh the scorched cries
Oh the floods cry
Oh we cry
You bring light

You bring light"

GAVI BENT DOWN, cupping his hands as though he was catching a frog, and placed his hands right on the fire. He felt the bitter taste of poison, smelled the burnt edges of it, and the fire went out. He stood up, gleeful, looking around, but they were focused on their own fires, so he went on to the next one, and they went on that way, their song floating around them, winding its way around the field until all the fires were gone. The sun was high in the sky.

All four of them sat on the side of the road, exhausted but jubilant, until Gavi shook himself.

"We need to take down the walls and release the people from poison so they can care for their lands and the fires don't come back," he said. His voice sounded hoarse from singing and smoke.

Ivy nodded and jumped up, clapping her hands. There was a long streak of soot down the side of her face. She grinned at them.

"What are you waiting for?" she asked, and Gavi was so thankful for her irrepressible spirit, the Ivy-ness of her, that he jumped up and hugged her. Soon he felt a little hug by his side—Aria—and a hand on his shoulder, and the four of them were clinging to each other. They turned—Gavi saw Ivy wipe tears away with the palm of her hand—and began attacking the walls, pulling them to dust, then pulling down the second walls which sprang up after, the shame walls, Jabari called them. It was hard work, after they had spent so much time on the field already. But they sang, and it made the work go faster.

"YOU BRING LIGHT.
You bring light."

INSIDE THE HOUSE, a family had been trapped in the poison for months, doing nothing but eating and sleeping. They were thin from exhausting their food stores. Three young children sat on a bed at the edge of the room, and Gavi had to hold back tears at the look in their eyes when he walked in. They knew immediately who the seekers were and ran to them, shouting and crying.

"You're here!" the oldest said. She couldn't have been more than nine. "We knew you would come."

Looking around, Gavi saw the mother sitting on the floor in the corner, rocking back and forth with her *ser* on her head. He saw the father in the other room, lying on the bed they shared. And there were more people! Perhaps the children were cousins, because there were also another man and woman, and two elder people.

He and Ivy went from person to person, touching their foreheads, calling them back from fear and shame. Abbas and Aria played with the kids and began cleaning, sweeping away the dust of the months of being locked inside with poison, uncaring and bleak. Gavi turned away from the last woman, who smiled at him, and threw open the wooden shutters that covered the windows on the earth walls. He was shaking with exhaustion.

The people knew what to do. They had been poisoned before, one of the men said, but a long time ago, so they had never met Gavi, though they had heard of him.

"You have?" he asked, incredulously.

"Oh, yes," the woman next to him said, holding one of the children in her lap. "Everyone knows of the rescued son of the elders, white-skinned, with a gentle, healing touch and hair like the sun."

"Gavling, you're famous!" Ivy said, laughing.

Gavi was floored. He had lived in Jabari's shadow all his life, and to be honest, he didn't mind it there. In Jabari's wake, things were a bit easier. Jabari plowed through everything and it was easy to walk behind him. To hide away in the vegetable gardens and let his brother do the work. But he had never known that people talked about him, knew who he was. He looked at Aria and her eyes were shining at him.

It was a strange feeling, to be recognized, to be away from Jabari and still be seen. He wasn't sure it was a comfortable feeling, but it flickered in his heart and didn't go away.

They slept there that night, barely making it through dinner before they were asleep. The healing from poison was complete with the offer of hospitality, so it was crucial that the family offered them food and a place to stay. This family was more than happy to. They recovered quickly, jumping to make things more comfortable for the seekers. When the seekers refused to take beds from the family, the family found mats that they cleaned of dust, and Gavi was asleep as soon as he lay down.

The next day, they set off, aching and happy, content to walk along the road, looking for another place to help. Right away, they put out a tiny ring of fires in brush that didn't seem to have a family attached to it.

They were at a crossroads, when Gavi saw it. Down the road was some sort of disturbance, dust kicking up and barely visible people, tiny in the distance. In the plains beyond, he saw more dust.

"Abbas," Gavi said, his voice low. "What is that?"

Abbas turned to look and his whole body tensed.

"That is a Gariah force," he said, his voice an intense whisper. "What are they doing on Maweel land?"

Ivy gasped and Aria's face paled. Gavi felt a swooping sick feeling in the center of his stomach.

"What do you mean a Gariah force?"

"The army of the Gariah," Abbas said, staring into the distance with one hand shading his eyes. "Soldiers, with horses."

"They're moving toward the city," Ivy said, panic in her voice. "What is happening, what are they doing?"

"I will go closer," Abbas said. "I want to see who is leading them. The leader of the force will give us an idea of what they are doing. An attack commander will let us know they mean to attack, but if they are a discovery force, we will know they are spying."

Gavi felt the blood leave his face at the mention of attacking and spying. In his lifetime there had been a lot of poison, but never a real battle. He felt dizzy, but stepped forward anyway.

"I'll go with you," he said.

"What about us?" Ivy said. "We just sit here?"

"Someone needs to stay with Aria," Gavi said. "She's not going anywhere. She's too young and not well, besides."

For a moment, Aria looked as though she wanted to argue, but she also looked a little pinched around the lips. After a moment she nodded. Ivy, on the other hand, spoke short, intense words with Gavi, telling him why she should go with Abbas instead of him, and in the end he won, but not without pulling out his leader status. He didn't like doing it, but he was sure of three things: Aria needed to stay, she couldn't stay alone, and he needed to see what was happening with that force.

Just before he and Abbas walked off, Aria spoke.

"There's something... I don't know. I don't feel at all well about this. Be careful, you two."

"What do you mean?" Gavi asked.

"I feel something... I don't know what it is. But something is seriously wrong."

Gavi and Abbas walked down the road until they felt they were too visible, and then they continued in a copse of trees that followed the side of the road for a long way. Abbas waited and watched every few minutes, but it didn't seem as though anyone knew they were there. As they drew close, Gavi got a clear picture of Abbas as warrior prince, trained for stealth and battle. It seemed that Abbas always knew where to step, how to get from place to place without being seen, especially as they drew nearer to the large cloud of dust that hid the camp.

Gavi felt strange things in the forest, movement and creaking, as though the trees were uneasy. And he could taste it himself, the horror of the Great Waste. He tasted intense fear and a great sense of loss. The nearer they got, the more Gavi felt as though he could hear the earth crying. He was puzzling over this when Abbas put a hand out to stop him.

"They are setting up camp now," Abbas said. "Stopping for the night, I think. If we watch, I may be able to tell who it is, just by the color of their tent."

They waited while the men on horseback dismounted and joined the men on foot. They gathered in a loose circle, unpacking and setting up short white tents. Abbas pointed out a couple of men who had left the camp and were walking toward them.

"Scouts," he whispered. "We'll have to leave soon, so they don't find us."

The scouts drew closer. Gavi could see their faces under their *sers*. He wasn't sure if the Gariah called their head coverings *sers*, but they looked the same as what Gavi had worn all his life to protect his head from the sun.

"We need to go," he whispered. He could see the satchel that one man had slung over his shoulder. It wouldn't be long before the men stumbled on Gavi and Abbas in the brush.

"Just a moment, they are raising the leader's tent, I can almost..."

Gavi waited, his heart beating in his throat as the Gariah scouts drew nearer.

Abbas drew a startled breath, suddenly, and said, "Let's go."

Together they turned and ran back through the brush, as quietly as they could, not daring to see whether they were pursued. After they had run a while, Abbas threw out a hand and they halted, crouching behind the trees. They heard nothing. When Abbas stood up to look, they could see the scouts heading back to the camp. Either they hadn't seen them or they were too lazy to pursue, or they didn't consider them worth pursuing. In any case, no one followed and Gavi was thankful.

They walked the rest of the way back to the others, Abbas deep in thought. Gavi was dying to know who the tent belonged to, but sensed that Abbas wanted to reach the girls, and talk while they were all together. They nearly tripped over Ivy and Aria when they reached them, sitting by the side of the road next to a well, in the shade of a *hoona* tree.

He and Abbas drank and they all filled their flasks, sitting and resting in the shade. Gavi felt that the wait was unbearable as the tension grew and grew. Finally Abbas spoke.

"I don't understand it and I hate to bear this news, but the leader of the force that is going to Azariyah is to be feared above all men."

"What? Who is it?"

Gavi knew it in his bones, as the earth shifted underneath him, crying out against the force of Mugunta in the world, knew it even as Abbas drew a breath to speak.

"It is King Ikajo, the Desert King."

Chapter 16

Jabari's aim was off. He stared blearily at the target, the area scattered with arrows that had pinged off the target, or hit the wrong bar. The targets were long, like trees, painted with dots that Jabari could usually hit, one after another, barely stopping to pause. He had always had a gift for true aim. But his nights had become crazy ever since he started having the dreams, and he wasn't sleeping.

HE HAD NEVER DREAMED at night, or at least he never remembered his dreams. His mother was a dreamer who sometimes had foretelling, but Jabari usually fell asleep and was dead to the world within minutes, sleeping a dreamless sleep and waking up feeling great. Things had changed. Over the last weeks, he had been dreaming every night. Night after night he woke up sweating when the sky was still dark, and owls swept through the trees. The dreams often started out differently, but the same one woke him up at the end. He sometimes went up to the rooftop of the palace to lie on the cool stone and let the bats and owls fly over him, watching the stars and waiting for the dream to fade. He was tired in the mornings now. What was happening to him? He wished that he could get back to being normal.

He walked to the target and picked arrows out of the grass. The earth was parched and the morning was already hot, so that moisture beaded on the back of his neck and back and his hands were slippery. He jammed the arrows back into his quiver, slung it over his back, and slowly walked back to the shooting area. The morning was just beginning; people starting to be up and around, doing the morning work. The birds called to one another, and he could hear the coffee sellers outside the palace, and the cooks in the kitchen calling out orders.

Jabari had always loved mornings at the palace. Everybody knew what they needed to do, they flowed back and forth, full of hope for the day. He loved seeing the housekeepers with their brooms in the courtyard, shaking out rugs, or the gardeners climbing trees to pick fruit, beginning the first watering cycle of the day. Growing up in the palace had been beautiful, he realized, as a thought of what Isika's mornings might have been like crossed his mind.

He stood with his feet planted and took aim at the target. He aimed for the circle on the very top, but his arrow went slightly shy of it. It thudded into the tree behind the target. What was wrong with him today? He gritted his teeth and shot arrow after arrow. Somewhere around the third or fourth arrow he began to get his skills back, and the arrows thudded into the centers of the painted circles. He sighed with relief. With the Gariah force in their front yard, Jabari couldn't afford to lose his archery gift. The sun was gaining heat, despite the smoky haze that covered the city. Sweat trickled down his forehead, along his face, and dripped from under his jaw.

What he wanted more than anything was Gavi beside him, so they could talk about the dreams. Gavi or Ivy, either one. Someone who had known him since he was a child, knew that he wasn't usually so afraid. Last night had been horrible.

The dream was faded, a world without much color, and Isika was in the mouth of a shark. The shark carried her swiftly away, and Isika screamed for him. He swam and swam but he couldn't reach her. And then the same ending to the dream, the one that woke him. The man.

Morning bells pealed out over the city. It was time for the singing to begin in the tower. The singers had been diligent, singing for the lives of the rangers who fought the fire. Singing to strengthen them, singing to fight the power of the poison of the fire. They had an important job, every bit as needed as what the actual rangers did.

The sound of the singing drifted out over the practice field and Jabari's throat tightened. It may have been the dreams that had him so tense, because he had never been a dreamer, but it could be something else. He hadn't been a night dreamer, but two dreams for his life had always guided him, leading him until now. The first, to be the Lightwalker of Nenyi. This was a pipe dream, because Lightwalker was someone he and Gavi had made up, not even a real thing. Still, striving for it shaped what he did and who he was. The other dream was to find the stolen queen. Jabari had spent his whole life daydreaming about finding her. He thought about what she would be like when he found her and how he would serve her forever. He had grown up hearing stories of her magnificence and beauty. But he hadn't found her.

She had died; she had died. The sorrow of it gripped his throat again. She was dead, and he would never be the one to find her. But he had found Isika, her granddaughter. Now he lived his life near someone who was the next queen. She was next to him as they ate, next to him as they walked, next to him as they created the barrier that was protecting the city even as he stood here shooting arrows into a target. She was with him; he had found her! He had been the one to bring her back, so this dream had happened.

But it wasn't what he had imagined. He wasn't sure who he was without these things driving him, because Isika was Lightwalker, not Jabari, and though he had found her, the future queen, he couldn't serve her. At least, not in the way he had dreamed of serving the stolen queen. When he had dreamed of a queen he had dreamed of someone older, more magnificent, ageless and perfect. He hadn't imagined his real-life flawed friend and he didn't know what to do now that his dreams were different. He didn't know what to make of himself. And now his nights were something he couldn't recognize.

He straightened. All his arrows were spent again. He walked out and began to pick them up, one by one, pausing to see if they were bent or if the feathers were crumpled. He had dreams of Gavi fighting off mud demons, of his father running over clouds as though he was made of air. He had dreams of a red-cloaked man and sometimes he was looking out through the eyes of the red-cloaked man, at the face of a beautiful woman who resembled Ben and Aria. She had pleading eyes and small children clung to her robes. He dreamed he was Aria in a boat, all alone, no one nearby, and the waves threw the boat around and soaked him to the bone, and he knew he would die.

He dreamed he was the red-cloaked man, and he ran and ran, though endless hallways, turning and never finding a way out, always searching, looking for the woman with the children. That was the end of the dreams, the one that always woke him. When he woke, his heart raced and he needed to get air, so he went to the roof to find it, but the smoke had begun to hide the stars. He wished his nights were still just for sleep.

After he had every arrow back in his quiver, he turned to walk back to the palace, going the long way to see out over the fields. On the way into the palace, he saw Ben, who was heading out of the palace after First Singing. He had his head down, hurrying toward something that Jabari couldn't imagine. He knew Ben was burdened in a way none of the rest of them could understand.

"Ben!" he called, wanting to catch him.

Ben paused, looking up, and waited for Jabari to reach

him. *He's grown,* Jabari realized. They were all growing up, on the cusp of moving into something new. He thought that the dreams might have something to do with this, that perhaps growing up was tangled with finding new gifts. Were the dreams even a gift? Or some poison sent to tangle his thoughts and keep him from focus? As he grew closer to Ben, Ben's face changed and grew troubled as he heard something of Jabari's thoughts through the music that came from him. *What does it sound like today?* Jabari wondered.

"What's going on?" asked Ben.

"I don't know how to answer that." Jabari said.

Benayeem stared. "Whoa, I never see you like this. You have such serious music coming from you, I haven't heard it sound this way since we got back from the Worker city."

Jabari grinned. "I should have known you would be able to tell. Are you walking home?"

"Just back to the house," Ben said. "I'm on my way to get something to eat before Second Singing. But it's barely morning, where have you been so early?"

"On the archery field. But I've been up since before dawn. I couldn't sleep."

Ben just looked at him, waiting for him to go on.

"I've been having dreams like I've never had before," he said. "They feel strange, like I'm seeing real things. You know dreams can be from someone's gift, right? So they see things that actually happen, or are going to happen? Or they see the truth of things?"

"Like Brigid?" Ben asked.

Jabari nodded. "Yes, in a way, but Brigid has dreams

when she's awake. She has feelings, or senses. Sometimes she can see things even when she's walking, and people around her have to help her, or else she could hurt herself. Mine are not like that. They happen when I'm sleeping and I don't know what they mean."

"What have you been dreaming about?" Ben asked.

"Oh, shapes and colors. Isika in the jaws of a shark. Aria in her boat. You as a small child, hiding under a table."

Ben stared at him, his eyes wide.

"Wait, sorry, Ben. I should have thought before I said that. Of course that would be hard to hear."

"No, no it's okay," Ben said, "I just... never mind. I wasn't expecting the dreams to be about us."

What isn't these days? Jabari thought, but there was no bitterness in the question.

They were going down the stone road now, getting closer to the hill where they would climb toward Ben's house.

"I keep seeing a man in a red cloak," Jabari said.

"A red cloak?" Ben echoed. His eyes were wide again.

"Yes. And small children, and there is a woman. I think she's your mother. Do you know anything of the red cloak?" Jabari asked. "It seems important, because I dream of him more than anyone else."

Ben shook his head quickly, his eyes darting away, so that Jabari knew he wasn't telling everything. He felt a pang of regret. He had hurt Ben somehow with this talk. It wasn't what he had intended.

"Listen, I'm sorry," he said. "I was looking for answers, but I should've thought before I spoke."

Ben shook his head again. "No, no. It's not... I don't know. Don't worry." He seemed shaken.

"Ben, you know if you need to talk, you can talk to me," Jabari said.

Ben nodded. "I know." He still wouldn't meet Jabari's eyes, looking off over the fields that were still burning.

THAT NIGHT the dream was different. He walked through a mile of tents, and the smells were so real, the smoke stung his eyes. Just ahead of him, the man in the red cloak hurried away. Jabari ran after him. He wanted to catch the man and ask who he was. He tried to reach him, but the crowd was thick on either side, and as Jabari looked around, he saw that they were warriors with white paint on their dark faces, rattling anklets around their legs. Gariah warriors, he realized. He was in the Gariah camp.

He wandered through the tents of the camp, Jabari always in pursuit of the man with the red cloak, always just behind him, his legs slower than he wanted them to be so that he could never catch up. He nearly sobbed with frustration. He knew that if he could just get to the man, grab his sleeve, if he could make him look, maybe he would finally get answers. Who was the man, and why he was following him through his dreams?

They walked and walked, and Jabari began to look more closely at the Gariah warriors. Maybe they would give him some answers. The warriors wore chains around their ankles to frighten their enemies. They rattled as they walked, and when they walked in unison it made a huge sound, making them seem bigger than they were. Jabari saw the men's faces, real faces, all different. This made him more afraid than anything had in the dream so far. Was he really in this camp?

He started to listen, he could understand their accents easily because of Abbas. They spoke of war and fire, and the Desert King, and a prickle of fear went up Jabari's spine. What were they bringing to his lands?

The man was getting away, as Jabari lingered, listening. Jabari ran, feeling as though he ran through water, and just before Jabari caught him, the man turned, as though he felt Jabari there. Jabari came to a halt suddenly, and everything became very quiet. The warriors disappeared, and all he could see was the man's face. The man stared at him, and Jabari knew he was looking into the eyes of a real person.

"Who are you?" he asked.

"Protect her," the man said. "Protect her."

There was a roaring sound, and Jabari looked up to see a tent with a flag. The king's tent. He heard a horrifying voice, bellowing. "Who is in this camp? I sense him!"

Jabari was afraid. The man in red looked at him with stern eyes.

"Young one, she is in the mouth of a shark. Protect her. Protect her. Protect her."

The king roared in his tent, and Jabari turned to run, but the man in red had tears in his eyes now.

"I have always... I have spent my life, I have spent my life trying to protect her. Protect her with your own life if you need to, she is my lovely one."

Jabari knew he had to leave or the warriors were going to come for him.

"Are you speaking of her?" he asked. "Or of her mother?"

And the man closed his eyes and he began to weep, and Jabari saw that he was melting with tears.

"Oh, but the mother is gone," he said. "I feel it. I feel it. She is gone, my lovely one."

Jabari woke up to find that his face was wet with tears.

Chapter 17

Isika stood on the upper rooftop of the palace, among the elaborate rooftop gardens her grandmother had commissioned. She held her face to the sky, running her eyes over the magic dome she had constructed with Jabari. She searched for answers with her mind. What was making holes in it, and how could they patch the holes so the protective magic would stay put? Jabari stood beside her, his face turned upward as well, and Ben lay nearby, his arms crossed under his head as he stretched out on a patch of grass in the rooftop gardens. Keethior dozed on a rock nearby. He didn't leave Isika's side lately, which was strange for him, the most independent, haughty servant in the world. Before, she could never find him when she needed him. Now he flew everywhere she went, sleeping outside her window at night, or sometimes even perched on her bed, and when she asked him about the change, he pretended he didn't hear her.

The palace was the heart of Azariyah city, and from the rooftop, they could see for miles. The houses of the city looked small and sweet from here, and the forest spilled into the feet of the mountain on the north side of the city. The palace was also at the center point of the dome, and Isika could see rivers of light pulsating along the crest and spiraling outward. The dome stretched over the woods beyond, in case the poisoner decided to try attacking the city from behind, sending fires through the woods. Isika shivered, thinking of it. Her beloved trees. She felt sick at the horrible possibility.

"I think we need screen magic again," Jabari said. "We can't put a molded patch over that, there's nothing left of the edges."

Isika nodded. "But where are the holes coming from? What is hitting the dome that has the power to make holes in such a strong force?" She knew it was strong. The two of them had crafted it with all the power in them. Even Ivram was impressed. She knew it because when he had come to look at their work, he had stared at the dome, openmouthed, for a few minutes before patting her on the shoulder.

"This is it, young one," he said. "This is exactly the kind of work we hoped for, during your trial."

She smiled at him sadly. Something told her it wouldn't be long before she would be breaking the rules of the trial again. She felt it under her skin, a burning that seemed it would sear holes in her, the way holes were forming in the dome. She felt torn. Pulled. She felt that one good option was to tear the barrier down and greet what came with fists out and bared teeth. But of course that wasn't right. She couldn't understand the urge, so she shoved it away. But she worried that it wouldn't be long before the pull was too strong to ignore.

Ivram had gone on to wander around the entire dome, muttering to himself. He threw a patch up in one place, and even gave some excellent advice on how it could be better supported at the center.

Jerutha, when she came to visit, was confused.

"But how is a dome different?" she asked. She had grown up with the sacred walls of the Worker village and was still unsure about why the Maweel hated them. "You don't like the walls. Isn't a dome a rounded wall?"

Isika glanced at Jabari, so he answered. "Walls are grown of poison, by Mugunta, or what you would call the goddesses, to keep people away from each other, to keep people out. The dome will only keep the poison of the fires away."

"But then, won't it keep the poison in, as well?"

Isika thought about that now, as she stood staring up at the top of the barrier, trying to get the energy to make a screen again, to paste it over the patchwork barrier.

"What if what Jerutha said was right?" She asked Jabari. "What if we can't hold this thing together because we're keeping poison in?"

Jabari stared at her, frowning, and she watched as his eyes grew wide and thoughtful. He nodded slowly.

"We need to make it permeable on the inside, so poison that makes holes and comes in can get back out. But that can only work one way. How is it possible?"

Isika shook her head. She didn't know how to fight a

poison so strong. How could she? She was so new at this. Apparently this part didn't come by intuition, the way so many other things had.

She saw movement out of the corner of her eye and turned to see Brigid walking to them, running her hands along the short hedge that formed the walkway on the rooftop garden.

Brigid had become a better and better friend. Lately Isika and Jabari went tree climbing often, and sometimes they invited Brigid along. The sky had been so smoky lately, and there was so much work to be done. Isika was exhausted, so she spent any free time she had in trees.

Keethior ruffled his feathers, waking up, then opened his wings once, flashing the deep red lights in his feathers, as Brigid approached. Isika watched the bird. Despite the calm of his presence and the sweetness of the Othra, his out-of-character behavior made her nervous. So did his silence.

Brigid drew near, and Isika started to greet her friend, but Brigid interrupted her.

"There is something," Brigid said, clearly distressed, her hair coming out of its long braid as though she had been in a windstorm. "I can feel... I don't know, but there is something big coming this way. I thought I should warn you."

Brigid's gift caused her to sense things in a way that made her very rarely wrong. She was wild-eyed, and as Isika stood there, speechless, not sure what to say to her or how to ask what she meant, a wind picked up and there was a loud, rushing sound. Isika turned in the direction of the sound and saw an impossible thing.

Below them, hundreds of animals galloped, ran, or flew along the stone road toward the palace from the plains. As Isika watched from the high place, people began coming out of their houses to stand along the road, open-mouthed at the sight. The stampede of animals moved as one, closer and closer, up the hill, and as they did, Isika felt a wave of their thoughts, their fears calling to her. She spotted the purple and silver shimmers of the Keerza among them, and then they were clambering, hoofing, and flying up the stairs toward her.

In the air were more Othra than she had ever seen, their feathers alight with all the colors of bright jewels. There were other birds: large eagles, the tiniest finches, little bits of blue and green that seemed as though they couldn't be flying so swiftly. And the running animals—she saw big cats and the fleet footed deer of the plains, she saw horses and cattle, and their cries, wordless and desperate, surrounded her and filled her mind. She sank to her knees, distressed because she wanted to help, but she was overcome, overwhelmed by the sheer number of them. She could hear Keerza speech but not what the Keerza were saying, and it was mixed with fox calls and bird cries, and the speech of the horses who had apparently broken out of the horse pens of nearby houses. She bent low over her knees, trying to find a quiet place.

Stop! she called, but her voice was tiny in the storm. *I can't hear you!*

Before she was completely curled in a ball, Keethior was there, fully, fiercely awake, and he flew to stand before her, taller than her as she knelt, his wings spread to block her from the multitude of animals. His Othra calm was a curtain of quiet between them. Slowly, slowly, the animals quieted, and Isika sat up, wiping at her face with her palms. She had tears running down her cheeks from the piercing noise of their pain.

Keethior was speaking into their minds in animal speech.

Pick a representative, he said. *One animal can tell us what has happened. The World Whisperer cannot understand when you talk like this.*

There was murmuring and then an old Keerza stepped forward; an ancient purple gazelle with massive antlers that rose from his head, gleaming like silver. Isika shook her head to clear it, and Jabari held his hand out for her to grasp as she slowly stood up to speak with the Keerza. The air was smokier than ever, and Isika was having trouble seeing which animals were actually there. Jabari stood right beside her, and Benayeem was next to him. Ben's face was tight with pain, and Isika suspected he had been just as blindsided by the music of the animals as she had been by their speech.

Lady, the Keerza said. *There is deep evil coming. We think it is Mugunta himself.*

What? How can Mugunta move? Mugunta is not a person.

There was murmuring among the Keerza and the Keerza who spoke corrected himself.

Maybe Mugunta cannot come here, but there is deep evil, deeper than any that has come to Azariyah before. We are fleeing because fire goes before them, burning everything, and we will go to the mountain. Nenyi has told us that we should warn you before we go. So we have come to warn you.

Isika's stomach dropped. *Warn me of what?*

Warn you that not all is lost. And tell you that you are Nenyi's own.

Isika was thoroughly confused now, because it didn't sound like a warning. She turned to look up at Jabari, and by the look on his face, she knew she wasn't the only one who was confused. She could see that he had been following the conversation, his brow furrowed. Now he spoke.

Honored Keerza, he said. *We know she is Nenyi's own. She has the mark of Nenyi on her, his magic is with her.*

Do not doubt! the Keerza said, nearly shouting in Isika's mind. There was more murmuring from the animals, and as one, the Othra opened their wings in a slow flap in the way they had, releasing feelings of calm and goodness over the group. Isika could count twenty of the Othra, and she was tempted to go to them and meet them, but the old Keerza was speaking again, fiercely, to Jabari.

Especially you, son of Andar, do not doubt. The World Whisperer needs you.

Jabari looked back at the Keerza, but his gaze was distant, almost as though he was looking beyond them into something deeper.

Brigid was there on her other side, then, slipping her hand into Isika's, and Isika leaned against her friend, her knees suddenly shaky. The walking animals began to go down the back stairs and range toward the forest on the other side of the palace walls. The Othra and other birds lifted up from the palace and followed. Keethior stayed on guard in front of Isika, though he let his wings settle back down.

Within a matter of minutes, they were alone on the palace rooftop. The gardens were trampled and eaten in places.

After a long silence, Jabari spoke.

"What," he asked, "was that? And how are we going to explain this mess to the gardeners?"

Isika smiled, but she was shaking. Her body felt like leaves in a strong wind. "I think I need to sit down," she told Brigid, who was still half supporting her. She sat in silence while Jabari told the others what the Keerza had said in animal speech.

Isika felt the way she did after a battle with the Great Waste, and just the fact that she had a familiar way she felt after a battle, made her feel that she could cry from who she had become.

She barely recognized the girl who spoke to animals and thought in terms of magical fights and how they wore her out. But she wasn't the girl from before either. She walked to the bench and sank down on it, bringing her knees up to rest her head on them. There was great evil coming and they all needed to not doubt. She didn't know what to do. She felt unmoored from her body, as though she would float away from it. As though she was nothing.

When was the last time I felt like myself? she wondered. And she knew the answer; it unfurled in front of her like a new leaf and she caught her breath.

She remembered being small inside her mother's arms, curled up while her mother hummed over her. Every time she was with her mother, she felt like Isika, loved, alive, precious. And she realized with a shock that it didn't matter where she was, if her mother was there she was Isika. Back in the foggy place, with the vague shapes and colors. In the desert. In the Worker village. The memory of being someone's daughter brought her back to herself. She raised her head and looked at the others.

Jabari lay back on the grass, arms under his head, staring at the sky. Ben sat cross-legged, watching her with a worried, quizzical look on his face. Isika had no idea what kind of music might be coming from her. Brigid was right beside her, one arm slung around Isika's shoulders, and Isika felt a flash of love for her friend.

Here too, she thought. *With these friends I feel like myself.* And like that, she came back, mooring herself again.

"Does anyone have any idea what they were talking about?" Isika asked.

Ben shook his head solemnly, and Isika could feel Brigid shrug at her side; the shrug lifted her own shoulder. Jabari sat up, his gaze meeting Isika's.

"They do that sometimes," he said. "Bring warnings. Though not usually all together, like that." He frowned. "So something intense is coming. But I don't understand their warning. What would cause us to doubt?"

"It could be the Desert King himself," Isika said.

"Yes. I've been preparing for that ever since the first fires came," Jabari said. "We recognized his magic. But why would that make us doubt? Make me doubt? Why would Nenyi think that we need a warning?" Jabari said. He ran his long hands over his hair, leaving pieces of grass in it. Isika found herself staring at his face and quickly looked away. She was distracted, restless, not wanting to focus on the trouble surrounding them.

Ben spoke, tearing a piece of grass to pieces while he did, looking at the ground. "You wouldn't ask that if you had been near him. He can make you doubt anything."

Keethior gave a low cry. "Watch now, children," he said.

He had barely finished saying it when a ranger came over the top of the stairs, reaching the garden where they sat, running toward them, breathless.

"The elders want you, young ones. We have seen the force that approaches," he said. "And Gavi sent a message that the Gariah warrior, Abbas, recognized the Desert King himself. He is coming."

All the rest of that day, while Isika went to many meetings with Jabari and the elders, she felt as though she was in a dream. Smoke was everywhere, more holes came into the dome but she didn't have time to fix them. She walked as though she was asleep, listening to the elders speaking of what they should do, but not understanding.

Everything seemed to whisper to her. She touched every tree she could, and they gave her bursts of strength, so she could keep standing. He was coming, he was coming, and he was looking for her. She remembered her name in the fire and shivered. Even the paintings seemed to whisper to her. Especially the one of Azariyah, the grandmother she had never met. *Remember us,* they whispered. *Do not forget. Do not forget.*

She couldn't understand the meaning behind what they were saying. It was always just beyond her.

And then they got word that he was in the plains before the city, and time seemed to stop.

Chapter 18

Gavi walked down a farmland road with Ivy beside him, thinking again about the faces of the rangers. They had been shocked, but there was a feeling beyond shock in their faces, and he couldn't place it. He tried to be focused on what he was doing, but their faces came back to him, and he looked for the word. He didn't understand it. They had been shocked. But what else?

He and Abbas had traveled closer to the city, looking for rangers to warn about the identity of the approaching force. When they found a pair of rangers, two men who had been rangers for decades already, people Gavi knew by name, the men were watching the force move nearer and nearer to the city. They seemed stupefied, almost as if they were still deciding what to do.

"Peace behind you and before you," Gavi said, and they responded, "Peace."

"The leader of this force is the Desert King," Gavi told

them, moving straight into the bad news. He didn't add, *don't be fooled, this is no small force, this is not usual, it is almost as if Mugunta himself has decided to come.* He didn't have to.

The eyes of the rangers flew to Abbas, standing beside Gavi. Abbas nodded.

"Yes, it is him," he said. "I recognize his tent."

The look on their faces. Like children's faces for one split second. He got the impression that he had presented these weathered, experienced rangers with the last information they would ever expect. But why? Why had they been so surprised? Surely it wasn't so strange that the King would attack them? Why hadn't they been expecting it all along?

But Isika. His mind insisted. *She's supposed to make things better. Why are they getting worse?* Wondering gave him a stomach ache; made him feel disloyal to a friend he loved. And that was the feeling behind shock, he knew, as though he had been searching for the last wooden block of a puzzle. It was betrayal. But why were they so surprised?

Gavi's little group were still seeking poison walls and fires and clearing them away. Still seeking, yet Gavi knew he was searching for something else, something beyond removing walls, some way to help. It was there, he just needed to find it. He glanced at Ivy, finally emerging from his own thoughts enough to become aware of where they were. The road was lined with trees. He'd been along this road many times before; it wasn't all that far away from the city and most often it was free of poison. Today would be different. He could feel the ache of approaching poison in his hands.

He had just spotted a distant haze of smoke when Ivy spoke.

"Gavling?" she asked. Her name for him always reminded him of their childhood, going back to when both of them could only babble along together. He couldn't remember a part of life that hadn't had Ivy in it. She was his sister-cousin. A smart, funny, annoying friend.

"Yes?" he replied.

"Do you think we should still be on our seeking journey?"

Gavi glanced over at her, walking with her long, swinging stride. He looked ahead to Abbas and Aria, much farther along the road. Abbas looked back at them, pointing to the distant smoke, and Gavi nodded, feeling a deep exhaustion that went deeper than the need for sleep. Abbas turned back to the road, and he and Aria sped up, marching toward the burning field.

"I have no idea what we should be doing," Gavi said. "This isn't something we have come across before." He thought for a minute, then turned to her.

"What do you think we should do?"

She looked surprised to be asked, although she shouldn't be, he thought. He'd been asking her advice for as long as he'd been able to talk.

"I don't know either," she admitted. "But it seems strange to keep putting out fires and tearing down walls while an army is marching on our city."

Not quite an army, Gavi thought. They weren't fighting as they went, though their fires burned before them. They seemed intent on getting to the city. But what did they want?

Was it a battle? It was what the rangers had asked, with their blank, surprised faces.

"We're watching because they seem to be approaching to talk, not fight," the taller ranger had said. They were both black-skinned and taller than Gavi. He had felt himself relaxing in their presence the way he always did with rangers. All was well when the rangers were there. Rangers always knew what to do. But their faces were so surprised.

Had the Desert King laid a spell on them? he wondered, walking beside Ivy. Was that where the confusion came from? It didn't seem like them, to allow a force to get all the way to the city. Something was very wrong. He made a quick decision.

"We'll work on this house," he said, as they reached Abbas and Aria, who stood gazing at the burning gardens and flowers around the little house. "And then we go to find a way behind the Desert King's force. We can learn something, or confuse them, help Azariyah in some way."

There was a gleam in Abbas' eye as he grinned in response. Perhaps he had been waiting for Gavi to say they could move in the direction of the Gariah force. If so, Gavi inwardly congratulated him on his restraint. For a prince, he was extremely supportive of Gavi on his first seeking journey of solo leadership. Or whatever this was.

They took care of the fires around the house quickly. It wasn't so hard anymore. They knew what to do, and the more they fought the poison fires, the easier it became as their fear faded away. Once you had put out a flaming sunflower with your hands, you knew that the next flaming sunflower wouldn't burn you.

The house was tiny, really, just a little thing surrounded by a fairly short wall and these kitchen gardens that were burning. Gavi straightened after putting out one last fire in a tomato plant.

The others were done, as well. They had soot on their faces, Aria more than they others, and he smiled. But then he realized she had more soot on hers because she had been crying and wiping her hands on her cheeks. His heart gave a pang and he jogged over to her.

"What is it, little bird?" he asked, laying a hand on her shoulder. He could feel it as soon as he touched her. The poison arrow was having its way again, burrowing fear and anger and pain deep into her.

"Why didn't you say anything?" he asked, already busy smoothing the hurt places, sending healing. Her tears slowed and the pain on her face eased.

"Because you just did this two days ago," she said, her voice broken. "And I didn't want to wear you out. Why is the arrow hurting again so quickly?"

Gavi didn't know how to answer. Why was there so much sadness in the world, why were there so many things going wrong? Why was his friend poisoned with this horrible arrow? He had come to hate the thing, it pierced her daily and made her life full of pain. She was so brave but he could see it wearing her down.

"We need to get you back to Azariyah," he said. "Back to the healing tents."

"They can't do anything," she whispered, crying again. "I'm so sorry, Gavi. I ruin everything."

"Hey now," he said. "What are you talking about, Little Bird? The last time I looked, you were one of my dearest friends and you made everything sweeter and more fun."

She smiled slightly, but the words didn't reach her. They couldn't get past the ugly arrow, piercing her saddest, smallest self. Gavi had seen the arrow, and he knew where it hurt her. It was the memory of the day her stepfather, Nirloth, had rung the bells and sent her away. He knew that she had mixed it up, and the arrow made her believe it had been Isika who had rung the bells.

"Let's do the wall," she said, straightening her shoulders.

"Okay, but Aria," he said. "It wasn't Isika with the bell."

Her shoulders slumped again. She was tall, this girl, like her older sister, but fragile. "I know," she said. "But that's what I remember."

This arrow had created a false memory that hurt her beyond belief. Gavi didn't know how to fix it.

They pulled the walls down soberly. Once or twice, Gavi tried making a joke, but it fell flat, which didn't feel right at all, and he wondered about the poison arrow, wondered about their strange mood. It had something to do with the air, and with this king and his strange force. For the first time since they'd left, he wished with all his heart that it had been Jabari who had led this seeking journey, not him. Because Jabari could triumph over anything. Jabari could make them laugh, strange air or no. He wondered what Jabari was doing right now.

ONCE THE WALL WAS GONE, nothing but dust around their feet, they walked up to the house, climbing a short set of stairs to the porch. Gavi noticed a couple of old stools, the old three-legged kind, and a loom, and realized that an elderly couple lived here. He felt a flash of anger at the poison targeting the elderly. But of course it targeted everyone. He touched the lintel and the sides of the door, feeling his gift radiating out into the walls, dispelling the remnants of poison, and then he opened the door, stepping inside. He had to duck a bit as the doorway was short.

Inside, the room was quite dim. Ivy immediately began to push out the shutters that had been pulled tightly over the windows, and Gavi looked for the people. There was an old man sitting by the fire. Gavi went to him. Out of the corner of his eye, he saw Aria walk to the kitchen. She would put a pot of water on the red rock stove, then throw fruit peels into the boiling water to drive the stench of sadness out of the room. Abbas was busy with a broom. Everyone was silently at work, a good team.

Gavi laid his hands gently on the man's head, and after a moment, the old man's eyes fluttered open and he smiled up at Gavi. His black skin was creased all over with wrinkles, as leathery as Gavi's satchel. But his eyes were clear.

"Thank you, young one," he said. "How did we come to this? But you're Andar's son, aren't you?"

This had been happening more and more often. Andar's son. Andar's son. Gavi thought it was a way for people to remark on how he looked different, so pale-skinned with this yellow hair, without saying it quite that way. Everyone knew Andar had a light-skinned son. He nodded at the man, who sat up in his chair.

"But where's Ava?" He asked. "Where's my lovely girl?"

Gavi straightened and looked around. There was only one room that led away from the main part of the little house. Through the open door he saw a bed, with a tiny shape under a blanket.

"I think she's there," he said. "Is Ava your granddaughter?"

The man stared at him with astonishment. "No, young one. Ava is my wife, my own heart's girl."

Gavi heard a snort of laughter and turned to see Ivy standing with her hand over her mouth.

"Forgive him," she said, pulling her hand away from her mouth. "He's never been too bright."

Gavi shot her a fake glare and walked back to the room, feeling a little uncertain. Was the woman okay? She lay so still in the bed. But as he approached, he saw that she was only sleeping, curled up and tiny under the covers. She really was as small as a child, but her hair was bright white against her black, black skin. He watched her for a minute before reaching out to touch her forehead, but even as he recognized the lack of poison, she opened her eyes. They widened for a moment, as she saw him reaching toward her, then they softened.

"Finally," she said. "I've been waiting for you forever."

SHE MADE them soup that tasted like heaven after the unending rabbit stew they ate every day. Even Gavi was getting sick of rabbit stew, and he had thought at certain times in his life that he would never grow tired of it. The soup was spicy, made with peanuts and a root vegetable he remembered from when his own grandmother, Laylit's mother, was alive. He watched the old woman, wondering.

Only a strong person could resist poison when it was layered in the walls around the house, burning the field, and taking over her husband's mind. This tiny woman was special. He had thought her frail-looking when she was lying in the bed, but the minute her feet touched the ground, it seemed as if she was spry as a child. She danced over to her husband and kissed him, gently, on the mouth. Tears sprang to his eyes and she said softly, "I missed you."

"I'm sorry," he said, but she brushed his apology away.

"Oh love. We ache for Nenyi together. She will make all things new."

Then the woman started to cook. And when they sat on their stools in the old way, eating the soup she had made, the last, lingering traces of poison vanished, and Gavi could feel the strength of the house, the love that was in it.

He found himself opening up, telling the couple about the Desert King, about him going to the city, about Isika's name in the flames. The old man shook his head and sighed and exclaimed but could give no answers. But the woman looked off into a distant corner of the room, her brow furrowed. She put her bowl down by her feet, and set her spoon in it.

"The World Whisperer, Isika... she must be precious to him for some reason," she said. "Has anyone thought to ask why?"

The words reverberated through the room, which had grown very, very still, as though people were afraid to breathe. Gavi turned the thought over in his head, and suddenly felt as though he couldn't get back to the city fast enough.

Chapter 19

Ben hardly knew what he was doing anymore. The days were tied together with a long thread of anxiety that hummed in his brain. He felt as if he were sleepwalking, and he sang constantly, trying to keep the outer music at a distance. But everywhere, always, in and underneath everything, he could hear the Desert King's music coming closer, growing louder as it approached the city. It was horrifying, doom-filled music full of wrong notes and ominous drumbeats.

The city was in a state of preparation, the Maweel fortifying their city and looking for wisdom. Everyone had their roles, and he and Isika came and went from their house to the palace, back and forth throughout the day. Isika had ceased to go to the pottery workshop at all, spending all her time fortifying the dome.

Ben walked to the uppermost tower of the palace, where the flat roof was hot under his feet. In times of need, the singers sang together to strengthen the rangers, their music forming a net of magic that they could send over to the fire, where the rangers defended the city. In their songs, they asked the Shaper for help. There were fewer singers than usual, as many of the singers were rangers, out fighting fire, singing as they worked. At first, Ibba had come to the singing tower with Ben, but when she started having nightmares, weeping in her sleep, Auntie put her foot down and said, "No more."

Benayeem sang as though he was in a dream. Singing kept him alive and in his right mind, but it was difficult for him, because he could hear the other music. One moment he was truly in his body, aware of the singers who stood to his left and right, the next, he was lost in a far-off city, a time long ago, small and afraid.

More memories came to him over the days that they waited and sang. Ben was thrust into them suddenly, as though a hand were plucking him away from himself and setting him in the past. He didn't seem to have control.

One moment, walking up the stone road, arm in arm with Isika, she on her way to fortify the barrier, he to sing with the others. The next moment, catching sight of his mother and older sister in a long hallway. He called to his mother, trying to run to her. She turned, halfway, and he caught sight of a baby in her arms. Who was the baby? How long had he been away? Screaming for her. Being pulled away by merciless arms, while she cried and called that she loved him, loved him.

He came to himself crumpled on the ground, Isika beside

him, holding the music off so he could come back to himself. It felt painful to speak about it, to tell Isika about the memories he had pushed away all these years, but she wouldn't let him go until he told her. He didn't want to lie to her, so he told her of seeing her with their mother, of how he was kept away from her, of how she must have had Aria in her arms, but he hadn't known she had a baby.

He looked up to see tears running down her face. She wiped at them with the back of one hand. Behind her he could see a few concerned people, and the tall silverwood trees that lined the stone road.

"I can't remember it!" she said, shaking her head, distressed.

"I have barely remembered it all myself," he said. "When we left, I was with Mama, and I was happy, so I pushed those memories far away."

"Why are they coming back now?"

"Because of the evil that is coming. Because the Desert King grows nearer," he said. "His fire scorches everything before him." He sighed. "And he is tied to that time. His music brings it back to me."

ONE MOMENT SINGING, another moment trying to balance a glass on a platter, holding it as still as four-year-old hands can. Fear in his heart and his mouth. The slap of a hard hand on his cheek, dropping the glass, sweeping up broken shards.

One moment singing, another sitting at the base of the king's chair, trembling. Holding a cloth in his hand that was used to wipe up any spills as soon as they happened. Too close to the king's feet, which he had seen kicking many slaves. Too close.

And then one day, he was there, at the plains on the edge of the city. Ben knew as soon as he woke up that he was there. He crept through the day half-cringing, cursing himself for his overwhelming fear. He sang with the others, drifting in and out of the present. The elders walked around conferring with rangers who ran in and out. Ben caught sight of Karah huddled with Jerutha in one of the palace hallways. To his shock and horror, he saw that Karah was crying, her beautiful face streaked with tears.

And then night came.

Ben could feel that the Desert King stood at the very entrance to the city, at the place where the plains met the horse meadow. The horses had already been led away, and the people evacuated from their farmhouses. Everything nearby was on fire and the city glowed orange with it in the darkness.

Ben, Isika, and Jabari stood on the palace rooftop, searching the dome, their barrier, with their eyes.

"Do you think it will hold?" Isika asked. Her voice sounded strange, as though she were choking. Her music was brave, sad, and scared, all at once, so poignant Ben could barely listen to it.

"We're not old ladies weaving a blanket," Jabari said. "Of course it will hold."

"Don't let Auntie hear you say that," Isika said. "I'm pretty sure her blankets are very, very strong."

Ben smiled, thinking of Jabari and Isika weaving away on giant magical looms, but the smile couldn't stay. It slid off his face as he heard the undercurrents of their music, the terror under their brave voices. They had been through scary things before; the poisoned bay water that killed a man, the priests in the desert sucking the moisture out of their bodies. But there had been a chance, then, that they would get away and get back to Azariyah, which beckoned like a kind and lovely light. Now they were fighting for Azariyah itself, and Ben felt that if Azariyah was gone, there would be nothing good or lovely left in the world.

They heard it then, a long, low hiss.

"What's that?" Isika asked, and Jabari started to speak, worry furrowing his brow, but he froze as he saw a brilliant orange flame on the horizon, brighter than any other, dancing with green light in its center. Ben shuddered with pain from the music that came from that fire. The flames came closer and closer until they lit up Isika, only Isika, in a circle of light that caught her. Jabari tried, but couldn't break into the light, and Ben either, though he pounded on the strange shield that kept his sister from him. Isika, inside, seemed stunned, her eyes narrowed and searching, near tears.

"There you are," came a voice, and the silence that fell over the three of them was so deep that nothing was able to penetrate it. Dully, Ben saw Jabari shouting, lifting his hands to beat on the light around Isika, but he couldn't hear him.

There was a wild roaring and a thousand arrows of flame shot from the green smudge on the horizon, flying toward the three of them on the rooftop, flying toward their beautiful city, and Ben knew with dread in his heart that they would be burned. But far away, the arrows hit their barrier, Isika and Jabari's beautiful, singing barrier, and fizzled out. Jabari stopped beating on the light around Isika and looked up, his mouth open.

Suddenly Ben could hear again, though the world seemed very quiet. Not a voice, not the call of a bird. But he heard Jabari whistle beside him.

"It worked," Jabari said, "it worked!" He sounded stupefied.

How could Jabari still be happy about the dome when all hope was lost? Ben thought.

He shook his head. When had he decided all hope was lost? Was it when he was wandering back and forth from the palace to the house, buried under the weight of his memories? Was it being thrust back into such strong fear, something he had thought behind him?

He searched then, did something he rarely did. He listened for the sound of his own song, and somewhere deep inside he found the tiniest note of hopeful singing. He caught the note and held onto it with all his might. He began to feed it, carefully, even as the Desert King spoke again.

The sound of his voice was horrible. That was the first thing Ben realized. The second was that Isika was still trapped in the light of his searching fire and though Jabari stood as close as he could humanly get, he couldn't break through. The third thing Ben realized, with a mind that didn't seem to be working very well, was that the Desert King was talking to his sister.

"There you are," he said again. "Ah, Isika. I've found you. Well, Maween, I'm afraid I must take your World Whisperer from you, and she will whisper and protect no more. She is not yours. She is mine."

Ben couldn't take the words in. What was he saying?

The voice went on. "With her beside me, you will not be able to stop me. All of Maween will bow to the power of the goddesses, will be possessed by the grand one, the mighty force, Mugunta. You will belong to him. You will belong to me."

There was not a sound in a deep, sluggish silence. *Please let it be a nightmare*, Ben thought, trembling. Flashbacks hit him so fast that it was all he could do to stay where he was, to remain beside Isika, while she stared, caught in the bright, searching light, her face lit with orange and green.

He was tiny, crouching before a sharp boot as it kicked him for leaving dust on the floor.

His sister was across the courtyard. He saw the bad man walking toward her. He tried to warn her but he was pulled away again.

"It has been a plan going on for a long time," the voice said.

On the other side of Isika, Jabari picked up his bow, stringing an arrow and holding the bow in front of him, loosely. He gestured, and Ben did the same with his own bow, feeling foolish, for the fire of the king was so far away, too far to reach. But wait, was it growing closer?

"It began, you might say, when my father stole your queen. Did you ever stop your blubbering long enough to wonder why he did it? Or did you simply begin writing songs?"

His mother was in the throne room. In the throne room! The king, the bad man, put a hand under her chin. Ben saw her flinch away. He sat down and covered his ears, closing his eyes.

Where were the others? Where were Andar and Ivram? Could everyone hear this? Why would nobody stop him? Ben desperately didn't want to hear what the man would say next.

"That theft was part of a plan. A majestic plan, I should say, involving lineage, offspring, and the blood of warriors."

Next to Isika, Jabari put a hand over his eyes, momentarily letting his bow go slack, then raised it again. Ben saw tears on his face. *Why?* he thought. *Jabari, why are you crying?*

Isika was crying too. Ben wanted to reach her, wanted to put the light out, wanted the fire to leave her alone. *She's been through too much,* he tried to scream, but somehow nothing came out. And underneath everything, the steady, horror-filled drumming went on and on. But Ben wasn't curled up on the ground. He glanced up, put another thread of hopeful music into his tiny bundle. The fire was definitely coming closer, beating at the edges of the barrier. He tightened his grip on the bow.

"You see, your beloved queen had a daughter. You remember the daughter, don't you? I know you do, Isika, because she was your mother. And in the daughter's veins ran the blood of the most powerful sorcerers in the world.

The whisperers. But the whisperers had given themselves over to the weakest power. Nenyi. The Shaper."

Ben could feel his stomach turning over as another flashback tried to break in on him. "No" he whispered fiercely, and this time, the sound broke a little of the fear in the wind.

"Ah, weakness. The blood of the whisperers practically begged to be joined with the blood of the warriors, the desert lineage that comes from the destroyers, the ones who sprint down battlefields, leaping over the bodies of their enemies. True power, outshining the weak light of the Shaper. Power to control, to destroy. To burn."

It was there, then. The memory. Dropping his hands and running toward his mother. The bad man was touching her face—he must never touch Ben's lovely mother. Then the man, hissing. Strong hands grabbing him. Hatred in the king's words.

His mother's broken voice. "How can you treat him this way? Give him back to me, if you don't want him." Ben's heart lifting with hope.

"I will keep him near me," the man said. "As you well know, Amani. Even if he is useless to me, he is my son, bound to serve me." Misery.

Ben opened his mouth to scream a long, resounding no, but Jabari shouted instead, and his voice was mighty, as though he wasn't fighting back the winds of fear. Ben could hear the whole city taking a long breath as Jabari's voice echoed from the palace rooftop, strengthening the barrier with its sound.

"You will never be as powerful as Nenyi! She is the first and the last, the Shaper, the Uncreated One!"

The fire in the distance flickered and blazed higher. Jabari bent in half suddenly, as though he had been forced, his face tight with pain. Ben could do nothing, say nothing as the Desert King kept speaking.

"Yes, I have come to claim you, Isika, daughter of Amani, daughter of the Desert King. Dear one, you are now the most powerful person to walk the earth, whisperer and warrior. Come to me. Join me."

It was as though all the world broke open with sorrow. Keerza music roared out in anger. Othra mourned with long cries. The trees wailed. The earth itself called out. And then the earth cracked open inside the barrier, and a nightmare oozed out.

Chapter 20

Isika was in a long, narrow tunnel. It was dark on every side, and all she could see was the green light of the fire that wouldn't let her go, far on the end of the tunnel. *Help me!* she wanted to call to Ben and Jabari. But she had no voice—had she ever had a voice?—and she could hear nothing except the roaring of the searching fire and the sound of the man's voice, going on and on about things that couldn't be true. Dimly, she saw the blackened ground in front of the city open up. Shadows crept out, and her skin tingled with alarm, her body wanted to carry her away, but she couldn't move her arms or legs.

She breathed a short, frustrated breath; something in her hearing shifted, and she heard the sound of wings beating the air, and long, haunting calls. The Othra.

She shivered as a dozen of the huge birds, flew past her overhead. Wingtips brushed her head. Keethior! When the feathers touched her, she fell out of the grasp of the searching fire. The fire flickered, then blinked out. The Othra swooped as one toward the man, who had fallen silent. They dove toward him, shrieking, and Isika, who had only ever been comforted and perhaps mildly chastised by the birds, felt a prickle of fear and hope.

She saw through Keethior's eyes, and she saw that the man was tall and kingly, with rich brown skin and a silver robe, not ugly after all. Just as she and the bird descended on the man, he shimmered and disappeared. Flying with Keethior, she could feel the bird's surprise and then his awkward turn midair as he tried not to hit the ground. All around, warriors lifted bows, and the Othra flapped their wings frantically to get away. *No!* Isika thought, horrified. They wouldn't shoot an Othra, would they? Surely they understood about the sacred animals?

But to one side of Keethior, the unthinkable happened. One of the Othra gave a heartrending cry and plummeted toward the earth, an arrow sticking out of his chest. Then Isika was shooting back into her own body and she couldn't see what was happening.

"No!" she screamed, opening her eyes to see Jabari's face, very near as he bent over her on the ground.

"What is it?" he asked.

She shook her head, frantic with worry that something had happened to Keethior. She reached out and found him with her mind.

Stay where you are, he told her. He was fine. She suspected he had pushed her away to protect her.

"An Othra," she said with tears pushing at the backs of

her eyes. Her hip ached on one side, as though she had fallen. Had it happened when she flew with Keethior? "They shot an Othra out of the sky."

"Oh, Shaper help us," he said, bowing his head. "So many horrors in all the world. We have trouble here, too. Look."

He helped her up and they went to where Ben stood at the railing around the rooftop, looking at the ground below the palace walls. She gasped. She looked up. The barrier held, and yet in front of her the ground was seething with long lizards, as large as a person, with skin like wood in a fire, but walking on four legs, hissing and rattling as they crawled toward the palace. There were only five of them, but they seemed to be everywhere and the rattling sound they made filled the air until Isika had to raise her voice to speak.

"What are they?" she asked, horrified.

"Baloto," Jabari told her. "Mud demons."

"They're real," Ben breathed, and Isika found that she was deeply relieved to hear him speak. She hadn't even had time to think about the horrible things the Desert King had been saying, but she knew the effect he had on her brother, and a part of her had been terrified that Benayeem would be harmed beyond help. He seemed okay, though, turning to look at her, eyes wide over the strangeness of the lizards.

She looked into his eyes then, searching. What she saw made her shudder. He had remembered. She saw in his eyes what she desperately didn't want to see. That horrible man, the dreaded Desert King was truly their father. There was a ringing in her ears—she thought she might faint. Life had been simpler with Nirloth! She couldn't bear to be the desert daughter.

Jabari made a muffled exclamation and grabbed her hand. She looked down to see that the line of five lizards was standing perfectly still. They began to sway and then spoke, simultaneously, in a monotone hiss that filled her with dread. The wind picked up, and it was filled with fear.

"Isika, we will wait for you. Come within the week, and join us. If you do not come, all of Maween will burn and be lost. Your little barrier will flame and die before the week is over and there will be no help for you. Mugunta will start over with cleansed and burned ground, destruction that is pleasing to him."

There was a ringing in Isika's ears. She shook her head silently. What? They actually thought she would come and join them?

Oh, but I cannot, she thought. *My heart belongs to Nenyi.*

But it will all burn, a small, hopeless voice inside her replied.

There was a buzzing in her ears that grew louder and louder, until she recognized it as a hum of discontent from her feet. From the palace rooftop. The palace was awake and angry. Isika shifted her feet and sudden warmth flooded her.

Beside her, Ben and Jabari moved, and swiftly shot the lizards; each of them straight in the heart. They fell, but instead of lying dead properly, they dissolved into dust like poisonous things. The dust swirled in the wind and left tiny flecks of heat when it blew against her, a residue of sadness.

Isika felt stunned. She stared at her hands, feeling a burn

of shame that began in her stomach and progressed into her ears, the back of her neck, down to her knees. She was rigid with it, until Keethior gently called to her from a tree just beyond the palace walls.

World Whisperer, he said, only to her. *Come and help us mourn.*

She realized she couldn't even take a moment to try to understand all that had happened. She needed to go with her friend, to help the Othra. And yet it was as though she had pictured her beginning, her early life, as the clean, pure roots of a tree, and now the rot of mold was on the roots. She was dirty.

I can't, she wailed to him.

He turned a look of steel on her.

You can and you must. Stop crying like a child and come now.

JABARI AND BEN went with her. The grove where the Othra was laid to rest was away from the palace, down a dirt path, and they slipped away quickly.

"We're going to need to go talk with my parents," Jabari said, his voice tight.

"Yes," Isika sighed. "I know. This time I didn't do anything wrong, but I feel like I did."

Jabari didn't say anything, and Isika looked at him as they walked. His brow was furrowed, and she hated knowing that he, too, was thinking of the horrors they had heard. She flinched away from the possibility that he might reject her after all. Her roots were rotten, after all. He noticed her looking and shrugged.

"I just wish Gavi was here," he said. "He'd know how to get us out of trouble."

"Or Ivy," Ben said. "She's good at that."

"And not one of the three of us are," Jabari said. "How could we let them all go without us? We were practically asking for punishment."

Isika didn't say anything, but the word "we" warmed her, even settling around the knot of shame that seemed to have set up camp in her stomach. Her hands and feet ached a little less and she was glad for it.

They reached the little grove where the Othra stood, wings spread, in a circle. There were eleven of them, the twelfth on the ground before them, and Isika nearly buckled under the sorrow she felt from the others. She looked around anxiously, spotting Efir, Nirral, and Eemia. Keethior was of course there, looking at her with a *why did it take you so long* look. She didn't know the bird who had fallen, then, but the sorrow in her heart didn't give way, and suddenly she knew what she was supposed to do, though she couldn't say how.

She sang. Jabari, Ben, and the other birds joined in.

Glowing star of distant hills
Star of heaven black of night
Light in the feathers light in the dim
Light eternal light forever
Guide his way dear Shaper oh Shaper
Hold his way dear Shaper oh Shaper
Fly him into your heart pull oh pull

Bring him home
Bring him home.

When they were done, the Othra flapped their wings, creating a great wind, and the dead bird burst into flames. The fire that enveloped him burned in the jewel colors of Othra wings, deep red, purple, and blue. Isika wept, then, and felt as though she couldn't be happy again, knowing who and what she was.

She had lived a hard life and done many difficult things, but walking back toward the palace after the Desert King's revelation was still one of the hardest things she had ever done.

Once, she almost turned to run away, but Ben caught onto her arm, whispering fiercely.

"No! They will think you are guilty. You are not. You are still Isika, World Whisperer of Maween."

And then they were on the stone road. The city was chaos. Jabari looked around with stunned bewilderment on his face, and Isika felt the same, though she had only lived there for a short time. She had never before seen people shouting at each other on the Azariyah streets, though she had of course seen it in the Worker village. There were so many people on the streets. They stood everywhere, talking at each other in doorways and in the market square. They were so bright in their robes, and their voices were so loud. A headache began to form behind Isika's eyes.

Someone caught sight of her, and said, "Oh, the poor child."

Another person turned to look and such a look of hatred came over his face that Isika felt as though he had hit her. She stumbled, dizzy.

"She needs to be imprisoned," he shouted. "If we cast her out, she'll just join forces with the Desert King." There were murmurs that rose to a roar, and people closed in, coming so close that the three of them could barely walk. Jabari held his elbow and went ahead, pulling Isika behind him to try and get through. He seemed scattered and puzzled.

"I've never had to fight my way into the palace before," he said eventually. "I guess there's a first time for everything."

The people were forming rows, shouting at each other.

"She's our World Whisperer! We protect her with our life!" said one enormous man, whose shoulders were as wide as most doorways.

"Let's protect her by putting her behind bars, where she'll never harm us!" cried another man, and then a little woman roared and moved toward him as though she would hit him with her fists.

But a voice rang out with such authority and anger that everyone froze. It was Auntie, bustling up the stone road, Ibba in tow.

"How dare you!" she shouted. "You should all be terribly, terribly ashamed of yourselves, fighting in the streets like poisoned ones. Don't you see? This is what he wants to do to us! He wants us to become weak, pitiable creatures who suspect each other and drive each other away! Stop it now.

Stop it this minute. Be Maweel. Maweel believe. Maweel accept."

In the middle of Auntie's speech, Isika had somehow hurled herself into her foster mother's arms, so that she heard the end of it as though it was coming from Teru's heart. She knew she should appear strong, that she shouldn't have run like a chick to a hen, but she didn't have any power left. After she had breathed the scent of Auntie's perfume and the fragrance of charred flat bread for a few minutes, her heart calmed down.

The people listened to Teru. Many of them walked away, shame on their faces, touching their fingers to their foreheads in a gesture of apology and respect. Isika felt the shock again, the one that told her what a respected, strong woman Auntie was, though she had become a woman who barely left the house. How surprising Auntie was. What had her life been before she was so hurt?

"Are you sure you're okay to be out here?" she asked.

"Don't you question me like everyone else," Auntie said, the warning thick in her voice, and Isika smiled. She turned toward home, but Auntie stopped her.

"Not yet," she said. "We need to go to the palace before anything else."

Isika sighed, but went without arguing. Jabari put a hand on Isika's shoulder briefly, and Ben touched her cheek. Auntie held her hand, and on her other side, a hand slipped into hers. She looked down to see Ibba, and smiled.

As they walked together this way, Ibba sang, and the song Isika heard melded with everything around them and filled in the spaces. But she listened harder to Azariyah and found something that had always been there, though she hadn't known it at first, when she had thought that Maween was perfect. It was brokenness. The earth was crying, the sky was filled with smoke, pierced with arrows of sorrow. Isika could feel the trees crying out for their lost brothers, and she could hear the mourning of the Othra. She felt that she could even hear it when she stepped into the palace, as though the floor was crying out. The paintings seemed to whisper to her, *we are waiting, we are waiting.*

I am so nearly dry, the waterfall told her from a far-off place.

I'm sorry, Isika told them all. *I'm so sorry. I don't even know if I can help you, after all.*

Chapter 21

Jabari didn't think Isika had noticed the gatherers, but he knew Ibba had. Her eyes were wide in her little face as they passed the group of people gifted with gathering, the growing and tending gift. These were the palace gardeners, or the people who knew all the plants that could be gathered from the forest, the ones who supplied the healers with fresh herbs. They stood near the palace, on the deadened ground where the Baloto had emerged and given their horrible ultimatum.

He had heard what the mud demons said. He had understood, though he didn't think anyone else knew what they said to her. He and Isika were the only Maweel with animal speech.

And she's only half Maweel, his mind told him.

Shut it, he said back, but he could feel the muscles in his cheeks and the backs of his hands tensing with the effort of not thinking about it. Half Maweel, half Maweel. It didn't matter! Look at Gavi! Gavi was born a Worker, and you couldn't find a better person in the world. Oh, Gavi. Jabari felt another surge of worry for his brother and ground his teeth. Jabari wasn't used to this at all. He was the seeker, the one on a journey ridding the world of poison. Not the nesting bird at home, worrying about Isika, Ben, Gavi. Aria. Seas and stars, he had grown a lot of complications.

The gatherers circled the scorched earth, a motley group of young and old. Not all of them were gifted in singing, but they were all doing it sincerely, with great effort. They were trying to sing the earth back to health. And the thing Jabari noticed, the thing that made Ibba's head swivel and her eyes widen, was that the song was not helping. The earth, with that many gatherers singing over it, should have been bounding back to life, the grass should have been springing forth, hurling itself up out of the earth. But though the gatherers sang and sang, the ground remained charred and dead. When Jabari squinted at it, he saw that behind the physical presence of the ground, it looked empty. There was no glow of magic, nothing there at all.

He said nothing, though he was growing a headache that felt like a Baloto had curled behind his left ear. Ibba looked up at him with questions in her face and he gave her a small shrug.

"Don't worry, young one," he said. "All will come right in time. Nenyi will rush in and heal all of this." He may as well have been talking to himself, it was so exactly what he needed to hear.

They walked up the steps to the palace, and down the

oddly silent hallway. The guards weren't at the door, which struck Jabari as strange, until he saw that they were all clustered around the back of the great room, where Andar sat on the regent's chair in full robed glory. Jabari sighed. The headache was getting worse. He didn't know if he had the strength for his father to get all weird and imperious suddenly. His dad was an excellent guy, but Jabari had known forever that the more fearful and worried he got, the more pompous he seemed. Once Gavi had told Jabari he did the same thing when he was worried, and Jabari had responded by mushing a jam tart into his brother's face.

But it was true. And it was why he had spent these last months making every possible effort to become Isika's friend. Truly her friend. Lastingly her friend. Something that would be worth the effort before the day was put to bed, as he realized his father was in his "judge" position. Isika would be on trial. The hairs on the back of his neck stood up, because he realized that if there was anything, anything at all he had learned over the last months, it was that Isika deserved their loyalty. Maybe more than anyone he had ever met.

Or half their loyalty, the voice said again.

Ugh.

Enough. It was all too serious, and that was what Mugunta wanted. He thought of Auntie ploughing in back there, sleeves rolled up, like the time she had discovered him putting paint on chickens when he was a little kid. He thought of how Isika had run and put her face right in Teru's neck, where the softest, most comforting place was. He felt a little touch and realized that Ibba was holding his hand, that she was holding Isika's hand on the other side, that Isika was holding Auntie's hand, and that Ben had his arm slung around Auntie's shoulder. *No*, he thought, looking at his father's face. They could get through this with some humor. And love. But what if they knew what he knew about the ultimatum?

No. The ultimatum didn't matter. All that mattered was that they were here and...

"Seas and stars, is that *carrum*? From garden chilies? Did you raid Gavi's pepper patch while he was away?"

He made his way toward a table set up on one side of the room, covered with plates of meats and bowls of fresh vegetables and *carrum*, Jabari's favorite spicy dipping sauce. He didn't let go of Ibba's hand, so they all just sort of trailed after him, unwilling to let go of each other, like a lopsided dance line. They broke apart slowly and, following his example, picked up plates and began loading them with food.

Jabari heard Isika's stomach growling, and she met his eyes with a grin when he cocked an eyebrow at her. At her smile he felt relief breeze through his body like a fresh wind, the kind he hadn't felt in a while, under this smoky sky.

Andar cleared his throat.

"We need to talk. I'm afraid it can't wait." Everyone froze and stopped piling food onto their plates.

Jabari turned. "Father, we have buried an Othra and broken up a very strange group of fighting, hissing Maweel. Respectfully, we need to eat."

With a sniff, Teru continued to pile grilled meat and sauce on her plate.

"You also shot those lizard things," Isika told him in a low voice.

"Yes," he said loudly, so his father could hear. "We also shot Baloto. We're starving."

He enjoyed the frustration he saw in the tightening around his father's eyes, but when he glanced over at Ivram, his old teacher, what he saw was like a punch in the gut, because Ivram's face was seamed over with sorrow. After a slow blink, while Jabari stared, he seemed to gather himself and sit a little straighter. His face didn't turn back to his genial Ivram self, but it wasn't so heartbroken either. It was calm. It was an act of calm, and Jabari's heart beat harder and faster.

They took their food and sat in one of the cushioned spaces to the left of the elders. After some intense whispering, the elders joined them. Jabari saw that his mother's face was as hard and angry as he had ever seen it, while Karah's face was puzzled, with deep shadows under her eyes that were dark on her pale skin.

He felt a clearer feeling of war within himself than any he had felt before, including in all the time since Isika had arrived and he had begun questioning where his loyalty really lay.

This is too big of a test, he said, and he realized it was a sort of prayer. He was speaking to Nenyi, who above all, should be able to test whomever he wanted. Right as he saw his father's face harden into readiness for the first question,

Jabari couldn't yet tell what it would be, there was a scuffle at the door and a girl ran in, all brown hair flying and tunic flapping. Brigid.

"Excuse me! I'm sorry, I just need to find out if I can come, I'm looking for... oh there she is, is this a bad time? I'm ready to wait, I'm coming to sit..."

"Come on in, Brigid," Jabari said, marveling as he often did that someone so gifted could be so scattered. She ran over to Isika and curled up at her feet, looking for all the world like she was offering herself as a servant, though she was just sitting near her good friend. *She's so much smarter than she seems*, Jabari thought, looking at Brigid's seemingly innocent face. And then Keethior swooped in, and Kital came in with Dawit, on pretense of worry for Teru, until it looked as though Isika had a little army around her.

Jabari sat back to enjoy what would unfold, still with that thread of worry running through everything like an ugly old snake.

Andar began the questions, and if he was at all intimidated by anything—anyone would be intimidated by Teru sitting there daring him to hurt Isika, Jabari thought—he didn't show it.

"Isika," he said, leaning out so he could loom over her a little. "We must know. Did you know about being the Desert King's daughter and keep it from us?"

"No," she said, and her sure, small word eased a bit of pain that had lodged itself in Jabari's chest, behind his rib cage. He turned his head to the side and coughed.

"How can we know if we can believe you?" Laylit asked.

Isika turned to her. "I don't know. But I have never known anything of this before today. I had vague memories of the place I had come from. I could see my mother's face there, but nothing else. Colors maybe. Gold. I've told you all this before, haven't I? We've had this talk."

Andar sat, rubbing at the side of his head, and as he watched, Jabari thought of how familiar the action seemed. He did it when he was distressed as well, just like his father, and suddenly none of it seemed funny and his father seemed like a real person again, upset and trying his hardest. *Don't make me choose,* he thought.

"Tell her," Andar told Ivram. "She needs to know how important it is."

Ivram blinked slowly and when he sat up a little straighter, he looked like a much older man. Karah sat forward as well, and Jabari noticed that Jerutha had entered the room at some busy moment, sitting on the floor behind Karah, holding baby Mesu, who was sleeping.

"I have told you a little about how our queen was able to be stolen. She was so powerful, Isika. More powerful than you, because she had been raised to be the World Whisperer, taught her whole life."

Truly more powerful? What about the mixture of warrior and whisperer? the awful voice in Jabari's head asked. He shrugged it away again, feeling the strain of trying to trust. Feeling like he would sleep for months after so much effort.

"She was able to be defeated because she was betrayed," Ivram said, and his voice was full of a thousand sorrows.

Teru gave a tiny sob, and when Ivram looked at her, she shook her head at him.

"Don't," she said.

"She needs to know the danger, why we need to know everything," Ivram told her. "I'm sorry, Teru, do you need to take a moment outside?"

Teru shook her head, and held Isika's hand very tightly. Jabari felt very confused, and felt a shock of worry when Ivram seemed to give him a look of apology.

"The betrayal came from someone we know well. We don't dwell on it, for many reasons. Because the person was often beautiful and kind and good. She hurt our whole land by what she did, and she couldn't have known how many terrible things would happen as a result."

Jabari was shaking his head. He couldn't understand where this would go. Ivram took a deep breath.

"The person was Andar's own mother."

There was a roaring sound in Jabari's ears. He blinked, and blinked again. "What do you mean?"

Ivram turned to him, his eyes deeply sad. "Your grandmother betrayed Azariyah and delivered her to the Desert King."

Jabari couldn't seem to understand. "Wait. You never told me this?" he asked. "My grandmother? She put us where we are now, with the Desert King so powerful and our own World Whisperer unable to put it right?"

Andar bowed his head. "It wasn't all she was. She was a good mother to me. She regretted her actions for the rest of her life."

Teru was openly crying. "She was so sad, Jabari. I knew her, she was like an older sister to me."

"You are right, young one," Ivram said, clutching his staff, which glowed blue briefly. "Betrayal is the worst kind of poison. It has put us where we are now. It is why we have to be sure. If you betray us, Isika, Maween will never recover."

No wonder they've always been so hard on her, Jabari thought. At least that made sense now. But looking at Isika's stricken face, knowing what they both knew, Jabari thought Ivram couldn't have put a harsher burden on his friend. The ultimatum of the Baloto was that Isika should go to them to join them, or risk all Maween being burned to the ground. Which was the betrayal? What choice would condemn Maween? He couldn't help it; he went to her and put a hand on her shoulder, and when she looked up at him, she searched his face.

I heard, he told her in animal speech. Her eyes widened slightly and she made a soft sound of despair. *Should we ask them what to do?* he asked.

She gave her head a tiny shake, eyes wide. Okay. They could wait; they had a week.

"She knew nothing," Ben said then, sitting straight and thrusting his chin out. "She forgot everything about that time. She asked me all the time, where had we lived, what had happened there, but I didn't want to remember. I pushed it far away."

"You knew?" Andar said.

"I knew we had lived in the Desert City. But when the fires came, I started to hear his music, and I remembered... I remembered that I was a slave in his palace when I was a boy. He likes to have children as slaves. He likes to make children work."

Jabari felt a flash of revulsion for the king. Was he that horrible? Children were meant to play. Beside him, Ibba uncrossed and recrossed her legs on her cushion. Was her father really someone so terrible? Isika, Ben, Aria, Ibba. Their father couldn't have passed anything to them. Ben was the gentlest person he knew.

"Why did you not tell us, young one?" Ivram asked. Jabari noticed again, how much softer they were with Ben. He wondered why Isika got their guard up so quickly, but one look at her clenched fists, and angry, rebellious face and he remembered why. *Oh Isika,* he thought. *You do yourself no good like that.*

"You can't understand what it was like," Ben replied. The words were soft but his face was hard and strong. *You're growing up,* Jabari thought, looking at the younger boy. "You hate him comfortably from the beauty of Azariyah. Imagine what it was like to serve him, to hide from him. Have empathy for us. It was horrible. I was separated from my mother to live in a place where I never stopped being afraid." Ibba left Jabari's side to curl up with her head on Ben's leg. He put a hand on her head, playing with one of her braids, swallowed and went on.

"Isika was always with our mother. So was Aria. Neither of them could have remembered. It was only me. Only me."

Jabari thought of children everywhere who suffered, and his heart ached.

"Please," he said to his parents. "This is enough. They didn't know. How could they know? We need to move on, make a plan. Please let me go find Gavi. I'm scared for him, now, out there alone." *And Aria*, he thought. Aria, who had been hurt so much as a child as well.

"No," his father said. "You're right. We will leave this now. But Isika, you will stay very close to the city, where we can see you." Jabari bristled, and saw Isika jerk suddenly, as though she had been hit, and knew she was thinking about her decision. Join the Desert King? Or watch Maween burn. "And Jabari, we need you here as well. Do not fear for your brother. Don't forget, he has the Gariah warrior with him. We need to stay together and make our next plans. Go on now, rest everyone. Peace be on you. You've had a long day."

He caught up to her, as she was leaving with her family.

"Don't go," he whispered.

She fell back so they could talk without the others over-hearing.

"How can I not go?"

"How can you go?" He hated to see her face so sad. "Wait, Isika. You have time. Let's tell the elders and see what they say. You don't have to be alone in this."

"No!" she said. "You heard them. It will be worse if I tell them. So much worse."

They stood near the portrait of Azariyah the queen. It was almost too much, looking at the old portrait and knowing the betrayal that had been her downfall, watching the result of that betrayal tormenting his friend.

"Just promise me you'll wait, that you'll think it through," he swallowed. "And that you won't leave without telling me."

She nodded, her eyes unfocused, far away. "I will."

It would have to be enough. But the weight he felt, watching her walk off with her little family, was like a large, heavy stone.

Chapter 22

The next morning, Isika was up and running the moment her eyes opened. She pulled her riding clothes on, laced up her soft travel boots, and stalked through the barely lit kitchen, bumping into Auntie on her way to the door. Auntie grasped her by the arms and held her out, searching Isika's face with her eyes. Isika looked back, despite the hard lump of pain near her heart that told her to run.

"I love you, my gift," Auntie said finally. "Every day, I thank the Shaper that you four beautiful children came to us."

Her words were the last thing Isika had expected to hear. She often felt that they had only brought trouble to Teru and Dawit, who were too fragile to bear all the trouble.

"Oh, Auntie. I love you, too. I—I don't know what to do. I feel crazy, as though I've never known my real self."

"You'll know. The Shaper will guide you," Auntie said,

though there was a furrow in her brow that gave her worry away. "Just promise me you're not about to do anything stupid," she said.

"It depends on what you think is stupid," Isika whispered with a smile that collapsed on itself. "But I'm not going anywhere really. I just need to go for a ride."

"That sounds like the right thing," Auntie said. "See? What did I tell you? You'll know what to do." And then she pulled her into a hug. Isika let herself rest there for a minute, smelling Auntie's lemon oil smell, then kissed her on her cheek and left the house and the smell of good food, the beautiful white earth walls, the flowers. It wasn't time for comfort. Isika needed to reckon with herself.

She ran down to the horse barn and found it charred and empty after the evacuation. She reached for Wind with her mind, throwing her inner voice as far as she could.

Wind! Wind, I need you!

Wind! Come to me!

After a moment she heard his voice, faint and reedy, as though from far away.

I am coming!

As she waited, there was a rush of wings, and Keethior was there. Then hoofbeats echoing over the earth, and Wind rode down the hill, with four other horses.

They wanted to come, he said, pulling up in front of Isika and pawing the ground. *I couldn't stop them.*

Isika reached out to the other horses and offered thanks. They shook their manes in a wind that still reeked of poison. Their eyes were wild, and she reached out to offer calm, until each horse was settled again. She didn't bother with a saddle, using the fence to clamber onto Wind's back.

Go, she told him, and he went. They flew over their normal path along the meadow, but it was black and devoid of feeling or life. The horses didn't like to run on it. Isika felt their fear, so she sent them waves of comfort, and Keethior called overhead as the five of them ran.

If they ran fast enough, Isika thought, they could outrun the shame she felt, at being the daughter of a monster.

No, Keethior told her, and she jumped, looking up. Keethior was rising and diving, rising and diving in the air.

I didn't realize I was thinking that so you could hear me, Isika said.

When you're like this, your thoughts are so loud there is no way I can't listen, he told her. *But young one, whose daughter are you? Think hard.*

She thought of the horrible man, his voice. She thought of Nirloth. But no, though they both had some claim on her as fathers, she was not their daughter. *Mama,* she thought. Her mother, frail in her bed, dying. Isika shied away from the painful memory, but surfacing, she heard horrible laughter in the air and smelled the smoke that hung over the city, so she dove back down.

Her mother, lying back on her pillow, so thin, her dark brown face still so beautiful against the rough sheets. Her eyes shiny with tears.

"Mama," Isika was saying in the memory. "Don't leave us. Come back to us."

"You don't understand, my girl. I don't want to go, but my

spirit is broken. I fought so hard to save us. And now Aria is gone. Nothing I did mattered."

"It's not true," Isika insisted. "Everything you did mattered." But Amani turned her face away. She didn't understand.

Isika rode, her horse's feet pounding the ground, tears streaming down her face. They ran, and she wept, and she looked at the ground and pleaded with it.

"You were a meadow!" she shouted, "You were grassy and filled with flowers! Remember what you were! Come back! Live!"

Keethior let out a long cry, and Isika turned to look back at him.

In their wake was a path of green, new, fresh grass, like a wide stripe across the blackened meadow, dotted with tiny purple and yellow flowers, nodding in the breeze. They ran to the end of the field and turned, running on the perimeter. Isika threw her hand out, pointing, and the grass sprang up, not only where the horses ran, but running into the center, to meet the long stripe of green that had come.

Her mother in the Desert city, holding little Aria, whispering to Isika.

"We have to go, little one. A kind man will help us. We have to find a new place to live, get your brother back and run away."

"My brother?" Vaguely, young Isika remembered the boy she saw sometimes, skinny and small, wailing across the courtyard. Was that her brother? Had she forgotten?

Running in the night, so so tired. The little crying boy

beside her, often crying, so skinny. Her mother, holding him and singing over him every night, until Isika was eaten up with jealousy.

"Shhh," she would tell Isika in their small tent. "He never had time with me. You have never left my side. There is plenty of love for both of you."

Staring at him by the fire in the night, so curious. One day, walking to him and taking his hand, bringing him over to the big rocks to show him how fun it was to jump off them. The little boy, his eyes big, flinching and looking at their mother as though they would be in trouble for jumping. Their mother nodding at him.

"It's no trouble, my sweet Benayeem."

The days, learning to play together, to be brother and sister, with the little one, Aria. Running and bringing back flowers for their mother. Ben's cries at night, the sound of their mother singing over him.

I'm her daughter, she told Keethior.

Yes, he said back to her, only a speck in the sky.

But I'm his daughter too. We don't get to choose to be only one.

You get to choose to be whatever you want.

I want to leave. I want to leave forever. I can't bear that I'm bringing them close to so much danger.

You can't leave. The speck in the sky was getting bigger now, it was coming closer, and Isika heard the humming coming off of the giant bird, a beautiful song of love and loss. *You are their hope. Look. What the gatherers and healers could not do, all of them together, you did.*

Isika turned from where she was still trotting Wind around the perimeter of the field.

It was green. All of it. Tiny young shoots of grass carpeted the ground, and the other horses had stopped running and bent to eat. She flicked her awareness toward Wind and heard him trying not to think about food because it wouldn't be polite if she wanted to ride farther. She laughed and dismounted, letting him wander over to the other horses. He tore mouthfuls of grass mixed with the tiny purple flowers.

Do the flowers taste good? she asked him, pulling at her braids, hot on her neck.

Spicy and sweet, he said.

Isika looked around and saw that they were close to a wooded area, on the far edge of the meadow, away from the city. She remembered walking through this grove to watch the rangers fight fire. The little stand of trees was blackened as well, with a thick layer of ashes that covered the ground. Isika wandered into it, her heart aching for the trees. A storm of ash erupted as she stepped in, and she closed her eyes, leaning one hand against a tree. The tree felt empty, as though it had left its shell behind, but when Isika leaned in, she found the humming she was looking for.

Come back, she breathed, and waited. After a moment or two, a gust of energy burst out of the roots of the tree, flowing upward, and the tree's heart buzzed with life again. With her eyes still closed, Isika could see light pouring into all its branches. She felt the ground humming and realized the tree was calling to the others in the grove through its roots, calling them back. She kept her eyes closed, lending all the strength she could to the trees, and when the air was still and the buzzing had calmed, she opened them.

She stood on a green, thick-woven carpet of grass, tiny flowers woven in the midst of the springy blades. These little wildflowers had more colors than were in the meadow, they were like a sunset in different shades of red, orange, and purple. The trees had lost their ashy cast and leaves had returned to their branches, forming a mixture of sun and shade in the grove.

Isika sighed as the ache lifted from her heart. She sat down at the base of one of the trees, suddenly weary. It wasn't enough to sit, so she lay all the way down, curling up at the roots of the tree, letting her eyes drift closed.

She thought she slept for a long time with the sun high in the sky. A tall, tall man came into the grove, someone Isika hadn't seen before, but when she turned her head to look at him, she saw that she did know him, this being whose dark brown skin glowed with an inner light, so when the sun caught it, he shone like gold.

"You've never come to me this way before," Isika breathed. "Is this what you look like?"

"You always ask me that," Nenyi said, and his voice was like every beautiful song Isika had ever heard. "And I always tell you the same thing. I come in a way you can see me. I can look tiny or big, young one. I am male and female. You cannot contain me in a shape." He laughed. "I have forms so terrifying you would perish if you saw them. So I come quietly."

Isika was weeping. The man came closer and Isika saw

that his eyes were very kind. He reached one gold flecked hand out, but Isika cringed away, still crying.

"Don't touch me. I'm dirty. Do you know who my father is?"

"Of course I do. I shaped you. I shaped your father."

"Why did you let him turn into this?"

Nenyi sat back against the tree and held a hand up, turning it back and forth so Isika could see that there was something else there, in his hand, glistening and dancing in the wind; a tiny golden thread, so thin it seemed it would break.

"Careful!" she said, without thinking of whom she was talking to. Heat rushed to her fact. The Shaper. She had actually just told the Shaper to be careful. He didn't scold her, though.

"It's very strong," he said, in that same beautiful voice. It was a voice that made Isika want to swim, to jump, to dance. When she heard it, she thought she could do anything. "Though it doesn't look strong."

Isika tried to see where the thread was going. It fell from Nenyi's hand and trailed along the ground for a while. Maybe it was why Nenyi had come. So Isika would find something at the end of the thread, something that would help her change everything, help her solve the problem. She could never join her father. But she didn't want the mud demons to burn Maween. This was the question: should she join them to protect Maween, take all her trouble away? Or stay and fight, knowing that if they burned the city, it would be her fault. She looked at the thread that trailed along the ground, a golden line draping over bits of grass between her and Nenyi.

"May I?" she asked.

"Of course. It is yours, too," Nenyi replied.

She picked it up and realized it really was stronger than it looked. It was warm to the touch, almost as though it was alive. She shivered. She skimmed her fingers along it, until she felt a tugging on her other hand. Slowly, she lifted the hand and stared at it. The thread was connected to her.

"It needs to be stronger," Nenyi said, his voice a warm buzz that somehow carried warmth and warning at the same time. Isika stared at him. Nenyi went on. "Though yours is stronger than most."

"How do I make it stronger?" Isika whispered.

"Trust. It's the only way. Every time you are afraid, turn your heart back to the earth, the singing trees, the simple birds, and remember that you are shaped. You are made to open your hands and receive. This is the kind of trust that changes your thread." Nenyi looked up and there was great sadness and kindness in his eyes.

"It's why your father is the way he is. I did not want it, but he cut the thread. If someone wants to cut the thread, I must let it be cut. But if your thread is intact, if it is stronger, no one can claim you, young Isika. Not your father, not even your beautiful mother or grandmother. You belong to me."

Chapter 23

Jabari stood in the pottery workshop doorway, his mind panicked and blank. He had dropped by Isika's house that morning, hoping for breakfast and a moment to think about what to do about the mud demons and their stupid ultimatum. Showing up was all that he could think to do. He wanted her to know he wasn't avoiding her, despite the revelations of the day before. But she wasn't at home. And Tomas didn't know where Isika was, either.

"She didn't turn up today, no," Tomas repeated. "Ben, you don't know where she is?"

Beside Jabari, Benayeem shook his head. Brigid stood on Jabari's other side. She had also turned up on Teru's doorstep that morning, looking for her friend. She turned to Jabari now, her eyes wide.

"What has she done?" she breathed.

"I'm sure it's fine," Jabari said, his voice decisive. "We'll just have to find her." He was having a hard time breathing. Did she decide the sacrifice was worth it? She wouldn't have left them, would she?

Keethior, he called.

Keethior was a long way off. His voice in Jabari's head sounded like it came from the other end of a long corridor, whispery and echoing, barely audible.

What, young one? I am busy.

Where is Isika?

There was a long pause. *Don't want to disturb her,* the dumb bird said. *Won't tell.*

So they ran, searching every place the three of them could think of;: the market tree; the palace library ("Never," Jabari said, not knowing Isika to spend any more time at the palace than she had to, but Ben insisted); Brigid's house; Jerutha's rooms (where they tried not to alarm Jerutha but failed); and the whole time, Jabari pestered Keethior to tell him where Isika was. He wrestled down fear that she had gone, that she had given herself up to save them, or some other foolish thing she had thought up. He never, even for one moment, considered that she had joined forces with the Desert King. She would never, ever do such a thing. He knew it like he knew that Gavi was his brother, like he knew he was destined to be a ranger, like he knew the sun in the sky. He trusted her, outside defending her to his parents, outside the courtroom. He trusted his friend. Isika.

All right, impatient son of Andar, Keethior said, his voice reedy, full of that strange humor the Othra had. *Follow the green and you will find her.*

Stupid, overgrown crow, Jabari thought, as he, Ben, and Brigid hiked along trying to figure out the cryptic message.

"Aria's gift for finding Isika would be nice just about now," he growled, looking at Ben. "Why can't you have that gift?"

"Why can't you?" Ben shot back.

Jabari hadn't told anyone the gift he suspected he had, which was to speak to Isika himself, with animal speech, through her mind. It was too creepy to tell. He had been trying as they searched, calling her name in his mind, but there was no response, just a deep, frightening silence.

They nearly bumped into Brigid, who stood staring into the distance.

"Follow the green, the Othra said?" she asked.

"Yeah."

She pointed, and then Jabari saw it too, a distant glimpse of brightest green in the middle of the blackened ruin of the plains before Azariyah. Past the horse barns. His stomach leapt into his throat and without saying anything, they all began running.

The whole field. The whole field had come back to life.

"I saw the gatherers," Jabari said, as they stood staring at the thick grass at their feet. "I saw them trying to bring it back. They couldn't!"

"This kind of magic doesn't come from the Great Waste," Brigid said.

"No, it doesn't," Jabari said.

"I've never doubted her," Brigid said, her face and voice clear and happy.

Jabari didn't think he could say that, but he didn't doubt her now.

They set out to find her. The palace horses had returned to the meadow and stood grazing. Jabari bent to look at the tiny flowers in the field. He'd never seen flowers like them before.

His heart was beating too fast. They needed to find her and he was still fighting panic. Jabari never worried. It wasn't like him. He didn't fret. He just didn't. But this time, even though Keethior didn't seem afraid, Jabari was terrified. He was worried that she was gone, and she would never how he felt; that he trusted her. That he wanted to follow her as queen.

"Here she is!" Brigid called from a grove of trees on the meadow's edge.

Jabari nearly staggered as relief cascaded over him. He and Ben came running and pulled up at a circle of silverwood trees around a hollow carpeted with grass and flowers that Jabari knew he had never seen here before. Isika was asleep, curled at the base of a tree, her long arms cushioning her head, her braids spread out behind her. Higher up in the tree, Keethior perched, his head under his wing. Ben rushed to her side.

"Isika," he said. She seemed to come from far away, opening her eyes and blinking up at them.

"Oh," she said, her eyes filling with tears. Her voice was endlessly sad. "It was a dream."

"I think," Jabari started, taking a seat on the grass beside her, "Well, I don't know what happened, but whatever it was, I don't think it was a dream."

She sat up and brushed at her cheeks with her palms. "Why do you say that?"

Brigid's mouth hung open, and Ben tilted his head to one side, the way he always did when he was listening to music none of the rest of them could hear.

"You're covered in gold," Jabari said. "You're glowing with it."

She lifted her long hands and stared at them, turning them over and over. Her dark brown skin looked as though it held a million stars, like it was covered with gold specks. She stared, rubbing at the shimmer, but it stayed. She stared at a spot on her palm for a long time.

"I can't see it," she murmured, "but somehow I can feel it's there."

They all huddled close as Isika told them all that had happened to her. Jabari felt awe, but also a sharp twist of envy.

"You saw the Shaper!" Brigid said.

"I often see him," Isika replied, "though he always takes a different form, and it's usually in dreams. But this time it felt like it really happened, like he really came to me. That's why I was so sad when I thought it was another dream."

She told them about the thread, touching her palm as she said it.

"He said we all have a thread," she said. "Everyone."

They were silent. She began to speak again, "I have to..." but before she could get it out, Brigid interrupted.

"I want you to know that I trust you fully," she said. "I always have, and I know you will never betray us."

Isika shook her head, her mouth open slightly. "How can you know that?"

"I just do. I know these things, remember?"

"I feel the same," Benayeem said. "But you already knew that."

Jabari wanted to say something, but he felt tongue-tied. It was already hard just to look at Isika, to see her lovely face transformed into something shining, otherworldly. He needed to say something, to agree, but he couldn't get his voice to work, it was too important. She looked back and forth between Brigid and Ben, tears clinging to her eyelashes. Jabari didn't want to scare her with the strength of what he was feeling. He cleared his throat.

"I'll never leave you," is what he ended up saying. Inwardly, he cringed, but he tried to keep his gaze steady as she turned to look at him. "I mean, I'll go and help you. Wherever it is that you need to go, I can help."

Thank you. Her voice in his head as she looked at him.

You're welcome.

She took a deep breath, still holding his eyes. Then she turned to the others and released the breath.

"I have to go and fight him. That man. The Desert King," she said. "But I am afraid to go alone. Will you go with me?"

They sat in silence for a moment, all of them thinking of the horror of facing the Desert King.

"Of course," Jabari said, at the same time as Brigid said, "Now?"

Isika laughed, and it looked as though some heaviness lifted from her.

"Not now. You're eager, Brigid! No, not now. But," she looked up at Keethior, perched in the tree above her, pretending to be asleep. "Tomorrow."

Tomorrow. Tomorrow they could die? Tomorrow they would fight.

"Tomorrow," Jabari agreed. "Then we have things to do. I know where we should go."

IT TOOK them a while to get there, because Isika kept stopping to bring trees back to life along the way.

"Later, maybe?" Jabari said, after the seventh tree.

"It hurts to see them that way," Isika murmured, and Brigid took her hand.

Jabari fell into step beside Ben, behind Isika and Brigid. It was no use walking in front of them; they kept having to stop and wait.

"What does it sound like?" Jabari asked, after a while.

Ben glanced up, surprise showing on his face. Then he smiled, his eyes crinkling in a way that was now familiar.

"Isika?" he asked.

Jabari nodded.

"She sounds the way she normally does. But back in the grove, she sounded like nothing I've ever heard before."

Jabari looked at Isika, who was touching another tree. "The gold is fading, too. Whatever it was, it wasn't permanent."

"It was something," Ben said. "Hopefully it will be enough to help her get through this. I think... I think we can help her, but she will have to face our father on her own."

Jabari was surprised that Ben could so openly call the Desert King his father. He glanced over at him and saw his face drawn and set. He nodded, reaching out to pat Ben on the shoulder.

When they reached the waterfall, Jabari was more than ready to get into the water. He was hot from a day of panicky searching, and gritty from the smoke in the air. They all plunged in, taking their outer clothes off, swimming in their underclothes. Jabari dove under the water. He sat under the falls and let the water crash the day's worry out of him. He soaked in the beauty that hadn't been stripped from this place yet. No fire had come here. It was untouched.

Isika swam in circles, diving to touch the bottom and coming up. Then she and Brigid swam together, talking quietly. Jabari couldn't hear over the roar of the waterfall. Ben swam for a while, then climbed onto a rock that had a bar of sunlight streaming across it, stretching out and closing his eyes.

Soon, Keerza began to drift in, pausing on the far side of the stream to stand like ethereal guards. Then Efir flew in, then Nirral and Eemia, so that there were four Othra perched in the tall trees that surrounded the waterfall. Jabari pulled himself onto one of the rocks and looked up. The trees stretched into the sky like needles, higher than he could ever hope to reach. He felt a stab of longing. He had felt this before, when he touched something beautiful, when he saw beyond the normal into the truly good.

"We should sing," he told Ben. Benayeem sat up and blinked, rubbing his head with a smile.

"I was nearly asleep," he said. "It's so peaceful here."

They sang, and the words tumbled out into the air and pulled them into a different kind of space, one where the sky was the bluest they had ever seen, and there were gentle, magical creatures, and no one would ever destroy Maween.

Light on high
Light on high
Burn within
Burn within
Light on high
Burn within

As they sang, Jabari thought about the words in a way he never had before. It was a different kind of burning, not the kind that emptied and left things for dead, but a soft burning that lit the way home. A candle. But then he thought about himself, how he had struggled over accepting Isika, and he thought, no, it's another kind of burning as well, one that is picky, that removes the unlovely and leaves something bright and hard behind. He had been through that burning. Maybe he would go through it again. Isika had been through it, surely. Ben too. Had Gavi? What about Aria?

"I wish Gavi, Ivy and Aria were here," Isika said, as though she had read his mind. "I don't like not knowing where they are, or if they are safe."

"Tomorrow we fight for them. Soon they'll come home,"

Jabari said automatically. Isika looked at him after he said it, and he realized she saw through him, straight to his own worry. The truth was that he had no idea whether they were safe. He was used to pronouncing things that he wanted to be true. He smiled at her, rueful, and she picked up a handful of water from the stream and threw it at him. He gasped at the cold, then jumped off his rock and pulled at her ankle until she fell in the water.

He didn't see the storm of arms and legs until it hit him, and Brigid was tackling him, pushing him under. Under that cold, clear water, nothing could touch any of them, no fire, no hatred. Ben joined them, and they played and sang, played and sang, readying themselves for tomorrow.

Chapter 24

When they grew tired of the water they all climbed out, sitting in the last of the sun to dry themselves. Jabari stretched out on on a large rock, soaking up the warmth of the day, preparing himself for the moment of going back into the thick of the chaos. Nearby, Brigid played with Isika's hair, coiling the braids in her hands and letting them go, then tying them into a crown at the top of Isika's head. As he looked at the side of Isika's face, two things became very clear to Jabari. He felt far more for Isika than a servant for a queen. He felt far more for her than a friend felt for another friend. Even a friend who had been on two long journeys with a beautiful, talented, funny friend.

He felt that everything else could disappear and she would still be more than enough. She stood on her rock, when Brigid was done, reaching up to feel the way Brigid had done her hair, laughing down at her friend. He watched the

Isika-ness of her, the way she shrugged to test how her hair felt, her brilliant smile as she teased Brigid.

Seas and skies, what on earth? Oh no. Gavi was going to roast him over a fire. Gavi would know within one heartbeat, when he came back, that Jabari was gone, more than gone. Jabari had disintegrated. This was the first thing.

The second thing was that he couldn't tell her. She was bearing the weight of Maween, the knowledge of who her father was, the rekindling of the earth's magic to heal itself, the thread to the Shaper. All of this in the time it took for the sun to rise and set twice. One more momentous thing might crush her. Maybe... maybe someday. Maybe in a peaceful time. His resolve strengthened, he could feel it tightening in his jaw and shoulders. He knew that what he had said yesterday was true. He would never leave her.

"Enough, children!" Startled, Jabari looked up. Keethior. He would need to be sure to keep his feelings well away from the animal speech part of his mind. When Keethior swiveled his head to stare at Jabari, Jabari narrowed his eyes. Maybe he was too late.

Too true, young one, the bird said. *Remember I can understand your Maweel speech too. But I will not tell her.*

Jabari felt heat rush into his face, swiveling his head to make sure Isika hadn't heard that. She was oblivious, gathering her clothing and wrapping it up in her *ser* to carry. She glanced up.

"Yes, Keethior?" she said, her voice wry. "You have our attention."

"I applaud your efforts to remain in the light, but, World

Whisperer, wake up and look around. The time for action is now."

Jabari, startled, looked into the forest, and sure enough, the bird was right. There were small fires in the forest, burning in the trees. He heard Isika draw in a breath sharply.

"Oh!" said Brigid. "When did that happen?"

"It doesn't matter," said the bird, imperious as ever.

The Keerza and other Othra were gone. They had left as silently as they had come, and Jabari hadn't noticed. Keethior flew down from his tree and landed in front of Isika, keeping his wings lifted and slowly waving them backward and forward. Light, brilliant red and purple, flickered within them.

"World Whisperer," he said.

"Isika, remember?" She replied, her arms wrapped around her middle.

"You heard me," the bird said. "Put out the fires."

"Myself?"

"World Whisperer. Put out the fires."

She stared at him for a few moments, then turned and walked over to one of the fires. She began by picking up dirt and tossing it on the fire, but it blazed up higher. She glanced back around to Keethior.

"Think, daughter. It is poison. How must you deal with it?"

She stood staring into the forest, then held her hands over it and after a moment, it winked out. Brigid and Jabari applauded.

"Now all of them," Keethior ordered.

"At once?"

"Are you World Whisperer or are you not?" Keethior asked. Jabari could hear Isika grumbling as she turned back to look into the forest, and he smiled to himself.

She looked out over the fires, into the sickly orange flames that lit patches here and there in the twilight. The fires disappeared. They all cheered this time.

"If you're finished bossing me around?" Isika said to Keethior, "I would like to go speak to the elders about our plan to face the Desert King tomorrow.

The mood grew serious quickly. Jabari cleared his throat.

"You're going to tell them?"

"I'm done with sneaking away," she said, and after a long moment, he nodded.

They walked out of the forest together in their underclothes, after gathering their clothes to carry.

"How did you do it?" Jabari heard Brigid ask.

"It's not there, really, just like the walls," Isika replied. "I sent it to nothingness."

They reached the palace just as the lights were lit, warming up the night, and paused to pull their clothes on before approaching the entrance. It was Jabari's favorite time of day at the palace. The soft, curved earth walls were glowing here and there from the torches and red stones that flickered against it. The guards bowed as they went in, but there was an air of suspicion hovering. Jabari sighed.

The great room door was open. Inside, the elders stood around a table spread with food. Jabari's stomach growled. Dinner. They hadn't eaten in a long while.

Isika grinned at Jabari.

"You heard that?" He asked.

"I heard it too," his mother said. "Come and eat," and then after a pause, "all of you."

They filled their plates with grain and spicy curry, flat bread and *kiri*, the long, green vegetable that tamed spice and cleansed the palate. Jabari missed Gavi more than ever, his cook of a brother, who refused to let foods touch on his plate so they wouldn't touch before the right time. He missed Gavi so much he would even risk his brother knowing he was over the moon for Isika, just to see him right now, laughing his head off at Jabari.

They reclined around a low table, and after they had eaten some, and the hunger in Jabari's stomach was starting to feel more comfortable, Andar spoke.

"Are you here simply to enjoy food with us? Or because you have something to say?" He looked at each of them. Isika looked up from her plate and cleared her throat. Karah leaned on Ivram's shoulder, Andar and Laylit were beside them, and the four friends sat on the other side of the low table. There wasn't as much tension as the night before, but Jabari still held his breath for Isika as she began to speak.

"I'm going out to face the Desert King in the morning," she said. "Out on the plains in front of the village. He has threatened to burn all of Maween, and I believe I am the one who is meant to stop him."

Silence. Andar's mouth was slightly open. Karah looked stunned and Ivram had his eyes shut. Jabari dared a glance at his mother's face and found that her eyes were shiny with tears. He stared. His mother never cried.

"How did he threaten to burn Maween?" he finally asked. "Have you had contact with him?" His face was fairly neutral but Jabari knew his father well enough to know he was worried and possibly angry.

"The lizards," Jabari broke in. "The ones Ben and I killed. It was in the message they came to give us. I heard it too, in animal speech."

The elders stared at Jabari, and Isika gave him a look of gratitude.

"I'm going with her," Brigid announced. "And so are Ben and Jabari. We're going to ask Deto if he wants to join us, and we're wondering if any of you want to come. Also, if you'll send some rangers with us, it would help immensely."

Oh, Brigid. Her voice was sweet as she invited the high elders to join them in a quest that the elders hadn't yet approved. They looked stunned, especially Jabari's father.

"I'm trying not to do anything secretly anymore," Isika said, and her voice was as near to humble as she could make it, Jabari thought.

The elders looked at each other.

"We'll confer," Ivram said in his gravelly bass. "And let you know in the morning. Let's meet here, at the palace steps."

In the morning the air was smokier than it had ever been. It was so bad that the sun was hidden, as though it had decided not to come up that day. The colors in the sky were nothing like the sky Jabari had known above Azariyah all his life.

He dressed and ran to the outer palace steps, wanting to get there before Isika so he could gauge the response of the elders. He was too late. She was already there, and his jaw dropped as he saw that Auntie and Ibba were with her.

"You're coming?" he asked them.

"Yes," Auntie said simply.

"I'm very tough," Ibba told him.

"Well, I know that," Jabari said. "But you're a child on a battlefield."

Auntie snorted. "You're all children. But I'll take her home if it gets to be too much."

Isika held Wind's reins, and Jabari noticed that she wore her circlet on her head, a bright strand of silver against her dark skin. Beside her stood Ivram and Karah, with Jerutha and the baby nearby. As he watched, he saw Jerutha kiss her sister, then Isika, and stand to the side to wave them off. He relaxed a little. It was enough that Ibba was coming, they didn't need an infant out there.

He didn't see his parents anywhere, but he figured he would find them soon enough. However, Ivram pulled him aside.

"They're not happy, but they agreed to stay inside rather than making a scene. You're going to need to help them, Jabari. Your father is terrified of betrayal, growing up under the shadow of your grandmother and her choices. If we get

through this, I think you might be the only one who can bring
them around."

Jabari nodded. He looked to see who else was with them.
Besides Ivram and Karah, Dawit, Teru, Ibba, and Deto, he
saw nearly twenty rangers. Ben had his horse, and Ivram
stood beside his own, leading Karah's also. The rest of them
were on foot. They wouldn't dare bring the horses out if Isika
wasn't there. Jabari realized that Karah and Ivram bringing
their horses was a display of faith in Isika.

Oh Mom, oh Dad, he said inwardly. *Don't miss out on this
because you're stubborn.*

Isika mounted her horse and spoke. "I don't know what
will happen," she said. "I know only that we will go to meet
him. And I know for all his posturing and armies, all his fire
power, he is missing something. We have a connection to the
Shaper of all things, the Uncreated one. That is greater than
this evil king. We can be sure of it."

They went. They left the road at the horse pasture, and
crossed the new green field. Jabari saw the others looking
around, murmuring to each other, pointing at Isika. He saw
them straightening their shoulders and sitting or standing tall,
seeing for themselves what she had done. And then they
came to the edge of it all. The green ended and they were
looking out at what used to be their fertile Maweel lands.
They saw an endless sea of blackened earth. Beside Jabari,
Brigid flinched at the sight of it, and Ben doubled over on his

horse. Isika rode over to him, put a hand on his arm, and he sat up again.

"All right, Ben?" she asked.

"Yes, I have it now," he said. Jabari thought that perhaps out of all of them, Ben was the strongest. He heard and overcame the worst things in the world, every day.

Isika wheeled her horse to gaze out across the plain, and after a moment, she pointed. Jabari saw a smudge across the horizon. Something was coming.

"Father!" she shouted, and the sound of her voice sent a shiver of awe across the little group. It was louder than it should have been. Keethior was there, suddenly, flying overhead with the other Othra.

"Father!" she called again. "Come and face me!"

Chapter 25

Isika sat on her horse and waited. She had called the Desert King and the words she shouted, summoning him, would possibly end her life. She knew that he was stronger than she was. She knew that he had cut his connection to the Shaper, and possibly given parts of himself over to Mugunta in exchange for power. She thought of the people she had faced in the past, possessed by goddesses, powerful and stricken. She shuddered. She knew she was probably no match for the Desert King.

But she couldn't help feeling optimistic, mounted on Wind's back with Ben and Night on one side, Jabari and Brigid on foot on her other side. Jabari had his bow at the ready, one arrow loosely notched. Brigid stood with her face to the sky, listening. She opened her eyes and nodded at Isika. He was there. He was coming. Ben was clenching his jaw, but his back was straight in his saddle. Ivram's staff, which would be Isika's one day, was glowing with a dull, pulsing rhythm.

Four Othra flew overhead, and Isika felt Keerza hovering on the edges of her consciousness, ready if she needed them. She felt confident, even. She knew her thread was golden and strong, and Nenyi wouldn't have sent her here if she didn't have a chance against her father.

All of those good feelings vanished the moment she saw him. The smudge on the horizon rippled and shifted like a serpent as her father and his army came closer. They moved faster than an army should, with strange undulations, and the reason became apparent as they grew nearer and she recognized the first row. Her father in the center on a horse as red as flame, Baloto, the mud demons, flanking him. Behind them were row upon row of men, marching, faces painted with white stripes, knives and shields in their hands. But Isika could only keep her gaze on them for only a moment, barely even a moment, because there her father was, and he had all her attention.

It was the first time she had seen his face. *Oh,* she thought. *This is what being torn apart feels like.*

His face looked like her own. She heard Jabari gasp, and out of the corner of her eye, saw him take a step back. The resemblance was so strong that she felt she was looking in a mirror. She had always believed she looked like her mother, but now she knew she was wrong. Yes, her mother's face was there, in her jaw and chin, delicate and strong at the same time. But her father's eyes, his nose, his brow. Ben looked like her mother, Aria looked like her mother. Isika looked like the Desert King. Maween's chief enemy had her face.

Sounds of dismay all around her. Everyone saw what she saw. How could the queen and king of these countries at complete odds resemble one another so closely? The proof of her tainted blood was right there in front of all of them. She thought she could weep, but she was caught by his triumphant, imperious gaze.

He's only a man, she reminded herself. But it felt like he had been looking at her all her life. He was the face behind the mirror that told her she would never be good enough, that she would always be wandering alone in old broken fields and on charred roads. He was the shame that swallowed her when she saw how flawed she was, when her jealousy and greed rose up before her. He was her cowardice. He was the bruised feeling in her limbs on a morning after Nirloth had beaten her. He was the taunting words from other children, telling her she was ugly, different, not accepted. He was all of those things, and he was the lack of hope, the utter defeat. She was frozen in place, or she would have fallen under it.

Then he spoke, and the world seemed to be on fire. His voice set fire to everything, everyone.

"Ah, my daughter," he said, and Isika heard sobs to her left and her right, but she couldn't turn and see who was crying. *Is it Auntie?* A tiny part of her thought. *I don't want Auntie to cry.*

"I have been waiting for you. You know me, don't you."

The world was blazing. Fire everywhere. It burned up around him and enveloped him. It ate her from the inside.

She would have screamed in pain but she couldn't say a word.

"You recognize me. I am your future. I am your past. Oh, Isika, I am everything to you."

The lizards on either side of him screamed and writhed in some kind of war cry. Her name was a curse on his lips. *Don't say that name,* she wanted to tell him. *That is for my mother only.* The thought of her mother woke her a little, and she looked up to see the Othra wheeling in the smoky sky. Keethior was trying to say something to her, but she couldn't quite make it out in the roar of the flames around her father.

Another sound broke through, though, and dully she turned her head. Shrieking. Auntie stood, her feet planted, pointing at the king on his horse. She was saying something, lots of somethings, but the noise of the inferno kept Isika from understanding. He spoke again, and her head was pulled back to him.

"It is inevitable," he said. "It has always been and always will be."

"Which goddess are you?" she asked in a moment of clarity. Her voice was only a whisper, but he heard her anyway. There was a sudden movement beside him and Isika's eyes turned toward it. A man, standing next to the king, putting a hand out to Isika, shaking his head at her. She was distracted, momentarily, but drawn back to the king when he threw his head back and laughed. The sound tore at Isika's insides.

"Can't you tell? I am everything and all, I am an end in myself."

Isika remembered Nenyi and the thread. *He cut it.* Independence. Four sisters, four realms, Fate, Power, Independence and Wealth. She faced Independence.

"You are wasting time. I will kill every last one of this pathetic group of people for every minute you waste. You recognize me, daughter. I am your past and your future. I am everything."

The fire would eat her. It was tearing the sky open, tearing the earth apart. She walked Wind forward, wreathed in flame. He didn't seem to want to go, and when she looked back, she saw that Jabari was clutching Wind's reins, dragged forward by the horse, his face twisted as though he was screaming. There were tears running down his face. Dully, she wondered at that. *Jabari crying? Why was he holding on to her?* But she couldn't hear what he was saying, because all she could hear was the sound of her father's voice. She nudged her horse forward, one more step, dragging Jabari with her.

Chapter 26

Herrith felt as though the earth had suddenly become unsteady, as he saw Isika for the first time since she was a young child. He stood beside his horse, knowing that now the world would come to pieces; it was crashing in on him. Surely King Ikajo would sense his guilt, standing close to him, gazing at his daughter as well. The girl sat tall on a horse that somehow didn't run away from the mighty power of the king, which shouldn't have been possible. Their own horses had to be brought up near to the king, to get used to his power, which frightened animals and children. Even then, they had spells laid over them by the stable magicians. But there Isika sat on a horse that seemed calm and in its right mind, not ensnared by spells.

Despite all that, it was her face that caught at him. She looked like her father, yes, but it was her mother that he saw, in the eyes and the set of her brow, furrowed in kind concern.

Herrith hadn't seen that face since that night, that dreadful night when he helped them escape an eternity ago. He had been sure that he would die, that the king would find out his betrayal and have him executed, if he could wait long enough. But somehow, he had been shielded. King Ikajo never found out that it had been Herrith, his servant and cousin, who had helped the king's favorite wife escape.

He hadn't died, but it had been worse than death to live in a palace without Amani, his friend from childhood, his one true love.

AMANI HAD COME to him secretly. She left the women's quarters and found Herrith as he was rushing to tell the kitchen workers that the king needed a second dinner. The first had ended up on the face of a slave who had angered the king, and Ikajo was still hungry.

When Herrith turned the corner outside the throne room, Amani was there, waiting for him. Her hair was braided and oiled, her flowing robes a deep ruby red. She wore gold bracelets on her wrists and a circlet around her throat. But her face was tearstained and miserable. He thought he knew why. The boy had been caned the day before, just ten strikes on the backs of his legs, but the boy was a young child, and not strong, either. The king treated him worse than the other slaves, despite all Herrith's attempts to shield him from the anger of the king. Herrith wondered at the king's anger toward such a small child. Ikajo carried what seemed like great disappointment in the boy, and Herrith only partially understood, as much as he ever understood the king and his emotions, anyway.

Amani had Isika and the little girl, Aria, with her. Isika played with the tassels of a nearby drapery as Amani caught sight of Herrith. She put the little girl on the floor beside Isika and strode toward him, her face furious.

"Amani," he said, and his hands came up. She backed him into a corner, her finger at his throat.

"You said you would take care of him!" she said.

She was trying to be threatening, but she didn't have it in her, and she only sounded heartbroken. Herrith caught at her hands and held them.

"I have tried, Amani, you know I have." Her face fell as he went on. "I cannot be everywhere at once, and lately Ikajo wants him close, right under his chair. And the boy gets so frightened..."

Her whole body slumped as the anger left her. She pulled her hands away and put them over her face, then leaned against the wall, sobbing. Isika looked up, her face creased with concern.

"Mama?"

Amani took a shuddering breath. "No, it's okay, young one. Mama will be okay." The sconces in the long hallway threw gleaming lights onto her hair and face.

Herrith remembered his kitchen errand. "Walk with me," he said. "I have to gather more food for the king, who threw a fit and tossed his dinner onto the nearest slave." At her sharp look he shook his head. "No, it wasn't Benayeem. He is sleeping now, in the slave quarters."

She grasped his sleeve as they walked, pulling on it, the little girl in her other arm. "We must leave, Herrith. You must help me escape." Aria looked at Herrith with huge eyes, and because she was perched on Amani's hip, pulling the dress over her belly, Herrith saw the new curve. Amani's belly rounded out in a gentle bell. He stopped walking.

"You're with child again," he said.

"I am." Her face tore at him. "What am I doing but supplying him with more slaves? When will he decide to take Isika? I cannot remain and see my children beaten! I must save Benayeem before he is gone from us, before it turns his soul bad. He is such a sweet, quiet boy. He won't last long. Herrith, please help us!"

Her face was so lovely, as though it was lit from a thousand candles. Their friendship was impossible, always had been. But he was caught, he would do anything for her.

"It's my life if I get caught helping you," he said. "And where will you go?"

"The Shaper will guide me," she whispered.

Herrith felt the blood leave his face. He looked quickly up and down the halls, hoping no one had heard, that the goddesses themselves hadn't heard, listening through the walls. Of all the things Amani had said or asked, this was the limit.

"That name," he murmured, still feeling faint. "You must not speak that name."

But he could not bear to see her so miserable. He knew she was right, that eventually the king would take Isika, and what he knew about the king's plans for Isika would kill

Amani, who upheld her mother's faith. As he looked into her beloved eyes, he knew he would help her, even if it meant his life. He had never been able to say no to her.

He gave her a slight nod. "There is a way. You must be patient and wait for me to tell you when. But we can get you out before the week is done."

She rewarded him with a brilliant smile, and when the little Isika saw her smiling, she smiled at Herrith, too.

"You ask for my life," he said, bitterly, meaning it in more ways than one, because if she left the palace, he would be lost.

"You could come with me," she said.

"If I do, he will move the world to find us and kill us," Herrith said. "Betrayal will feed his magic. You will be safer if you go alone." He put a hand over his face.

"I will miss you," Amani whispered. "But the Shaper will watch over you, too."

"Don't say that name," he said sharply.

He pulled his sleeve out of her hand and strode away, leaving her standing there. He ignored her as she called his name. He was afraid to look at her. He didn't want her to see the tears on his face.

ALL OF THIS, and he had gone without Amani's friendship, her light for so long. He stood opposite Amani's daughter, shaken by the way he saw the mother so clearly in the girl's face.

He could see that the girl was stronger than Amani ever

had been. He was caught in a nightmare. He had given every-thing to help Amani, so many years ago, and now he was here to hurt the girl again? It was a waste. His efforts had been such a waste. He should have known Mugunta would have his way, no matter what. Herrith knew Amani was dead. He could feel her absence in the world like a missing limb. Herrith had saved the little family, and now the king was intent on destroying them.

Herrith took a deep breath, and then blinked. It was the boy! Benayeem sat on the horse beside Isika, but he looked different. He was stronger. Perhaps leaving had saved more of him than Herrith had thought possible. He hadn't held out much hope for the small, terrified boy, when he carried him from the slave boys' quarters and put him in Amani's arms. Amani had saved the boy, he thought. With her love.

"Brilliance," he said, unable to stop himself, "why don't we leave them be?"

He cringed after he said it. The words were so bare, with no mask, no hiding, no double meaning to shield his true heart. The king turned and stared at Herrith with disbe-lieving eyes.

"Have you turned so soft, Herrith? Shall I send you to the place where old horses go?"

Herrith shuddered. "No, Brilliance, I only wonder if they are worth it. Look at them on those old horses, with crows flying overhead. Why must we pursue such unpromising chil-dren? You remember them in the palace. They were nothing, even then."

The king looked long at his children on the horses. "I see

what you mean," he said finally. "And I grant you that the boy is still worthless. But she will be magnificent, with the strength of the desert and the whisperer in her. She is a warrior. I have not come to take her a moment too soon, because they would have ruined her. We will take her and keep her for our own."

Herrith's heart sank. He watched as the king shouted at the girl, watched the words take hold of her, the fire of the king's power paralyze her. He couldn't stand by, he just couldn't, as she began slowly walking her horse toward the king. He saw the boy on her right pulling on the horse's reins. He shook his head and held his hand out, telling her *no, no, go back, no*. She glanced at him for a moment, and he saw her almost pause to listen, but the king's power washed over her again, and she kept on walking toward the king, like a woman entranced.

"Amani, forgive me," he muttered under his breath. "I tried, oh I tried."

Chapter 27

G avi felt something sinister in the air the moment he woke up, a faint discomfort, his heart beating faster, but it was Aria who drove them to run.

"Isika!" she shrieked in her sleep, sitting up in her bedroll as the sun was getting ready to rise, staring over the fields to the north, in the direction of the city. Gavi sat up as well, turning to look at Aria. She was shaking.

"Gavi," she whispered, then frowned. Her hands shook like leaves in a stiff wind. "Abbas!" she shouted. "Ivy! Wake up! We must go now. Now!"

Ivy sat up, rubbing at her face. "Gavi?" she asked. He saw the confusion in her face. "What?"

Aria wrapped her arms around her stomach. "Sorry, Gavi. But I feel her, something is wrong. She's preparing for something. Someone is planning to hurt her, and it feels like she's going to let it happen." She shut her eyes tightly. "I don't understand what I'm feeling."

Gavi thought quickly. They were far from the city, and to reach it quickly, they would need to run. The last days of putting fires out and tearing down stubborn walls had taken a toll on all of them, and he hated to make them run. But as he felt the unease at the base of his neck, prickling in his wrists and ankles, he knew Aria was right. Something was horribly wrong. They needed to run.

"Breakfast is leftover soup. We can be gone before the sun is above the horizon," he said.

Ivy blinked, but Abbas was already standing, packing his satchel and pulling his short, curved sword out to check the sharpness of the blade, though he had checked it the day before, and the day before that.

Gavi ladled bowls of cold stew and they ate quickly, washing the bowls in a nearby stream and pausing for a moment to look around and make sure they left no trace. Then they ran.

Despite his nervousness, Gavi felt a spike of joy in running. They had been traveling slowly for a long while, stopping at nearly every house to put out fires. It felt good to have a destination and go like arrows. They ran all through the early morning, stopping for water and to catch their breath once. It was mid-morning when they saw the army.

At first it was only a smudge, like a bruise on the horizon. But it soon became more visible and Gavi saw the dust it raised. He halted at a well to refill flasks. None of them could tear their eyes away from the foreign organism that was the moving army.

"Four goddesses," Abbas breathed. "The king's army."

"What are they doing?" Gavi asked. "They're nearly at the city gates!"

Aria shook her head, rubbing at her arms, covered in gooseflesh. She looked frail, and her eyes were shadows in her face. "What should we do? What is happening to Azariyah, that the king can get so close?"

"We need a plan," Abbas said.

It was easy enough to see what they should do, what their part was in the whole thing.

"I have a plan," Gavi said. "But it is very, very dangerous. These seem to be dangerous times. I wasn't prepared..." he trailed off.

"What, Gavling?" Ivy demanded. "Enough with the rambling."

"We need to cut them off from behind," he said. "Harass them. Perhaps we can distract them, break their mass up."

"I don't know," Aria said quickly. She shivered. "Isika is at the other side of that army. Maybe we should go to her."

It occurred to Gavi to be annoyed at the way she contradicted him and talked over him, in a way she would never do to Jabari. He could see that Ivy's eyes were narrowed. She was annoyed too. But as he watched her, her eyes trained on the front of the army, he knew she carried a heavier burden than the rest of them. She could feel the danger to Isika. Of course she was torn.

"She'll have people with her," he said gently. "Jabari is there, the elders and the rangers. We'll be more helpful if we help from behind."

Slowly, she nodded, and he saw she had tears in her eyes.

"Enough talking," Abbas declared, fidgeting with the blade that hung at his waist again. "We fight."

They ran toward the army, sticking close to the trees that stood beside the roads, buildings, anything that would be cover for them. And as they ran, something clanged in a metallic shriek, and the sky turned to fire. The burning was strongest at the front of the army, where Gavi assumed the Desert King was. The fire spread, though, through the whole army, and into the fields surrounding them.

Aria shrieked in terror. Abbas muttered a steady stream of curses under his breath, an angry hum.

But they kept running, and then heard noises, jingling and clanking of shields, the sound of many sets of feet, and they were very, very near. They stopped to catch their breath. Aria was still vibrating, her whole body shaking, but this time it seemed less like fear and more like magic.

"I think..." she said. "I think I know what to do,"

Nearby, a grove was burning, the flames oppressive with heat, and Aria began to move toward it. Slowly, she moved her hands through the dry air, calling every bit of moisture she could and breathing over it. To Gavi's utter shock, her breath turned it to something like ice. She threw a sheet of it over the grove. The fire went out.

The sheet wrapped around the trees and disappeared, and though the fire lapped at the edges of the trees, it couldn't enter the grove again. Aria pulled water from the air again and threw it. It froze midair and sailed over the heads of the army, turning to hail that pelted their hands and faces. Great cries erupted, and some of the soldiers broke step, looking around wildly to see what was attacking them.

"Now," Gavi said. Abbas, Ivy, and he moved quickly. Abbas was a whirling, fighting vision. He was everywhere at once, attacking half of the people who turned back to fight them. The men died quickly under his blade, and Gavi felt as though he would be sick, but plowed into one man, who fell when Gavi's staff hit his arm. On his other side, a man stabbed upward with a knife, but Gavi spun and wasn't there when the knife reached him. Another spin and that man was also down: a short blow to the back of his head with Gavi's staff took care of him.

"Try not to kill them!" he shouted to Abbas. At first he thought Abbas didn't hear him, but lightning quick, Abbas changed his sword for a staff and began fighting like Gavi, blows to the sensitive parts of the head and neck that would incapacitate men for a long, long time.

Ivy fought with her hands, the way Ivram had taught her. She threw men easily, as though they were toys, her slight figure whirling, grappling, throwing. She laughed, the sound stabbing holes in the flames, which withered and died out around her.

Hope, thought Gavi. *It can't survive hope. Oh Shaper, come to our aid.*

And the whole while, Aria threw hail and wrapped giant sheets of ice around trees, houses, and plants, making a circle of protection that fire could not destroy. They moved farther in as more of the army scattered, and then Aria wasn't throwing sheets anymore, only hail; small hard pellets that hit the Gariah soldiers in the eyes and face and the hands that held shields and knives, causing them to fumble in time for Gavi to knock them out.

Sweat ran down his back. The whole world was fire and smoke and strangely, ice. The magical ice that Aria made. He had time, as his body took over and he fought in a rhythm that seemed as though it couldn't be broken, to wonder about her gifts, what other amazing things she could do quietly while all of Azariyah was focused on Isika. He breathed heavily and heard a familiar roar beside him. A knife had gotten through Abbas's guard and he was bleeding from the shoulder. But he picked up the man who wielded the knife and threw him far away. The man fell and was still, and Abbas roared again and kept fighting. Gavi began to wonder how long they would fight. There was some commotion going on at the front of the army. He blinked. He could see to the front swell of the army because it was more thinly spread. Sparse from all the work they had done. It had never been so big to begin with, he told himself, disarming and knocking out another man, but he couldn't help but feel a swell of pride.

That pride made him falter and he leaned back to avoid a sword swipe, not quite fast enough. Blood ran down his cheek from the scratch. Putting his hand to it, Gavi knew he would need a healer's help. He thrust the thought out of his mind and pushed toward the man who had cut him, but Ivy got there first and tripped the man from behind, grinning. Gavi delivered a blow to his cranium, a little harder than necessary.

A scuffle again at the front, and a voice, a man talking.

The voice was like nothing Gavi had ever heard. Suddenly they were all listening, arms at their sides, no one fighting anymore. The man's voice had paralyzed them. In the stillness, Gavi saw that most of the army was either on the ground or had fled, and he could still see the backs of some of them, running, ice melting on their tunics as they went.

The spot where they stood was very near the horse meadow, nearly in the city. He had a sudden longing for home and bed.

The words, the voice. He listened as the Desert King called to Isika, calling her daughter, asking her to come to him. *What?* What was he saying? Isika was the Desert King's daughter? But what about Aria? Gavi turned and saw Aria. Her eyes were glazed, and as he watched, she began taking slow, stuttering steps toward the king. He ran to her, calling her.

"Aria!" he called. "Aria, don't go to him!"

She seemed as though she was in a trance. She didn't respond to anything he said, and though he held her arm, planting his feet, she dragged him slowly forward.

The voice went on, and for the first time, he felt despair.

Chapter 28

Jabari held onto Wind's reins, calling Isika, shouting at her until his voice broke. She didn't even seem to notice, riding blindly forward, but Wind began to resist her, refusing to move. She looked down at him, confused, then drove her heels into his sides. Jabari tried to stop the horse, but couldn't. Wind was strong, and he was going where Isika wanted him to.

"Isika!" Ben screamed, "Isika, stop this! Come back!" He had dismounted, and walked along the other side of Wind, holding on to a corner of Isika's tunic. She didn't even glance at her brother.

"Isika, don't you act like you can't hear me!" Jabari shouted. "Get back here, your horse is distressed. Don't drive him into this poison."

Isika inched the horse forward, step by step, eyes vacant, as though she was in a trance. And the Desert King's horrible words went on and on, poison words that crowded out sensible thought. Jabari looked around wildly for help, but everyone was tied up with something else. Mud demons tried to make their way into the city, curling their long tails and hissing from their small, wedge-shaped heads, but Ivram fought them with Karah and Brigid by his side. He held the World Whisperer's staff out, but though it buzzed and sent sparks toward the lizards, it wasn't strong, the way it should be, because the World Whisperer's power was dim. She wasn't with them. She was somewhere else, listening to poison words.

"You are nothing!" someone shrieked from beside him. It was Auntie, facing the Desert King. Some of her hair had escaped her *ser,* usually wrapping her hair so neatly. Her eyes were wild. Beside her, Ibba gripped her hand, feet planted apart, glaring at the King. *She isn't fooled by him,* Jabari thought.

"You are nothing!" Auntie said again, "You are nothing but a child against the greatness of the whisperers and the Shaper. 'They walk as light shadows in the world, and nothing will cause them to fall. They walk through fire and water, tall as giants, bringing the earth rest.' These are the words of the old poets, and you are a sad little upstart trying to build your own story. You cannot change the ancient ways. You are nothing!"

She lifted her hand and sent a streak of light toward the nearest mud demon. It disintegrated as soon as the light touched it, turning to dust that wailed as it flew. Its companions seemed to grow angry, and more of them came out of the ground, oozing like mud, crawling on all fours. Their eyes were red and angry, and they hissed as they moved toward Auntie, standing there with Ibba still at her side. The two of them looked defenseless against the Baloto; an old woman and a young girl, but as Jabari started toward them, still holding Wind's reins, Ibba raised her hand the way Auntie had, and the same light streaked away from her, destroying the nearest lizard.

"What on earth?" Jabari whispered.

The two of them stood hand in hand, shooting light at mud demons, and Jabari realized they didn't need his help at all.

He looked farther out, all the way to the back of the army. He looked again. It seemed thinner, scarce of people when it had been dense with bodies before. He squinted. Something was falling out of the sky, striking the people at the back of the group, scattering them. He caught sight of a staff spinning and a gleam of gold. *Abbas*. His heart swelled with hope. Gavi was there.

He pulled harder on the rein, because he still had this other problem. Isika was gaining ground on the Desert King, slowly. If she managed to break away and run, she would reach the Desert King, and Jabari couldn't let that happen. Ben kept yelling at her to stop. The horse grew more and more nervous, kicking and tossing his head. He would throw Isika and hurt her, if she didn't come back to them and calm her horse down. She was like a shell, there but unreachable.

He looked up and saw Keethior flying overhead.

What do I do? he asked. *How do I get her back?*

It's only poison, the bird replied. *Use your training.* Then Keethior dove and plunged straight into one of the lizards. The lizard writhed and disappeared in a cloud of dust. The sight gave Jabari courage, and he let go of the reins and grasped Isika's ankle, pulling her from the saddle and catching her before she could hurt herself on her ground. He placed her down on her feet. She wouldn't look at him, and her eyes were glassy and unfocused. She tried to walk toward the Desert King, but Jabari held her hands.

Isika, he said in animal speech. *Come back to us.*

Isika!

He began to sing.

"Water flowing between earth and sky
Bright day, old night, gentle and wise"

Jabari held onto Isika's hand and bent close to her. She blinked at him, her eyes coming into focus.

"Birds on the wing, fire in the stars
Oh high one, earth is in your hands
Oh true one, we are in your hands."

She blinked again slowly, and she was back. Jabari saw her there, knew she was truly in her own skin, not in the distance, lost to herself anymore. Ben stood beside them, and Jabari heard him draw a breath in, almost a sob.

"Welcome back," Jabari said.

"What under Nenyi's skies is happening?" she asked. "Why are you holding my hands?"

He grinned at her, gave her hands a squeeze, and let them go. She frowned and looked down at her hands, shivering all over. A shadow crossed her face and he knew she was remembering whatever distant place she had traveled to. She looked at Ben and for a moment her face was like a lost child's. Jabari felt that he and Ben needed to take her away from this horrible place, before she lost herself in poison again. He looked around, feeling panicky. Why was poison so close to their city? Where could they go? Maybe the trees, the waterfall. He squatted down and picked some of the wildflowers she had brought to life the day before. Orange, purple, yellow. The faintest pink. He stood up and piled them in her open hands, a little heap of color. She looked at them and stopped shivering.

Then the voice started up again. Jabari had barely realized it stopped until it started again and his head rang with horror.

"Isika. My daughter."

This time the voice was velvety and nauseating. Jabari turned, unable to stop himself, and looked into the face of the man who resembled Isika so strongly. He flinched again, seeing that familiar face, but he forced himself to keep looking, to find the differences. He needed to, to make sure he never believed they were one and the same. No one could help their parentage.

"My eldest, incomparable daughter. I care about nothing beside you. Look what I have brought, look how far I came, how much I have lost, looking for you."

Isika stood with her head high, holding her hands out,

cupped, with the flowers still in them. Her circlet shone and the look on her face was unreadable.

"Come, my dear one. I care only about you. Leave the others, your useless siblings. They are nothing to me; I only want you. Together, you and I will rule over all of these lands. My beautiful daughter. My World Whisperer."

Isika's face blazed then, and she took a step forward.

Chapter 29

Behind the army, Aria focused on ice, pulling it out of the air, raining hail on the army. She could see that she was succeeding. The army was thinner, more spread out, not the solid mass it had been before she and the seekers had started their attack. She turned to grin at Gavi, then froze as an impossibly loud voice rang out over the force.

Aria went as cold as the ice she had been throwing.

It was the king. She couldn't move. Desperation, longing, and hatred swam in her head as she heard his words. He spoke to Isika and the cruelty of his words stabbed through her.

She fell where she stood. The man—her father—kept speaking, and his words were unceasing, they were swollen around her, a cold, raging river that she couldn't escape. He spoke to Isika alone. He didn't even seem to know that Aria was there, back among his men, doing magic even she had never known she could do. He spoke to Isika, not to Aria.

I only care about you. The others are nothing to me.

Nothing,

Nothing,

Nothing.

She was seven years old again. The bells rang out in harsh, jarring clangs, sealing her fate. Nirloth's face was hard, like flint. "We're sending her over. We can't be the only ones who don't send a child to stop the famine. The other villagers will revolt."

Aria's mother cried and fought him, screaming that sending a child away wouldn't help anything, telling him that he couldn't take her child.

"Aria is mine! You cannot send her. She has never been yours!"

In response, he locked her in the house.

Aria remembered. She remembered. There was the long procession down to the harbor, the icy black water. She remembered her fear, a constant ache in her stomach, screaming for her mother. Then Isika pushing her into the boat, her hand hard on Aria's arm.

It wasn't Isika. But she couldn't help it. She remembered Isika's face near hers, laughing at her, sending the boat into the water. Casting her away. Then a ripple, a shudder and the memory changed. She was staring at the Desert King's face, and she didn't know how she recognized him, because she had never seen him before. She only knew that he was sending her away, his eyes like black chips of stone in his face.

They mean nothing to me.

Sharp pain made her cry out as the poisoned arrow lodged deeper inside her body, very near to her heart. If she moved at all, it would kill her. She lay very still but as the Desert King's words went on, the arrow responded to his voice. It knew him. He had made the poison of this arrow, and it moved again. Aria screamed as the point pierced her heart. The pain was so terrible she knew she was dying. She lay sobbing, waiting to die. Maybe it would be best after all. Better if there were no more surprises, no more moments like this one. No new ways that she could be rejected.

She remembered the cold faces, the shrieking voices. The bitter tea that she spat out when she got a chance. The boat pitching in the waves, how she nearly froze in the icy water that sloshed over the sides. She sobbed and sobbed, calling for her mother, screaming for Isika, who had always looked out for her, to come get her. Isika didn't come. Aria remembered lying there for what felt like forever, wet and alone, waiting to die.

The pain was horrible.

Aria.

She remembered the long boat full of rescuers, pulling up beside her boat. The rescuers exclaiming aloud at the sight of her, dark-skinned child, far older than the other cast away children, eyes open. She couldn't speak, couldn't tell them who she was. They had warm hands, warm eyes. They had black skin, but she was so tired she couldn't feel anything about that. She didn't know who they were or what was happening to her. She didn't care.

No, leave me, she thought. *This time I don't want to be rescued. Let me die in the waves.*

Aria.

No.

"Aria!"

She opened her eyes to find herself lying on the scorched grass, her cheek pressed against the ground. Through the earth she could feel something, faintly, and she closed her eyes again to hear it better. It was her sister. Isika was in distress, and Aria always knew when Isika was in distress. Never mind. She wanted to go back under. All the way down and down. She let her eyes drift closed. *Leave me. This time I don't want to be rescued.*

"Aria! It's not time to take a nap!" She opened her eyes again, angry this time.

It was Gavi, not the rescuers, who had his face close to hers.

"I'm not taking a nap," she protested, her voice weak. *I think I'm dying,* she thought, but couldn't be bothered to say it aloud. She blinked again. She wasn't in the boat; she was lying on burned grasses in a field that teemed with warriors. And it seemed that her sister needed her. A wave of despair hit her. How long would she be confused about past and present and where the pain came from, who had betrayed her?

Gavi looked at her anxiously, scanning her face. His hair stuck up as usual, and he was on his knees by her side, holding his hand out for her to take so he could help her up. His eyes looked very blue in his face and she stared into them for a long moment. Blue eyes. When she was younger, she had asked Nirloth if it hurt to have blue eyes. He laughed his empty laugh and asked her if it hurt to have skin that looked burnt, like bread too long in the fire. She held her hand out to Gavi, noticing how dark it was against his skin, though he was tanned and golden, living and real, not pale like her stepfather. Not cruel. One father dark, one light. Neither of them wanted her.

They mean nothing to me.

She faltered, trying to sit up, breathing in sharp pants.

"What is it?"

"Something changed with the arrow," she said. "It's making it hard for me to breathe."

Gavi stopped trying to pull her to her feet. They sat close together on the ground, and somewhere, the man's voice went on. There were cries, sounds of fighting, but Gavi leaned his forehead against hers. He gasped and drew back in shock. His face drained of color.

"What happened, Aria? This is really bad—I..."

"I don't know," she said, though she had a pretty good idea.

He shook his head, looking into her face. "No, Aria. You can't listen to him. He's evil. You're *ours*. We rescued you. We want you. You don't belong to him."

"He's my father, Gavi."

"He's not. He doesn't deserve it. Don't listen to him."

She glanced away. *He's my father.*

"Don't you think we'd better do something?" she asked. "We can't sit here in the middle of a battle."

Gavi looked up. "True," he said. "Abbas has been giving us space, but we should help him."

As soon as he said it, Aria saw what he meant. They were huddled in a little stand of trees, hidden on one side by the thick bushes beside them. Abbas was on the other side, dancing a wide half circle around them, teeth bared, knocking down men who were lunging at her and Gavi. She frowned. The warriors all seemed to be pressing toward them specifically.

"Why are they all coming to us?" she asked, feeling dazed. Her heart hurt so badly that every breath felt like a knife. She watched as the warriors pressed in, their own faces dazed, only to meet Abbas's whirling staff with their heads.

"I have no idea," Gavi said, frowning at the persistent warriors. "But what do you think about getting up and away?"

"Let's keep fighting," Aria said.

Gavi shook his head. "No, we need to get you away. You're not able to fight."

"We need to keep fighting," Aria insisted. "Isika needs us."

"Are you sure?" Gavi asked, his face unhappy and unsure.

"Yes," Aria said, nodding. "It seems to be the only way we'll be able to get home and sleep in our own beds. One last push. Let's harass them enough that Isika can deal with the Desert King." Pain took her breath away. She paused, panting in little gasps, the arrow aching inside her chest. After a moment, she could continue. "Right?"

Gavi looked at her for a long while. Then he nodded.

"Okay," he said. "We can do that."

They stood and joined Abbas and Ivy in the fight. Aria pulled more hail out of the air and threw it over the warriors in the plain where they stood, and beside her, Abbas used his staff to incapacitate nearly every person who ran their way. She noticed dimly that the warriors still all hurtled toward her, and she found this curious, but the pain in her rib cage was so all encompassing that all she could do was hurl hail, over and over, trying to push farther in, to where Isika stood on her horse. Fires still burned around them, and she began experimenting with water, trying to throw ice on the fire. She found that she could also throw cold water on the fire, and this was vaguely interesting to her, but her attention was elsewhere.

She wanted her sister. The single-minded magic that told her where Isika was and whether she was safe wanted her to be near Isika. Lights flickered at the edges of her vision as she pressed forward, exhausted. The whole world seemed to be made of smoke, fire, and men with leering faces trying to hurt her. She pressed toward her sister, fighting the hurt and hatred she felt. She was angry, livid with fury. She was heartbroken and wounded. Still, her magic wouldn't leave her alone. *Get to her. Tell her not to go to him. Make her stay.*

The warriors ran toward her, though, a sea of faces and masks, dark-skinned people with paint on their faces, people who looked like Abbas, with braided hair and strong brows. They ran toward her with shields and spears out. She turned them back with hail that dropped against their foreheads and hands. Her friends swirled around her, protecting her. They were all confused by this attack, Aria could tell, but they focused on keeping Aria safe. Abbas and Gavi fought with staffs, knocking men out and leaping over their prone bodies as they slowly advanced on the king, and beyond him, Isika. Ivy fought hand to hand, and she always won. Aria fought the deathly pain in her heart, pushing thoughts of it away until she was only a machine, moving steadily, doing the same things over and over with her hands. She pushed thoughts of death away, of simply lying on the ground and allowing them to come to her. She noticed dimly that they were in a different section of the force now, where men had swords instead of spears. *Interesting,* she thought.

Then one of those swords flashed toward her, and she couldn't move. Time seemed to slow and she knew she would die, but then Gavi was in front of her, and the sword still moved toward them, striking Gavi across the shoulder and upper chest. Aria screamed as he fell. Abbas became a whirl-wind, pulling out his own sword and killing the other swordsman in the next breath. Aria threw herself on the ground beside Gavi, placing a hand over the bleeding wound. It was not good, large and bleeding steadily. She pulled her *ser* off her head and bound it around his chest. It was immedi-ately soaked through with blood. She pushed her hand down to stop the bleeding. Gavi was pale and unconscious, all the golden color drained out of him.

Still Abbas and Ivy had to fight people away from them, and Aria knew that if this battle didn't end, if they didn't get Gavi to a healer, he would die. Abbas was a storm of arms and legs, sword flashing and long hair streaming. Ivy leapt on warriors before they even caught sight of her. All of them were trying so hard, but Aria bowed her head. It felt impossible. They couldn't do this alone. The battle raged on. Aria tied the *ser* tighter around Gavi, tears running down her face.

Chapter 30

Isika stood holding the flowers out in front of her, cupping them gently in her palms. She felt sick, as though something had her by the stomach and was tugging it slowly, leading her somewhere she didn't want to go. What was happening? There was so much shouting, and at the edges of her vision, she could see scuffling and flailing, as people fought each other nearby. The man was vaguely interesting. He looked familiar to her, as though she had always known him. He was saying interesting things. But... something was wrong with the familiarity, as though she was walking in circles. And something was wrong with the man's voice. *Your voice has poison in it,* she wanted to tell him. *You should really do something about that. I'm sure the healers have something that can help you.* She could help him, if she went to him, she knew it.

Isika.

She shrugged, irritated. Every time someone called her,

she was plucked away from the world of the man and his words, and she didn't want to leave him.

She looked down at the flowers and blinked, confused. They were so beautiful, and looking at them, she had a little nudge of memory. Another man. Or was it a woman? Here, not far...just... she looked around... over there.

Nenyi, a voice said. *It was Nenyi.*

Someone was talking to her again. She grimaced, trying to block out the voice. It was the bird again. That annoying bird.

When we are out of this, you are going to be in so much trouble for thinking of me as the annoying bird. I am an ancient, otherworldly creature. I am an Othra, Isika, and you know it. Snap out of it!

The annoying bird was persistent.

She looked at the man again, tugged by his voice. He seemed to be demanding her to look at him, and she so badly wanted to do what he said. But she couldn't hold his gaze very long, because there was something wrong with his face. He had so much anger behind his eyes. He needed help. She took a step toward him, holding the flowers out. Perhaps the flowers could help him.

"No," he said. "Put down the flowers, Isika."

From Isika's right side, another man lunged forward. She turned and recognized her friend. *Jabari,* she thought. *I didn't realize you had grown so much. I thought you were a man. But what are you doing?*

Jabari was angry, vibrating with fury. *What's wrong?* thought Isika. *Why are you angry?*

"Enough!" Jabari shouted. "We have been merciful to you, but now you will leave. Leave our lands." His voice sounded very harsh after the softness of the man's voice, but Jabari's voice was clear of poison. That was nice. Isika saw the flowers again. She lifted them to her face and breathed the spicy fragrance. When she looked up, she was surprised again. What was going on? There were so many people fighting.

Jabari still shouted at the man. "You are not welcome here and she is not yours, she is not your World Whisperer, she is ours, and you may... not.... have her!"

The man began to laugh. He laughed and laughed, and his laughter was infectious—it made Isika want to laugh as well, but her friend was upset, so she waited to see if Jabari would get the joke and join in. She didn't want to laugh first if it would hurt his feelings.

"So that's how it is, little boy," the man said. "You poor thing. Son of imposters, makers of false positions and weak magic. She will never love you."

Me? thought Isika. *But I do love him. He's my friend.*

She held out the flowers again, as though to offer them, but just then the king raised his hand and threw something at Jabari. Halfway through the air, the thing became a roaring mass of fire, blazing heat that reached them from a long way off. It howled toward Jabari's face, and Isika felt a stab of fear; the thing would eat her friend. But just before it touched him, Jabari held up an arm and threw the fire off him, sending it straight into the sky, where it fizzled and went out. He swung his hand in a large arc and a strong wind came up. He threw the wind toward the man, and—Isika could barely believe it—the man fell.

Several things happened all at once. The fires around them blazed up higher. The remaining mud demons rushed toward Jabari, and Abbas appeared in the distance, holding a bleeding, limp Gavi in his arms, and Isika woke up to find that she had been under a spell during a battle, surely the most horrible thing Azariyah had ever seen. She'd been staring wistfully at a man who had hurt her brother horribly when they were small, a man who surely didn't want mercy from her. He stared at her again from where he had fallen, but she was finished with his spell.

She shrieked, and the sound was a long heartbroken, angry sound like a cleaver through the air, and then lifted her hands and threw the flowers toward the Desert King.

All the fires went out.

The flowers expanded as they flew through the air. They grew, changed color and formed into clouds that filled the sky, shielding the people from the relentless sun. It started to rain. Isika lifted her face, overwhelmed by the happy buzzing of the earth as its longing for water was answered. The rain was light and steady. It ran down Jabari's face as he sprinted toward Abbas and Gavi. Isika saw Aria at their side, holding tight to Abbas's arm as though she would fall if she let go. The sight distracted Isika, but the Desert King was getting up, helped by the man in red beside him, and Isika knew she couldn't go to Aria and Gavi yet. She needed to finish this work with the Desert King, before he got over his tumble and came at her with his poison again.

As she watched, the man in red looked at her. Even from far away, his eyes were so familiar, and it was as though he was sending her a message. She could almost hear it. *Do something.* Who was he? Why did she have the feeling that he was an ally rather than an enemy?

She sighed. This could not go on. But what could she do? She thought of her thread, strong and golden before her, spinning out to an unseen power. And her heart leapt as she remembered her allies.

Keerza! she called. *Please drive this horrible man away!*

She waited. She heard nothing, not even a whisper in reply. The Desert King stood and wiped the rain off of his face, holding her eyes, but Isika no longer felt deceived by him. She thought he looked more human as he stumbled to his feet, but the facade crumbled as he turned to look at her with demon hatred in his eyes. He didn't look as much like her anymore. There was no kindness in his face. She knew, suddenly that her kindness had come from her mother. The king saw that she was not fooled by him, and he held his arms out again in attack. Heat rolled off him, the same horrible desert heat that Isika had faced before. It rolled before him like a tall wave, and though Isika planted her feet, when it reached her, it knocked her down. She gasped with pain as it sucked the moisture out of her eyes, burning her eyelashes and hair. She screamed.

I told you to come, the Desert King said, and his voice had no poison anymore. It was terrible to listen to, a shriek of hatred. *Daughters are meant to listen to their fathers.*

Isika was sobbing now. Her skin hurt, every inch of it, and

she was lost in the need for water, the need to get away from the heat. But she heard him, nonetheless.

I am not yours, she said in reply. The heat wavered, growing cooler, and Isika saw that she was holding it away from herself, pushing it off her shoulders. She held her father's eyes with all the defiance she could put into a look.

You forfeited the right to call me daughter when you hurt my brother, she said.

Your brother! the Desert King scoffed, and the contempt in his face tore at Isika's heart.

Oh, Benayeem, she thought. *He doesn't deserve you.*

She heard a roar, as though from far away, and turned to see what it could be. Suddenly, the heat lifted, and Abbas tore through the remaining warriors, running straight for the Desert King. The roaring came from him, matching a look of fury on his strong face. The king stared at Abbas with dread and anger. He bared his teeth as Abbas came at him, sword drawn. Abbas laughed.

"Now you will pay for what you have done to my people," Abbas said. His face was damp with sweat and covered in ash. He hollered and lifted his sword. The king met it with an invisible force meant to thrust the sword back into Abbas' face, but Abbas danced away from it.

"I meant to squash you long ago, Desert Dog," the king said. He threw another blast of air toward Abbas, who once again leapt over it and laughed.

"Waste like you can't squash a Karee prince."

"I see no prince," the king said, spitting on the ground beside him. Isika saw a flash of alarm in his eyes as Abbas roared again, advancing on the king with death in his eyes, hatred in his movements.

"You took everything from us and had us running from hole to hole in the desert," he said. "But your poison cannot touch us forever, because we are under the protection of the World Whisperer now. I give her my allegiance and say that she will be my queen."

The king's face twisted with fury, but he missed a step as he moved back to avoid Abbas's whirling sword. He faltered, and Abbas moved in. Isika realized with a feeling of unease that Abbas was going to kill the Desert King.

Keerza! Isika called. *We need you!*

"Abbas!" a voice called, but it wasn't Isika who spoke. From somewhere to her left, she clearly heard the voice of her stepmother, Jerutha. "Abbas! Do not do this thing. His life is not for you to take."

Abbas turned, looking toward the voice, his eyes searching the people. He must have found Jerutha in the crowd, because he held her eyes for a moment, then turned, just as the king was advancing on him. He danced out of the way of another blast of air, pulled his staff out, and swept it behind the king's knees, knocking him to the ground again.

There was a long rolling sound like thunder, and Isika smiled.

In the distance Keerza spilled out of the forest behind the city, and galloped down the hillside, toward the plain where they stood. They were like a waterfall of purple and silver, long lithe animals with brilliant hides. There were at least a hundred of them, and the sight of so many, running together like a river, filled Isika with awe. She looked back at the Desert King, who had clambered to his feet and was looking at Abbas with murder in his eyes. A moment later, he saw the Keerza running in his direction. A flash of anger and fear changed his face, and he leapt onto his horse, wheeling it around. He shot Isika one more terrible look before riding away, across the scarred plains. Isika watched him go, hoping he would ride all the way back to his city and never return.

To her left, the last lizard disintegrated as Ivram drove his staff through it. The Gariah warriors that were still able began to run slowly after the Desert King, who was a dot against the horizon. He was gone before the Keerza were halfway down the hill.

Exhaustion fell on Isika's head and shoulders as she stood waiting for the Keerza. The strength left her bones and her legs shook. Wind came close and she leaned on his shoulder. He let her, though she could feel his weariness through his humming muscles. She lifted her face to the sky, closing her eyes and feeling the rain run over her cheeks. It was warm and felt oddly alive. She could hear it humming. She sensed most of the Keerza running past her, following the ragged group of warriors who trailed after the Desert King, but she felt a few of the oldest Keerza surrounding her, including the ancient one who had spoken to her in the rooftop gardens. When he put his nose on her arm, she opened her eyes to smile sadly at him.

Why are you thinking that you have failed? the great Keerza asked. He nudged her with one of his massive antlers.

Isika was close to tears. *I was so susceptible to his voice,* she told the beautiful animal. *He kept me captive for so long. If it hadn't been for Jabari, I wouldn't have snapped out of it. Even Keethior couldn't bring me back.*

You called me an annoying bird, Keethior added helpfully.

Isika shook her head at him, but her heart felt heavy.

You will never do anything good completely on your own, the Keerza said. *Don't be susceptible to the shame of the Great Waste now. Go to your friends. Go without shame. They need you.*

She nodded, and the Keerza elders left, running into the plains to follow the rest of their herd. Isika did want to rejoin her family and friends. Everyone was with Gavi, so she knew he was being cared for, but anxiety twisted her stomach into knots as she remembered how limp he had looked in Abbas's arms. She turned to go, but then the strangest thing happened.

The red-robed man appeared at her elbow, holding his horse by the reins. Isika looked around, slightly panicked, to see if anyone was there to help her, but besides the two horses, they were alone, standing in a little pocket of quiet. Isika's hand came up, as though to ward off a blow that was coming, but she remembered her old sense of the man being an ally, and lowered it slowly. He was so familiar, and as he began to speak, she heard that his voice was gentle and human, nothing like the Desert King's voice had been.

"Isika," he said. His face was similar to the Desert King's, but much older. He had lines around his eyes and mouth, and there was gray in the beard that covered half of his face and spilled over his robe.

"I knew your mother," he told her. "And you... and your brother, also, when you were small. I knew your grand-mother. You are very like her. You..." He closed his mouth, and acted as though he would leave, but then he coughed a little and spoke again. "I don't think he can beat you." He began to walk away, leading his horse.

"Wait!" Isika called. "What is your name? Are you the one? Are you the one who helped us get out of the walled city?"

The man smiled, "I'm Herrith," he said, but he didn't say anything else. He mounted his horse and set it in the direction the King had gone. Isika stood watching, tears that she didn't understand on her face, until he disappeared on the horizon, just as the king had.

Chapter 31

There was a little group of healers around Gavi, who was propped under a tent a healer had hastily thrown up.

Isika walked toward them, leading her horse, terrified of what she would find. Her fear must have shown on her face, because Jabari caught her eye and spoke to her right away.

"He's not dead."

It wasn't all that comforting. Gavi was ghostly in the rain, his clothes soaked with blood, his eyes shut.

"He lost a lot of blood," Ben whispered to her.

Aria sat on the ground, slumped beside Gavi, leaning on Ivy. Isika went to her. She looked terrible, but she tried to smile at Isika. She only managed to twitch her lips up, and Isika's stomach dropped.

"Aria," Isika said. "What happened to you?"

Aria stared at her for a moment, then looked away, over Isika's shoulder, at Ben.

"You heard what he said," she said to Benayeem. "Did it matter to you? That we are nothing to him?"

"Aria—" Isika said. "He was only saying that to poison—"

Ben interrupted. "I have always known I was nothing to him, sister. Today was no surprise. He hit me and terrified me as a child. He kept me from my mother, he made me live in fear. I would never want to be anything to him at all. You should beware of anything that tells you that you need to be anything to him. Do not trust those feelings."

"He is our father," Isika could barely hear Aria's whisper. She reached out to touch her sister and yanked her hand back at the festering wound she sensed within her. Tears sprang to her eyes.

"It's still so bad?" she asked.

"It's so much worse," Aria whispered.

The healers around Gavi straightened. "We can move him now," one of them said. She looked at Abbas, who stood half a head taller than even the tallest of the Maweel. "Can you carry him again?"

Abbas nodded and gently reached out to pick up the unconscious boy, just as Andar and Laylit came running. Jabari rubbed his hands over his face.

"What did you do?" Laylit asked Jabari, before running to Gavi and kissing his face. Jabari raised his eyebrows at Isika.

"How can this be my fault?" he whispered. "I wasn't even with him." The worry on his face showed clearly through his light words.

"Aria needs to go to the healing tents, too," Isika said.

"Her parents are coming," Ivy said then, looking up from where she sat with Ivram and Karah. "They'll take her." Karah had a dark smudge on her cheek, but her arm was wrapped around Ivy's shoulders and she looked happy. Everyone looked exhausted.

Isika looked at Gavi again. She could barely stand to see him this way, limp and without color. There was a burst of energy from the healers.

"No!" one of them exclaimed. "Put him down, quickly." Abbas laid him down as softly as he could.

"What's happening?" cried Laylit, trying to push herself closer, but the healers closed in and worked furiously over the boy.

Isika felt a tug toward him. Her circlet tightened and buzzed on her head, warming her with a rush that washed from her head to her feet. The pull was very strong now, like iron to a magnet. She sighed a breath of prayer to the Shaper and handed the horse reins to Ben. She drifted through the crowd, slipping past Jabari, who made way for her.

The healers worked at Gavi's hands and chest, but one of them sat back and pressed her palms to her eyes, shaking her head.

"No," she said. "There is nothing more we can do."

The healer looked up as Isika drew near, and there must have been something in Isika's face, because the healer moved out of her way, drawing the others with her.

Isika ignored the shouts and wails behind her and bent over Gavi, who was stretched on the ground, as still as a pond. *Gavi,* she thought, and touched her forehead to his.

It was like being submerged in deep water. She was tangled in the roots of a tree that went all the way down, down beneath the ocean, beneath a thousand miles of water, and she was diving, diving, pulling every horrible thing away from her friend. *Gavi.* She missed him. He had been gone for far too long, so long that she could barely remember what his roasted potatoes tasted like.

Come back, my friend, she said to him. *Your brother needs you. Aria needs you. We all do.*

She blinked, moving her arms and legs through the water, warmer now. She wasn't in the depths anymore. Then she saw Gavi floating just beyond her, eyes closed. He was motionless, pale in the water, his hair swaying like rippling grass. She swam to him, lights trailing her, and grabbed onto his hand. Immediately she felt the malevolent poison the blade had slashed into him, felt his despair over her sister, over his place in the world.

No, my friend. It is not like this. All will be well. You are loved. There are so many sunrises for you. You can poke the fire and make us soup. The fires are over, the land will be healed. There are so many reasons to wake up.

And then Nenyi was there, as the whale, swimming around them, streaming bubbles, circling them, over and under, until the whole ocean was filled with light. Isika's heart felt as though it would burst with love. She looked down and saw a cord that stretched from her hand to the whale, thick, golden, a living thing. She wanted to swim away with Nenyi, to tumble over and over in the ocean with her.

Breathe in the quiet, find the streams of bubbles. But she had something to do.

With Nenyi there she had the strength to pull the poison out of her friend and send it out into the ocean where it disintegrated, then disappeared, like pieces of ash floating away. *The fires are out,* she told Gavi. *It's raining.* Gavi opened his eyes and Isika smiled at him.

Moments later, she found herself bending over him on the grass, and there were tiny flowers growing around his head. His eyes were open, blinking and confused, and she was jostled out of the way while Laylit rushed to him and Jabari grabbed his hands.

She stood, light-headed. She was so tired that she ached with it. In a moment, Auntie Teru was beside her, her arm around Isika's shoulders, supporting her. Isika blinked fast, terrified that if she looked at Auntie, she would burst into tears. But she squeezed the older woman's hand, and then Ibba had her other hand. Ben turned toward the horse barn, leading Wind and Night, and Isika sighed with relief. She could go home.

Isika gave Jabari a long look before turning to go, a look that tried to say *thank you* and *I'm sorry* and *what just happened?* And then she remembered that she could say those things, so she said them into his mind.

You're welcome, he said, *though I don't know for what. And I agree, what just happened? You did well, though.*

She smiled. *So did you.*

She turned to Teru again, feeling as weak as a baby.

Together they walked home, and her front door opening for her felt like everything.

Chapter 32

The rain fell and did not stop. There was something in it, too, something that felt good as it sprinkled Isika's face. The raindrops felt like they contained something more than water. Isika asked Kital about it, one day when they were walking outside, looking at the fresh grass that was shooting up everywhere, always tangled with the new wildflowers that seemed to have come to stay.

"Do you feel something special in the rain?" she asked.

He stopped and thought about it. She watched him as he looked up at the sky. He and Isika both wore cloaks made from charmed cloth from the weavers, to protect from rain. The rain fell on Kital's face, running off his soft brown cheeks and making his eyelashes wet and spiky. He looked very serious, considering the rain. She smiled. He would start school soon—her baby was growing up, and he wasn't hers anymore. He was all of theirs: hers, Jerutha's, Teru's and Dawit's. Even Jabari came by occasionally to take Kital on little hiking journeys. They all loved him, and now that they had Mesu, he passed the love along, telling him stories and playing with him when Jerutha came to visit. It was so good to have little ones around, Isika thought. Especially now, when things were troubled and though the Desert King was gone, his echoes seemed to linger in her mind.

"It feels like it is watering us," Kital said, "not only the trees and grass and plants. Maybe we could grow taller in it, too."

"Exactly," Isika said. "I couldn't have said it better."

There was something healing in the rain. It brought hope to her heart, hope that there would be good days ahead, despite the fact that the man who was her father was their worst enemy. She could worry over the facts of her parentage for hours, hurting for her mother, who surely hadn't wanted such a man as her husband, and aching with shame over the sound of his voice, calling to her, naming her. She could spend sleepless nights worrying over Aria, still so sick. But when she walked in the rain, she felt trust again. The Shaper would work it out. Isika could breathe again, and believe in a life that didn't center around fear.

"Come," she said to Kital. "We need to go back. The others will be there for dinner. And your cake must be ready."

It was Kital's birthday and he was six years old, hard to believe. He had lengthened and lost his little boy roundness, but he was still Kital, enthusiastic and innocent, always ready for fun and adventure. Auntie was making him a birthday dinner and had invited lots of friends. She had asked Isika to get him out of the house and out from underfoot because he still jumped around when he was excited, and Auntie was going to start throwing pots, she said, if the boy hopped into her one more time.

They took one last look at the new plain, covered in the greenest grass. Again Isika felt as though the rain had changed it, making it more complete. Then they crossed the field to go back to the house.

The injured Gariah warriors who hadn't managed to hobble away had been rounded up on the day of the battle and sent back to the Desert City with provisions for the journey. The Maweel were merciful people. Three men had asked to stay, and after much discussion that Isika had to sit through, the elders had decided that they could stay and go through a year of apprenticeship in a trade of their choice. One had chosen to be a weaver, one a gardener, and one had chosen to work with the horses. All three were Karee tribesmen, people who looked like Abbas; tall, with long black hair and fierce faces. He had vouched for them, and they revered him as a prince, touching their fingers to their foreheads as a gesture of respect when he came near. Two were married and would be sending for their wives soon.

During the meeting that decided their fate, Isika had seen the mixture of emotions playing out. The Maweel opened their doors to castaway children, but if all of Gariah started pouring into their borders, what would happen? Still, the values they held for those without safety in their homes made their decision clear, and she smiled to see the sheer happiness on the faces of the three men.

"This will be your problem to deal with, someday," Ivram said to her at her lesson the next day. "And it is not simple."

But Isika's mind was already buzzing with solutions, and she smiled. Just then she felt up to the task. Possibly it would overwhelm her again the next day. But more and more, she felt she was growing into her place. She no longer shrank away from it. She was not the girl she had been at first, lonely and unaware of her powers. She had friends on every side, now. And a family.

They reached the house and heard the laughter even before they turned up the path to the front door.

"Sounds like Abbas is here," Kital said, and he dropped Isika's hand and flew up the short flight of stairs into the house. He adored Abbas, and was pretty sure he wanted to be a Gariah warrior when he grew up, an ambition that could be a little tricky once Isika was queen. She paused to cup a giant rose that was at full bloom, lowering her face to it. More laughter from the house.

"Do you whisper to it, to make it grow?" She jumped.

Jabari stood behind her, grinning. He was holding a large basket.

"Do you whisper to walls, to tear them down?"

"Is that all I'm good for? Tearing down walls? You have so many talents, and I'm nothing but a wall crasher."

"Well, you knock evil kings down too."

He smiled at her. "I didn't think you had noticed that."

She grimaced. "I had to remember it later. But what are we talking about, anyway? It's time to eat and forget all that. What's in the basket?"

"Gavi made me pick beans from his garden for the party. He actually had a harvest, during this crazy time. Maybe they need smoky skies to grow."

Isika shuddered at the memory of smoky skies. Rain fell gently on her face and hands, comforting her. "Is that why you're late?" she asked.

"I was cleaning up the workshop," he said, then paused. "I'm only going to be coming in once a week now."

"What?" She stared at him.

"I'm beginning ranger training. Not leaving for a few more months, but you know they do this brutal physical training, right? I have to run up mountainsides and stuff like that. And learn to wield an actual sword, and more herbal learning, and it's going to take most of my time."

Isika was surprised at the wave of sadness his words brought her. She had grown used to his company in the workshop. She liked listening to him sing in the other room, loved the way he teased Tomas in a way no one else could get away with. Who would meet her eyes when Tomas did something that only Tomas would ever do? It would be lonely without him there.

"One day a week," she repeated. "And after that, you'll be a ranger. Working way out there."

"Eventually."

She really looked at him for the first time in a while, noticing the way he had grown over the year. He was taller, so that she almost had to tilt her head to look at him. Almost, but not quite. His shoulders were definitely wider. She saw his nostrils flare slightly and realized he was laughing at her.

Something had changed between them, and she searched his face for understanding. But all she saw was laughter, so she narrowed her eyes at him and turned to walk into the house, slipping her shoes off as she went.

"I'll be happy to return to the quiet," she said. "No stupid singing or jokes."

"Sure you will," he said. "You can tell yourself that story. I'll still be there one day a week to make sure you don't all die of boredom."

It was then, right before she made it through the doorway, that she felt it, his hand on her shoulder, a thousand of those magic sparks through her, and she turned to look at him again. "Isika?" He said. His eyes were very serious.

"Yes?" She asked. Her voice came out in a little squeak and she could have drowned herself in the nearby vase of flowers.

"I—I'm glad we had this year. And I'm glad I decided to trust you. You've more than lived up to it. Thanks for being such a friend to me."

Isika felt two things. A sudden wave of happiness. Trust. He was her friend, on her side, and he trusted her. And she felt a tiny shard of disappointment. She nodded back at him and went into the party, chastising herself as she went.

What did you think he was going to say, stupid? she asked herself, but she didn't have much time to stew over it, because first there was Mesu to hold and play with, and then Abbas whirled her into some kind of wild tribal dance. She ate and ate. She sat with Jerutha and they talked over the past weeks and the coming days. The elders had asked

Jerutha to take over managing the palace housekeeping and kitchens.

"Really?" Isika asked, shocked.

"You know I've always loved to run a house," Jerutha said, her blue eyes crinkling in a smile. "The palace is just a bigger house."

"Much bigger," Isika murmured, searching her friend's face.

There was a big difference between menial labor at the Worker village and running a large staff at the palace. For a minute, Isika couldn't even find a way to respond. But after a minute, she realized with surprise that she could picture Jerutha running the palace perfectly. She looked at her step-mother now, like a sister to her, her pale cheeks rounded and rosier than they used to be. Jerutha was wearing a pale pink tunic over rich brown pants, and her hair was tied up on her head. She had become beautiful here, cared for and somehow important.

"It was Teru's idea," Jerutha said. "After she saw how much I loved helping her here. She mentioned it to Karah, and the old palace manager is retiring, so they asked me. Mesu is getting older, and one of the palace cooks has a teenaged daughter who can help me with him." Her eyes were shining, and Isika saw that the work was giving Jerutha a sense of belonging that she hadn't found in Azariyah before now.

"That's wonderful," Isika said, kissing Mesu on the cheek and handing him back to his mother. "You'll be like nothing they've ever seen before."

There was sadness in the evening. Isika had brought Gavi back from the brink, but he was still weak, and the healers said it would take him a long time to recover. He lay curled on the seating mattresses in the corner of the room, smiling at the dancers. Kital brought him food throughout the night, and Gavi ate what Kital brought until he had to hold up a hand, laughing, because it was too much. It hurt Isika to see Gavi wounded.

And Aria wasn't there. She was so sick now that she spent all her time alternating between her home and the healing tents. She wouldn't be going on any more seeking journeys until the healers could find a cure for her. Isika felt a familiar stab of pain at the thought of her sister, the one she had been helpless to save when they were both young.

This time, she vowed, *I will find a way to heal her.*

Ben had shocked the family by announcing that he was training to be a seeker, on his way to becoming a ranger. Ibba would begin training to be a gardener. Brigid would continue weaving with her family, occasionally going on seeking journeys. They were all celebrating different moments in their lives: Kital beginning school, Isika becoming second potter within the year. But things felt as though they were moving too quickly, somehow. Isika wanted to put her hands out and stop the scenery from racing away from her.

She couldn't stop time, so she tried to enjoy the party. She ate, and drank, and danced, and chatted with guests and friends. She cleared empty plates when she got a chance. And always there was Jabari, somewhere on the edges, meeting her eyes to share a laugh, watching her from across the room. It was nice to have a friend like him. A friend who could knock an enemy down, and also make her laugh. A friend whose touch sparked a bit. And this, then, wasn't moving too quickly. How could she complain, when she wanted to slow everything else down?

Later, when she was clearing plates, Andar and Laylit arrived, causing a little exclamation at the door as everyone complimented them on their gorgeous clothes. They were a sight, bright and almost too perfect in the homely room. Laylit walked straight to Isika and embraced her. Isika was stiff with surprise.

Laylit pulled back and looked into Isika's face. No matter how many times Isika saw Laylit, her beauty was always a surprise. Today she had tiny silver jewels glued around her eyes, and her hair was piled into a silver net. Her deep indigo robes shimmered with more jewels. Honestly, it was too much.

"This is all so complicated," Laylit told Isika in a low voice. "We have many things to learn and search. We don't know what to think about any of it. But first, before anything, I want to thank you for saving my son. I will love you forever for that."

"Oh," Isika said, unsure of what to say in response to gratitude that seemed slightly threatening, but before she could answer, she found herself whirled away from Laylit.

"Jabari!" Laylit scolded, "I wasn't done talking to her," but they were already across the room, and then outside with the dancers, under a canopy of red rock lights.

"You looked like you needed to be rescued. Dance?"

It was a high-energy dance; they responded and impro-
vised to the drums. Isika couldn't stop laughing at Jabari's
face when he danced. It was as animated as his arms and legs.
They tried to outdo each other in the dance, and there were
his eyes, and there was his smile, and when it was over he
squeezed her hand for a moment.

"She should be distracted by now," he said. "You're safe."
Then he disappeared and Isika went to the table to get herself
a drink, meeting Gavi's smug eyes across the room.

She glared and shook her head at him and he rounded his
eyes innocently.

And so they celebrated Kital's birthday, while the rain
continued to fall.

It was still falling the next day. And the day after that.
It fell for a month, then two. Then one day Isika got up to go
to the workshop. She stretched and found some clean work
clothes, standing to pull her tunic over her head. She stopped
short. She didn't hear anything but the birds. No rain on the
roof. She went to the window and laughed, staring. The sun
was shining, sparkling on everything. As far as the eye could
see, everything was green, blooming, and growing. The land-
scape was woven of a thousand colors. Isika opened the
window and felt the warmth of the sun on her. She turned
her face up to the sky, welcoming the new day.

~

What is the most important ingredient for a book's success? Besides, of course, the book itself?

It's what you, the Reader, says about it. Social proof. Reviews.

When people are out there, in the wilderness of the book jungle, looking for something to read, the main question they ask is, "Have other people read this? Did they like it?"

So if this book is your kind of book, and you think it might be someone else's kind of book, I will be over the moon if you leave a review on whatever site feeds you your books. Reviews can be the key to a book's success. Thank you!

~

ACKNOWLEDGMENTS

My heart says thank you to so many people. I don't know, the longer I write, the more I realize that this is all so dependent on so many things. A listening ear, readers who care about what I'm writing, a husband's support, kids who love me and love my writing. I think I could have *started* writing without support, but I don't think I could have continued for this long.

So thank you. Chinua Ford, you are a dreamboat. You are kind and very supportive of this stormy, emotional artist girl. Your enthusiasm for this series feeds me. Thank you.

Leaf Reilly, you dropped into my life right when I needed you. I'm so thankful that we are going to grow old together, being better and better friends.

Kai, Kenya, Leafy, Solo and Isaac, thank you for your interest, your questions, your cuteness, your quirk. Thank you for making me a mom. You make life interesting and you make me young. There is no way I would have written this series without you in my life.

Sara J. Henry, you know me and my writing and I'm so thankful for your keen eye!

Unicorns, especially Rebeca, David, Dorcas, and Melony, you have made this book mostly mistake free, and saved me from typo shame. Thank you!

Ro Ro of my heart, thank you for being the first reader of this book.

Tj and Mark Chapman, Diane Brodeur, Brittani Truby, and again Rowan Tree Keyzer, you are magical creatures. I pray that you will be stumbling into beauty every way you walk. Thank you for being my rockstar patrons.

Mom and Dad, you let seven people come rolling into your house. You are the epitome of support, loving and true. I love you.

And to my readers at Journey Mama. Thank you for helping me grow. I couldn't do this without you.

ABOUT THE AUTHOR

Newsletter

If you want to join Rachel Devenish Ford's Newsletter and learn about books and new releases, sign up here. Your address will never be shared!

Bio

Rachel Devenish Ford is the wife of one Superstar Husband and the mother of five incredible children. Originally from British Columbia, Canada, she spent seven years working with street youth in California before moving to India to help start a meditation center in the Christian tradition. She can be found eating street food or smelling flowers in many cities in Asia. She currently lives in Northern Thailand, inhaling books, morning air, and seasonal fruit.

Works by Rachel Devenish Ford:

The Eve Tree
    A Traveler's Guide to Belonging
    Trees Tall As Mountains: The Journey Mama Writings-Book One
    Oceans Bright With Stars: The Journey Mama Writings-Book Two
    A Home as Wide as the Earth: The Journey Mama Writings: Book Three
    World Whisperer : World Whisperer Book 1
    Guardian of Dawn : World Whisperer Book 2
    Shaper's Daughter: World Whisperer Book 3

Reviews

Recommendations and reviews are such an important part of the success of a book. If you enjoyed this book, please take the time to leave a review.

Don't be afraid of leaving a short review! Even a couple lines will help and will overwhelm the author with waves of gratitude.

Contact

Email: racheldevenishford@gmail.com
  Blog: http://journeymama.com
  Facebook: http://www.facebook.com/racheldevenishford
  Twitter: http://www.twitter.com/journeymama
  Instagram: http://instagram.com/journeymama

ALSO BY RACHEL DEVENISH FORD

Rachel has spent twelve years writing about life on her blog, Journey Mama. She has collected the best of these posts in the Journey Mama Writings series. If you love to know everything you wanted to know about authors and their children, you might like The Journey Mama Writing Series.

Book One: Trees Tall as Mountains

Book Two: Oceans Bright with Stars

Book Three: A Home as Wide as the Earth

If you like literary fiction, you might like A Traveler's Guide to Belonging.

"A beautiful, beautiful book." -Sara J. Henry, Award-winning author of Learning to Swim

> *Twenty-four-year-old Timothy is far from his home country of Canada when his new wife dies in childbirth. Stunned, he finds himself alone with his newborn son in the mountains of North India and no idea of what it means to be a father. He begins a journey through India with his baby, seeking understanding for loss and life and the way the two intertwine.*

Set among the stunning landscapes, train tracks, and winding alleys of India, *A Traveler's Guide to Belonging* is a story about fathers and sons, losing and finding love, and a traveler's quest for meaning.

www.ingramcontent.com/pod-product-compliance
Lightning Source LLC
Chambersburg PA
CBHW031026120726
47905CB00007B/2065